LETHBRIDGE-STEWART

THE SCHIZOID EARTH
I, ALASTAIR

Robert Mammone

CANDY JAR BOOKS · CARDIFF
2021

I, Alastair © Robert Mammone 2021

Characters from The Web of Fear
© *Hannah Haisman & Henry Lincoln 1968, 2021*
Lethbridge-Stewart: The Series
© *Andy Frankham-Allen & Shaun Russell 2014, 2021*
Benton was created by Derrick Sherwin
The Vault was created by Gary Russell

Doctor Who is © *British Broadcasting Corporation, 1963, 2021*

Range Editor: Andy Frankham-Allen
Editor: Shaun Russell
Editorial: Keren Williams
Licensed by Hannah Haisman
Cover by Richard Young & Will Brooks

ISBN: 978-1-913637-03-3

Printed and bound in the UK by
Severn, Bristol Road, Gloucester, GL2 5EU

Published by
Candy Jar Books
Mackintosh House
136 Newport Road, Cardiff, CF24 1DJ
www.candyjarbooks.co.uk

CHAPTER ONE

EVEN NOW, I am no leftist, but a part of me regrets the death of the Bolshevik Revolution amidst the chaos of the Russian Civil War in 1921. Without the strong bulwark of a resurgent Left, the militarism and conservatism of the Continent ran amok. While the mainstream parties in Britain attempted to hold the line, the economic havoc unleashed by the Depression in 1932 fatally undermined their legitimacy. And into the gap stepped men and women who formerly occupied the fringes of acceptable discourse, thrust into the mainstream by violence they fostered, and took advantage of. In time, the democracy and liberty that marked Britain as a beacon to the world began to gutter...

From 'An Unpublishable Memoir' by [redacted]. Retained in the Security Directorate Archives.

The sun had guttered into the horizon hours ago and darkness clung to the land. Britain slumbered uneasily through another long night, weary and wary in equal measure. Those who ruled raised another glass to their stranglehold on power, while those who couldn't sleep dared dream of better days. And there were those who did more than just dream.

As Britain slept, so did the little village south of the great estate. A patchwork of homes and other buildings, it was a sizable community made up of hardworking farmers and tradesmen. Another scheduled power cut had sent most to bed.

A soft breeze, warm with the coming of spring, sighed through the night. Newly budded leaves, thick and green, hissed like waves on a beach. A crescent moon, sharp as a

1

sickle, rode the sky, its faint light insufficient to penetrate the thick darkness clinging to the landscape. A night for poachers, then, assuming anyone would be as foolhardy as to be abroad during the rural curfew after sunset.

North of the village, beyond a series of low rolling hills split by a narrow stream, and at the end of a long gravel drive, stood a large, Georgian building. Its rectangular frontage and columned portico frowned down on a broad sweep of lawn, punctuated by a trio of silent fountains and rows of watchful elms. Several dozen windows glittered in the pinpricks of starlight, but there were no interior lights to shine out onto the estate. The building, at least above ground, was entirely dark.

Nevertheless, dark didn't mean dead. Like the nearby villagers, the staff was abed, and glad to be so. The local Auxpol Militia policed the curfew, intent on keeping the citizenry safe from threats external and internal. After all, the Party counselled vigilance and no matter how long you had known your neighbour, did you know the dark secrets of the heart? And beneath the grand house, far from the ruthless vigilance of the black-shirted militia, figures stirred in secret places.

Had someone been foolish enough to venture into the night and make their way along the verge of the drive, and then stolen across the lawn and up the steps to the entrance, they may as well have completed the quadrella and entered the main building. Inside, they would've seen a broad swathe of black and white tiles, stark in the faint moonlight glimmering through the door. A marble staircase swept to the upper levels, the highest portions lost in a gloom so black to be almost treacle. There, the intruder would have found shuttered room after shuttered room. Furniture draped in white sheets, thick with dust and cobwebs. Cloth covered paintings adorned the walls and a heavy scent of disuse lingered. It was, all told, an edifice to ambitions growing by the year. None of this, of course, would be obvious to an intruder, alert instead to the first sound of reproach at their presence. The real beating heart of the house rested well below ground level, where an intruder would find their steps taking them down, down into the tunnels and chambers excavated in the decades and centuries before.

In a ground level room off the main entrance, behind oak panelling hiding a priest's hole, stands revealed narrow basalt stairs winding deep into the earth. With the aid of a torch or lamp, the keen observer might see the graffiti scratched into the brickwork the further they ventured: history in reverse. Modern English at the highest levels, then some rhyming verse Shakespeare might've recognised, before plunging into the runic language of the Vikings who once pillaged the lands around the estate, terrorising the local people while setting up a temple to Thor on the grounds. Like iron filings to a magnet, that temple sat above yet another, far older and Roman in origin, its squat altar blackened with stains that might be age-old blood. Here, the journey into the past juddered to a sudden halt. Smashing through the mossy, marble-lined walls yawned an opening as welcoming as a lion's maw. Added to its incongruity in that noisome place, was the lighting strung along the tunnel's length as it burrowed into the native rock.

What awaited at the end of it? A rectangular room, carved from the rock by men jailed for political crimes and afterwards sent to a swift death in a punishment camp to ensure their silence. Banks of lights sat recessed into the ceiling, all blindingly bright. A mirror ran the length of one wall and, in its reflection, sat a figure in a metal chair. The chair was bolted to the concrete floor, but the figure was in no way restrained. After all, once summonsed, he knew he could not be anywhere but there. He would never forget the punishments for not following orders.

With his one remaining eye, he dimly saw his reflection in the mirror. He was aware of the awful itch that resided behind the patch covering his ruined left eye, an itch that only rose when he was anxious and afraid. The patch was too big, and the strap binding it around his head was too tight. His father said he will grow into it. With that itch came an awful desire to lift the patch's fabric and burrow his nails deep into the hole. It reminded him of the day, not six months before, when his father and he came across a fox caught in a trap, frantically chewing at its leg to escape.

His fear stayed his hand. Instead, he scratched at the

pinprick scabs high on his right bicep. He was young, in his teenage years, but the weight of what his life was rested heavily on him. His hair was black, and cut short. There were hints of the man he would become; in the anger marring his face, in his glaring, remaining eye, in the way his shoulders slumped. Hysteria prowled at the edge of his self-control. He was aware that to give into it, was to commit something approaching a sin.

He stiffened at the rattle of metal and squeaking wheels. A figure appeared, dressed in a suit and tie, pushing a trolley while whistling an aimless tune. There was something incongruous about his manner, but the boy knew beneath the bland mask of that face lay a monster.

'Here we go, my boy,' the voice said. Never his name, only 'my boy'.

There was a rustle of fabric and the man placed his jacket over the trolley. The boy saw the man unbutton his sleeves and roll them up, revealing brawny forearms, corded with muscle and thick veins.

'How is your eye? Hasn't been playing up, has it?'

The boy shook his head, the movement like a sparrow spying a cat and readying itself to lunge for the sky.

'Good. Good.' There was a moment of silence, then a long sigh. 'You know I'd rather not do this, don't you?'

Again, those nervous movements of his head, this time signalling assent.

'Well, needs must. The nation requires dedicated and able men, and this... medication will ensure that is the case. No child of mine will fail when the moment calls his name. You are a trailblazer, my boy, for a better and brighter future.'

The boy didn't feel like any sort of trailblazer, but he knew his father sensed negativity like a shark scented blood. He froze as his father dipped his hand into a metal dish, emerging with a metal hypodermic, its point glinting in the light. The boy heard the faint prick as it punctured the seal of a small dark bottle, then the bubbling hiss as the liquid drained into the barrel. The shadow of his father fell over him.

'Remember, this is for your benefit, not mine.'

His father said that every time, but the boy never quite believed it. On one occasion he even asked his brother, who always seemed older than the boy remembered, and his brother would agree.

'If Father says it is needed,' James would say, 'then it is needed. I'm not one to question him.'

But the boy never believed that either. James was always questioning their father. Oh, he was careful to never do so in their father's presence, but the boy had heard him several times.

But not him. No, the boy would never question his father. Not ever.

After.

Left alone, the boy lolled in his chair. He found it difficult to focus; his thoughts ran away like beads of water down a pane of glass. The image amused him, but before laughter betrayed him, he clapped a shaking hand over his mouth. It is in that pose that he heard a click, and felt a new tension coil tightly within his chest.

Directly in front of him, a white sheet descended from a recess in the ceiling. The room dimmed and the clatter of machinery started, then sped to a spinning whir.

WHAT WE WERE PROMISED.

The words on the title card were stark. Crowds, many waving tiny flags, line both sides of a road. His eye widened as he attempted to focus on the swimming features of children caught up in the excitement. The piano playing over the images was bright and gay. His drooling smile attempted to mimic the smiles of the excited people as soldiers marched in lockstep home.

WHAT THEY GAVE US INSTEAD.

The music turned grim, a thunderous denunciation. The cheering figures dissolved into long queues of men, women and children in front of a series of mobile kitchens. The children were dirty, their faces blank, their mothers' long suffering. However, the men caught the boy's eye – the sullen rage, the muttered, silent conversations between knots of them as they inched towards a handout of food.

A MARTYR IS BORN.

The Free Trade Hall in Manchester appeared on the screen. Lines of people waited to enter. The image shifted jarringly inside, and a tall, thin figure with a moustache gesticulated wildly behind a lectern while the crowd stared in rapt attention. At the height of his speech, with his face approaching ecstasy, there was a flash. The man slumped forward, and men swamped the stage.

A SAVIOUR TAKES UP THE MANTLE!

A different figure appeared, moustachioed and vibrant, standing at a lectern in another hall. The image cut between the angry denunciations his vigorous movements indicated he was delivering, to the adoring attention he received from the audience arrayed before him. At the end of the speech, the crowd rose as one and the image blurred with the fury of their clapping and hand waving.

A DAY OF GLORY read the next title card.

A stark image, wavering and clouded, appeared. The man operating the camera must've been drunk, the boy thought. The camera lurched from side to side, before it steadied. At the far end of a room, which had no windows and might have been underground, stood a family of four. A man, a woman, and two teenage girls, dressed in clothes that were stained and torn, but were undoubtedly once fine. They were dirty, hungry and scared, and the boy's heart grew heavy. Of all the images, those fragments of time disturbed him the most. He focused, as always, on the older of the girls, and felt a familiar dislocation in time and space. But the film sped on, and his attention was dragged along with it.

To the right of the camera, just visible, stood several men in uniform. With a thrill, the boy saw the black and white armbands each wore on their left bicep. Three arrows; one pointed left, another right, and the last upwards. The film was silent now, but there was no mistaking the response of the soldiers to a shouted command off camera. He saw the man at the far end of the room step forward in a vain effort to shield the woman and the two girls, but his chest blossomed black and smoke filled the room.

The boy had often wondered why the man, evidently the father, would do such a thing. It remained forever a mystery to him.

The man collapsed in a heap, followed by one of the girls and then the woman. Only the older dark-haired girl remained, her eyes terrified, her pale features stark in the wan light. That sense of dislocation jarred him one more time before she fell as well, half her head disappearing in a blurred fountain of brains and blood.

CLEARING OUT THE VERMIN read the next title card, and the music turned martial, commanding. Images of dishevelled, confused looking men wearing frock coats being harried down a tunnel, before armed men opened fire. The picture dissolved to reveal the Palace of Westminster ablaze, with a surging sea of people near the main entrance. Then, the same moustachioed man from earlier, haranguing the crowd as they surged around him.

ONWARD TO VICTORY.

Images of men at a table, headed by the same figure, applauded. Dignitaries walked up steps, to shake the hand of the Leader. More music, more people, more applause, more motorcades and speeches, ships at sea flying the flag of a great nation, diplomats making obeisance, soldiers under arms, squadrons of fighter planes in the air, ending with a card that displayed a map of the Continent, with the British flag unfurled in each capital city. Beneath the image, the title proclaimed what the image showed:

TOTAL VICTORY. EUROPE IS OURS.

The film rattled to a halt, plunging the room into darkness. The boy sat bolt upright, sweat lathering his face. His heart galloped along and his breathing was ragged, edging into ecstasy. Though he found some of the film disturbing, his overriding sensation at the end was one of triumph, of victory against an old regime that deserved to die choking on its own blood. The film, a frequent visitor in his life, and always viewed under the influence of the cocktail of drugs pumped into him. His response was always the same. Feverish ecstasy for the longest time, then the effect of the drugs abated, leaving him rung out and exhausted.

He heard footsteps, felt a hand clasp his shoulder. Waiting, the silence a kind of demand.

'Hail the Republic,' Alastair Gordon Lethbridge-Stewart said, his lips slack. 'Hail the Republic, Father.'

CHAPTER TWO

THE MURDER of anyone is a horrifying and unwelcome crime, even for those whose conduct and ideology are antithetical to good government and democracy. Under ordinary circumstances, though, and in spite of its rarity, the assassination of Oswald Mosley in 1936 should've resulted in nothing more than an investigation for the local constabulary, with a brief of evidence handed up to the district prosecutors, for initial action in a Magistrate's court.

1936 wasn't a year conducive to ordinary circumstances. Oswald Mosley, and the movement he created, was not ordinary in the slightest. With the effects of the economic downturn entering a seventh year, the situation in the United Kingdom had become particularly dire. While Imperial Preference smoothed the sharper edge of the conditions, this applied only to those fortunate to exist in the upper echelons of society. Everyone else, as Mosley pungently stated in an address to his local constituency, had to 'make do and enjoy the damned taste of it'.

His death ushered in worse things.

From 'An Unpublishable Memoir' by [redacted]. Retained in the Security Directorate Archives.

'Section Leader Du Plessis? You and Klaasen block the exit at the rear. I don't want any of these toffs thinking they can escape out the tradesman's entrance.'

Du Plessis, like his partner, was a deeply tanned bullock of a man. He nodded, and the pair, belying their bulk, moved smoothly away, disappearing into the dark with barely a boot scuffing the ground.

8

'They'll crack heads, Alastair, if you don't watch them,' said Platoon Leader Benjamin Knight. A solid figure with an open face marred by scarring across his right cheek, he wore plain clothes, like the others in the small team. 'Our South African friends think every problem is a nail, and they are the hammers.'

'Maybe, Benjamin.' Alastair moved out of the shadow of a doorway. A hand strayed up to his face, brushing the edge of the eyepatch in what had long been an unconscious, habitual action. 'We're sending a message, here, as much as anything else.'

'What's the message, Column Leader?' Unlike Knight, whose relationship with Alastair was an easy going one informed by years of serving together, Platoon Under Leader Frieda Lewisham maintained a stricter line of formality.

A wiry woman with black hair cut in a severe bob, wearing dun-coloured jumper and trousers, emerged from the shadows and joined the men. If Alastair prudishly thought the jumper a touch tight, he could at least admire the practicality of her trousers.

'The Republic tolerates dissent, Lewisham, within reason.' Alastair took his pistol from the holster on his right hip. He pulled back the slide and checked the magazine. Satisfied, he returned it to his holster.

'And our pampered friends upstairs are pushing the limits how?' Knight rubbed his jaw, staring up at a set of windows, where lights blazed and from which the low rumble of music was audible. Shadows moved on the high walls and across the ceiling.

'The warrant I obtained says they are,' Alastair said.

A soft burst of static issued from the walkie-talkie riding on his left hip. Lifting it to his mouth, Alastair thumbed the switch.

'Cyclops One,' he said. Alastair had baulked at the designation when assigned it, but appreciated, after beating up the Section Leader in an alley behind HQ, the implicitly mordant humour.

'In position,' responded a voice, the thick accent a low growl.

'Any trouble?'

Du Plessis' low chuckle issued from the walkie-talkie. 'Nothing we can't handle. Good thing there's a scheduled power cut – it's black as hell back here. Perfect for surveillance, and a bit of knife work.'

'I bet,' Knight said humourlessly.

'Let's keep the bloodshed to a minimum,' Alastair said. 'Unless circumstances dictate otherwise.'

'Sure thing, boss,' Du Plessis said shortly, before a burst of static signalled he'd ended the conversation.

'I'm assuming you're venting tension, and not questioning the reason we're here, Ben.' Alastair returned the walkie-talkie to his hip. When Knight nodded tightly, Alastair said, 'Good. Let's leave the morality for the ethics class. Let's put the frighteners into these idiots.'

Alastair stepped into a quiet street lined on both sides by Italianate style villas. Old money, money that pre-dated the Revolution of 1943, lingered behind tastefully designed porticos and thick curtains of superior quality. These were the residences of Party apparatchiks and their families, located not far from the Republican ministries circling like satellites around the New People's Parliament. The understated wealth was a silent rebuke to the austerity of the Republic. *Their day will come*, Alastair mused as he crossed the street.

He passed under an unlit streetlight. Du Plessis wasn't wrong. The energy cuts reached even into this bastion of privilege. If not for the thin moonlight, the street would've been swathed in darkness.

'Economies,' he muttered to himself, though glad for the darkness. He ignored Frieda's arched eyebrow.

Alastair checked with the South Africans one final time before he climbed the steps to the entrance. He disliked raids like this. It was all about politics, of that he was sure. Someone was sending a message, and he, to his resentment, was the messenger.

If there was a real suspicion of subversion, there was no way he and his team would be entering the house this way. The door would be smashed open, with Alastair tossing in gas canisters as his team stormed the entrance. Instead, Alastair stood in front of the double doors and rang the bell.

A distant chime sounded. Music drifted down from the

second story.

'How've they got power?' Knight asked.

'Batteries, probably,' Lewisham said. 'Or a wind-up player.'

After a few moments, the music upstairs quietened. Despite his annoyance at being used to send a message, Alastair let an anticipatory smile creep across his face.

The door rattled. Alastair stepped back, his hand straying to the butt of his pistol. Behind him, Knight and Lewisham did the same. The walkie-talkie at his hip droned quietly to itself.

The lock banged heavily as it was disengaged. Alastair saw the door drift inwards, framing a tall shadow in the gap. Flicking on his torch, Alastair shone it into the figure's face.

'For God's sake, put that down,' snapped a plummy voice, raising a hand against the bright beam.

The cut-glass accent immediately raised Alastair's hackles. He kept the torchlight trained on the figure, revealing a man.

'Look, I really must insist...' The voice trailed off when it saw the armed men. Alastair's torch lit up his shock of blond hair. Thick lips stretched in an approximation of a grin.

'I have a warrant to inspect the premises.'

'Is this a police raid?'

'Something better,' Alastair said. 'We're with the RSF Security Directorate.'

'The Leader's rat catchers?'

'That's enough of that,' Lewisham said, quietly.

Ignoring her, the figure nodded at Alastair. 'And you are?'

Nonplussed, Alastair stared at the man for a moment, as if unable to understand the question. It was his job to ask the questions, not the other way around. Unwillingly, aware that Knight and Lewisham were staring at him, he answered. 'Column Leader Lethbridge-Stewart. I have a warrant.'

'You already said that, Column Leader Lethbridge-Stewart.' The man broke into a grin, evidently feeling more comfortable now that he had got an answer out of Alastair. 'That's quite a mouthful, when you think about it.'

Alastair felt a familiar anger kindle itself. He cleared his throat. 'You are?' he said again.

'Oh, do forgive me.' The fellow stretched out his hand, as if Alastair was being introduced to him. 'George St Simeon.

All my friends call me Georgie.' St Simeon leaned forward and winked. 'You can call me George.' Before Alastair could respond, St Simeon stepped back. 'You have a warrant, yes?'

'Of course,' Alastair said smoothly.

The young man stared at him. 'Well, where is it?'

'What?' Alastair said, genuinely puzzled.

'Your warrant. I assume you obtained a warrant. After all, the rule of law still applies, even in the Republic.'

'You want to see it?'

'People I've never met want to enter my house, interrogate my friends, and generally toss the furniture around. Of course I want to see the warrant.'

Alastair glared at the young man for several long seconds. He wanted to smash the boy's face, bury the impudent grin under his fist. Instead, he turned to Knight, beckoning for the warrant.

Knight pulled a stamped page from a folder and handed it to Alastair, who presented it to St Simeon.

By the light of Alastair's torch, St Simeon perused the piece of paper at his leisure, making a show of checking the stamped seal and signature at the bottom of the page.

'Is that Sooty's signature?' St Simeon said, an eyebrow raised.

'Sooty?' Alastair said, with the hapless feeling the situation was rapidly slipping from his control. He imagined Du Plessis and Klaasen in his position – they wouldn't have shown the same patience with this silver spoon reared toff.

'Justice Samuel Ashes. Or "Sooty" to my father. They play bridge a lot.'

'Really?' Alastair's hold on his temper loosened, and the itch behind his eyepatch stirred again.

'Really,' St Simeon said, grinning impudently. 'Well, if Sooty has signed off on this, I suppose it's all right to let you in. Do mind the furniture, though. My father will be awfully displeased if there's any damage.' He looked around Alastair and nodded to Knight and Lewisham. 'Do the hired help understand?'

Alastair bristled. St Simeon waved a hand, as if swatting away a fly.

'A little joke. Don't mind me. The times being what they

12

are, some levity never goes astray, don't you think?'

Alastair's glower was his only response.

'Suit yourself,' St Simeon said, clearly enjoying himself immensely. 'Well, then. Card.'

It took Alastair a moment to understand. 'Pardon?'

'Card, I said. Are you hard of hearing, man?' St Simeon grinned at him, his teeth white and straight. 'The 1966 Registration of Security Forces Act requires that all personnel tasked with surveillance activities must carry identification with them.' He cocked his head, looking at Alastair as if he was a strange species of insect. 'You haven't left your barracks without identification? Your commanding officer would be most displeased.' St Simeon tapped his cheek, thinking. 'Who is your commanding officer? Father might know him.'

'You spend your spare time reading the statute books, do you?' Alastair shifted slightly and turned to give Frieda a warning glare.

St Simeon's grin widened. 'I like to know my rights, as determined by the New People's Parliament. We are still a nation of laws, yes?'

Lewisham's face hardened and something in it gave St Simeon pause.

Alastair took his identification from inside his coat pocket and presented it to St Simeon.

'That really is a lot of names,' St Simeon said, looking from the card to Alastair's face, and back to the card. 'Column Leader Alastair Gordon Lethbridge-Stewart.'

That grin again, that impudent grin. The urge to punch St Simeon in the face was almost unbearable. Alastair slipped the card back into his pocket, aware that the situation seemed to have escaped his control.

'Well then,' St Simeon said, stepping aside. 'You might as well come in. But I can assure you there is nothing untoward happening upstairs.'

Alastair bulled his way inside, Knight and Lewisham following behind. The door closed with a heavy snick, and a thick silence, of old money and heavy furniture, descended over them in a solemn hush. Upstairs, music thudded distantly, a reminder of the size of the building.

'Where are your parents?' Alastair asked.

'You mean Father?' St Simeon said. 'With the People's Parliament not in session, he's at our family estate in the south east. Helping to increase the productivity of the agricultural sector, as per our Leader's requirements. Something about artificially inseminating cows, or such like.' He leered at Lewisham. 'He's also into inseminating the housemaids, if you get my meaning.'

Her glare would've frozen the sun, but only served to increase St Simeon's delight.

'We'll want to check the identification of everyone here,' Knight said.

'Absolutely.' St Simeon turned his gaze to Alastair. 'I take it the Column Leader will want to do so personally?'

'My team will assist,' Alastair said.

'I think not,' St Simeon said. He spread his hands. 'After all, we aren't under any suspicion, are we? I don't think a little music constitutes a threat to the Republic?'

'Is there something you'd rather we didn't see?' Knight asked.

'I'm an open book. But I think you strain the limits of your warrant if you think you can simply march in here and question everyone.' St Simeon rubbed his chin, attempting to look thoughtful. A smile of delight crossed his face.

'There is a middle ground. Perhaps the Column Leader would like to come upstairs. He can take a look around, see that the most revolutionary act on the premises is the alcohol content in the punch.'

Alastair took a hard look at St Simeon. He sensed, or perhaps hoped, that his smile had become more brittle.

'That seems a... reasonable proposition.' He raised a hand to forestall a protest from Knight and Lewisham. 'My people will remain here.' He let his hand rest on the holster of his weapon. 'I think I can take care of myself.'

He lifted the walkie-talkie to his mouth again and thumbed the switch. 'Cyclops One. Remain in place. We are beginning our search.'

A grunt of acknowledgement came through amidst the static.

'The South Africans we have recruited to the security services in recent times are a great help and comfort,' Alastair said.

If St Simeon was impressed by mention of the mercenaries, he didn't show it.

'I'll be sure to relay that to my father.'

'See that you do,' Alastair said. He smoothed his jacket, then indicated the stairs. 'Well then, do lead on. I am anxious to meet all your friends.'

The young man mounted the stairs, as Alastair spoke to his colleagues.

'Remain alert. These children think they're smarter than we are. We'll see.'

Ignoring the unhappy looks on their faces, Alastair turned from Knight and Lewisham and began climbing the stairs.

Heavy chairs surrounded a small table at the far end of the upstairs hallway, and paintings hung from the walls.

'All your guests are inside?' Alastair asked. He tried to ignore the portraits frowning down at him.

'One or two may've snuck off to... get to know each other a little more, but I'm sure everyone is well accounted.'

Alastair's remaining eye twitched. He jerked his hand towards the door. 'Let's get on with it.'

St Simeon stepped forward and opened the twin doors, pushing them forward with an extravagant heave. Cigarette smoke and music billowed out. Candlelight flickered in the new draft. Faces turned towards them, and it wasn't just the portraits that Alastair felt were judging him.

Men and women, roughly St Simeon's age, filled the room. Many held drinks, while all the men and a good proportion of the women smoked. *European cigarettes, no doubt*, Alastair thought. Their decadence increased his annoyance.

'We have a visitor,' St Simeon said, stepping aside to usher in Alastair.

Suddenly wishing Knight and Lewisham were with him, and increasingly aware how his pride had made him vulnerable, Alastair stepped into the drawing room.

He felt himself being sized up and found wanting. He cleared his throat, but before he could say anything, he heard a woman's soft laughter. As if that were a signal, the room erupted into conversation once again. The beat of a fast-paced song from a player in the corner rose into the dense fog of cigarette smoke.

'You'll have to forgive them, Column Leader,' St Simeon said.

He stood at Alastair's shoulder, uncomfortably close, on his blind side. That had to be deliberate, Alastair decided. He shifted, so he could see St Simeon fully.

'I have a valid warrant in my possession to interview each of your guests,' Alastair said, fuming silently at his treatment. 'I am doing you a favour by not ordering my people in here to conduct those interviews. Count yourself lucky.'

'Lucky?' St Simeon's smile dropped away. The effect was so startling Alastair nearly took a step back. St Simeon leaned in. 'My friends are accused of subversion on trumped up charges designed merely to insult my father. No doubt, a Party apparatchik dreamed them up. Is this what the Republic has become? Factional arguments that don't feed our people, or give them meaningful jobs, or allow them the freedoms their grandparents had?' St Simeon stopped himself with a visible effort. 'Stress reveals character, don't you think, Column Leader?'

Startled, Alastair nodded his agreement.

'Good. You wanted to interview my friends. Well, they're all yours.'

Alastair looked around the room. Tight knots of men and women talked avidly to each other. *They are young*, he thought, as he stepped into the room.

His repeated efforts to confirm the identities of the people in the room were rebuffed. Some simply turned their backs on him, while others claimed they couldn't hear his questions above the music. Around and around he went, growing increasingly frustrated, aware, oh so achingly aware, that behind their spoiled faces, they were laughing at him. He imagined Knight and Lewisham downstairs, and realised it was now too late to ask them up. The loss of face would be unbearable.

His frustration dissolved into a rising, familiar anger. Old despair swept over him, a feeling of being apart from everyone else. More and more the desire to scratch at his eyepatch grew. He suppressed it, and turned to the last knot of people, aware

16

that St Simeon's coolly cynical gaze was on him.

'I have a warrant to interview you,' Alastair said for the dozenth time.

'A what?' shouted a young woman into his ear. Her hair was swept up, and a cloud of cigarette smoke and strong perfume clung to her in a fragrant cloud. Her eyes were the brightest blue he had ever seen, and he found himself captured in them for a moment. A snort of laughter from someone in the group brought Alastair back to himself.

'A warrant,' he said, somewhat lamely.

'Fascinating,' drawled a man in a black suit standing opposite him. 'Under whose authority?'

'The Party,' Alastair bawled into the silence as the music, which had ascended into a long, crescendo, abruptly ended.

'Why, the Party is here,' some wit said. 'He's just a little man with a smaller gun,' said another voice. There was a moment of shocked silence, then gales of laughter filled the room.

Something snapped, then. In trying to be reasonable, to take into account the political sensitivities clearly inherent in the issuing of the warrant, Alastair had soft peddled the entire situation. Now it was out of hand. Now they were laughing at him. He couldn't tolerate that. He would never tolerate that. Ever.

'I will have your attention!' he shouted, his face flushed bright red.

'Where's your thugs?' The atmosphere in the room tightened, and Alastair felt the gaze of the men and women bore into him.

His earlier bravado in coming up with St Simeon by himself seemed to drain away, as water from a holed bucket. He felt a familiar sensation of panic scrambling around in his chest, a fox trying to claw its way free of a trap. Sweat broke on his brow, and Alastair saw a forest of faces grinning impudently at him. Somehow, his pistol was in his hand and he swung it side to side, a scowl consuming his face. The maddening itch behind his eyepatch worsened.

'Back,' he shouted, his control beginning to dissolve. His finger tightened on the trigger. 'Back, damn you, or I'll shoot.'

'He won't shoot,' St Simeon drawled.

17

Alastair saw the cocky look on his face, under that shock of blond hair. The sheer gall of the fellow was enough to break the dam in his chest. Alastair pointed the pistol to the ceiling and pulled the trigger. A shot rang out, and the pleasure he saw at the looks of shock around him was almost sexual. *This is control*, a voice whispered in his head, a voice that ominously sounded like his father's, as panicked cries rang out.

On hearing footsteps at the door, Alastair turned and saw Du Plessis and Klaasen enter, their weapons drawn. Knight and Lewisham followed at their heels.

'Just in time,' Alastair said, feeling his heartbeat slow. 'You've saved me from making a frightful mess.' He pointed his pistol at St Simeon. 'Take this one into custody. I want the names and addresses of everyone else.'

The atmosphere in the room took a sudden turn. The wave of derision that had almost swamped him hurriedly receded. The arrogance went with it, leaving behind a group of frightened partygoers. Du Plessis and Klaasen moved into the room, and the crowd of people bent away from them, like a tree in a storm. The two men made St Simeon look like a child. Almost tenderly, they each took him by an arm and led him, his feet nearly lifting off the floor, out of the room and downstairs. Lewisham and Knight remained, ready to take details.

'I trust no one will make this more unpleasant than it needs to be?' Alastair said, roughly holstering his pistol. His hands shook, so he jammed them into his trouser pockets. He began to walk around the room, as his companions collected information.

'No one? Not a one of you? Very good,' he said, something of his old confidence and control returning. He noticed the look of unease on Lewisham's face at his outburst, filed the memory for future reference.

'I assume some of you are wondering what happens next, yes? Good. It is always smart to wonder about the future. The Party requires forward thinking people to contribute to our continued standing in the world. It wouldn't do to dwell on what happened here tonight, or even to yearn for what some might call a past glory. That would be a very bad mistake. My colleagues are taking your names and addresses. Do be sure to be accurate with the information you are supplying. We do check, after all.'

Lewisham took a camera from her bag and began to use it. The camera clicked and clicked and clicked, the flash sending shadows crawling up the walls as blank faced participants stared at the lens.

'As for your absent friend. Well, don't count on seeing him any time soon, if you get my meaning.' Alastair barked a short, harsh laugh.

The woman nearest to him jumped in fright, and he felt a savage sense of satisfaction at her reaction. He went up to her and cupped her chin with one hand, now thankfully still. Her skin went white where he gripped her.

'Yes, I think you do, don't you?' He looked at Lewisham to gauge her reaction. Her face was carefully blank.

Alastair turned to the woman in front of him. Tears filled her eyes. The fox was back in his chest, though this time it wasn't panic that made it claw at him, but a savage need to strike out, to punish someone, anyone, for the way he had been treated.

With an effort, Alastair composed himself. He released the woman, who stumbled back to her friends, clutching her face. At random, Alastair pointed to five men and women.

'Knight. I want this sorry lot in the cells, pronto,' he said, his voice raised.

There was barely a murmur from the room. Knight nodded, and with Lewisham, began corralling the people Alastair has chosen at random towards the stairs and the waiting wagons below.

'As for the rest of you, I suggest you pack up and head home,' Alastair said into the silence.

Downstairs, the sound of doors slamming shut and engines starting drifted through the open front door.

'I also suggest that you think long and hard about the sort of people you associate with in the future. And the things you talk about. Your gilded lifestyles can quickly become gilded cages.' Alastair's lips quirking at his joke. Turning his heel on the sullen group, he descended the stairs at a clip.

He felt refreshed, invigorated.

19

CHAPTER THREE

LATER, ALONE in a narrow gallery behind a two-way mirror, Alastair took a moment to compose himself. Away from the party and the hyenas who had dared laugh at him, he felt renewed, his familiar uncertainties vanquished. He glanced at his reflection in the glass. A moody face stared back. He blinked, then focused on St Simeon.

Slumped over the table, St Simeon's face was a study in confused misery. Fluorescent lighting buzzed in a cage overhead, the flickering light sending St Simeon's shadow sprawling headlong across a wall. Alastair smirked. After the intolerable embarrassment he had suffered, he would get his own back tonight.

The door leading into the gallery opened on well-oiled hinges. The thump of distant generators echoed in the corridor. While the general population of London endured another scheduled power cut, the Security Directorate made sure the lights stayed on. Lewisham stood framed in the light from the corridor for a moment, before entering and closing the door. She stood beside Alastair and silently watched St Simeon through the glass.

'Not so impressive now, is he?' Alastair said, chest out and chin up.

'He's small fry,' Lewisham said, dismissively. 'Tonight was a waste of time, an exercise in intimidating a politician through his son. We're better than this petty nonsense.'

Alastair froze, his hands clasped tightly behind his back. His head turned, tracking like the turret on a tank. Lewisham glanced at him, but she didn't look intimidated.

'You know it's true, Colum Leader,' she said.

'I don't know anything of the sort,' he retorted. 'Nothing is too small to escape the notice of the Party.'

'Save the propaganda for the RBC,' Lewisham said, sighing heavily.

She reached into her jacket and pulled out a battered packet of cigarettes and a lighter. Without offering one to Alastair, she shook a cigarette loose and lit it with practiced ease. Drawing heavily on it, she closed her eyes and tilted her head back. Lines of exhaustion cut deep into the sides of her eyes, the corners of her mouth.

Smoke crawled from her nostrils as Lewisham exhaled. 'We're sitting on top of a volcano, Column Leader. We run around, plugging holes here, there and everywhere, hoping we can keep it under control long enough so we can hand the problem off to someone else. Someone brighter. More enthusiastic.' She sighed again, then pointed at the window with her cigarette. 'Look at him. He's nothing but a waste of space. He won't bring down the Republic. He's certainly no threat to the Party. We're just adding fuel to the fire.'

When Alastair refused to answer, Lewisham flashed him an unreadable look, then ground the cigarette out in the ashtray on the window ledge. The door opened, and Knight stepped inside.

'The other detainees are in their cells,' he said, grinning enthusiastically. 'Some of them blubbed for their mothers before we got them out of the wagons. There's a couple there who are ready to sell their own families out for a chance to see the sunlight tomorrow.' He saw Lewisham's look of disgust. 'Don't be a bleeding heart.' He exchanged a glance with Alastair. 'She's gone soft again, hasn't she?'

'Don't you start, Knight,' Lewisham said, stabbing a finger into his chest. His face tightened. 'I do my job just as well as you boys. Better, I reckon.' Lewisham glanced at Alastair. 'If you don't need me here, sir, I'd best be conducting one of the other interviews.'

Alastair nodded. 'I agree,' he said. He glanced at the mirror, watching the boy slumped at the table. 'I'll take a swing at our friend Georgie.'

'He doesn't look happy,' Knight said, grinning.

'Let's see if I can cheer him up, then,' Alastair said.

Lewisham shook her head, and stormed out of the door.

'Why do you keep her around?' Knight said, after the door had slammed shut.

Alastair shrugged. 'She reminds me of my brother's second.'

'Column Leader Kyle? Isn't she in Eastchester?'

'Yes, with James. Overseeing the installation of something called Operation: Mole-Bore.'

'Didn't you want that post?'

Alastair glanced at Knight. 'Be careful, Ben. I go where I am ordered. As do we all.'

Knight didn't respond, but Alastair saw his thoughts clear enough. Knight knew, as well as Alastair did, that he wouldn't let it go. Alastair wanted that command, that prestigious position. And he would have it. Just like he eventually had everything that once belonged to his brother.

Alastair looked at the closed door. 'And that's why Lewisham reminds me of Kyle. Both are damned good at their jobs. Their loyalty is unimpeachable.'

'Loyalty to the Republic.'

'Of course. Is there any other kind? Problem with Lewisham, though, is she just thinks we can achieve our aims without breaking the furniture.'

'But I do so love breaking the furniture,' Knight said, staring intently through the glass.

Alastair chuckled. 'Which is why you can watch.' He raised a hand to forestall Knight's complaint. 'Lewisham's right. St Simeon is a little fish in a big pond. His father will better heed the message the Party is sending if his son is still alive. He'll be more pliable in future, knowing how close his boy came to a stretch in a labour camp.'

Reluctantly, Knight nodded. Alastair left him in the viewing gallery and went next door to the cell.

'You're a damned bully,' St Simeon said, eyes red and face drawn, as Alastair entered the cell and closed the door. Despite his evident fear, St Simeon retained some of his bravado. 'You're the best the Republic can summon. A one-eyed thug?'

'What was it you said earlier, St Simeon?' Alastair made a show of rubbing his jaw, then broke into a smile. 'Oh yes, "stress reveals character". I've got that right?' He slammed both hands on the table, making St Simeon jump. 'How's this for stress, eh? Take a look around. Take a good look at where you are.' Alastair glanced around the stained concrete walls of the interrogation cell to emphasise his point. 'You're a no one, caught in no man's land, with no friends, no father, no money.' He smiled, watching St Simeon's eyes widen in fear. 'I've met men like you; brave fellows who think their privilege gives them the right to do and think whatever they want. The Republic doesn't need people like you, with your money and your contacts. The Party certainly has no time for indolent children. No one would notice if you vanished, not even Daddy. Despite his inexplicable affection for you, he knows well enough to keep his trap shut.' Alastair leaned in, smiling. 'Unless he feels the pressing need to end up in the same shallow grave as his son?'

The blood drained from St Simeon's face. Alastair felt a surge of satisfaction that was almost blinding. He felt ten feet tall, and St Simeon just a child, cowering before him with tears in his eyes.

This is power, he thought. *This is... control.* His voice dropped, becoming almost conversational.

'You're nothing, did you know that? A nobody. No one would miss you, not really. Even Daddy would come to terms with it. After all, what choice would he have? Think on this, while you rot in here. I can make you disappear, did you know that? Just. Like. This.' Alastair raised his hand before St Simeon's face and snapped his fingers, the sharp sound like bone breaking.

St Simeon blinked, and his shoulders sagged. He looked away, the fringe of lank blond hair falling into his eyes. 'What do you want to know?' he mumbled.

'What do I want to know?' Alastair glanced briefly at the two-way mirror. He sensed Knight behind the glass, and favoured him with a triumphant smile. 'Everything, my boy. Everything.'

Despite the power cut, and the lateness of the hour, Benjamin Knight knew where to go to burn off some excess energy. Alastair had turned his offer of a drink down, and truth be told, while he liked the dour column leader, Knight could do without his presence tonight. There was something about him, some deep-seated sadness that made Knight wary of him. Certainly, he thought they got on well, but the look in Alastair's eye while he worked over the boy didn't make him a fit companion.

And Knight remembered. Remembered nine years ago when he first met Alastair; only back then he had two eyes and a moustache. He'd been different. Barely a hint of the man he had since come to know. Knight had heard rumours, rumours of an imposter posing as the brother of then-Major James Lethbridge-Stewart. Knight assumed that's who he had met, it was the only thing that made sense. Knight wasn't privy to the details, but he'd pieced a few things together since being assigned to the column leader's team. That imposter, that other Alastair Lethbridge-Stewart, he was long gone. And without him, finally, the real Alastair Lethbridge-Stewart had risen through the ranks. Of course, and Knight would never speak this out loud, there were still discrepancies. Not least the age; Alastair as he was now was the same age as the imposter had been *eight* years ago.

Knight put it down to one of those things he'd never truly know the answer to. And that was okay. He was an officer in RSF, he didn't need to know the answers to everything. As long as he did his duty and remained loyal to the Glorious Leader.

Knight considered dropping in on *The Revolutionary Arms*, but decided he wanted something a bit more fast paced. There was a nightclub, only for security forces, that he knew was open despite the power cut. A brisk ten-minute walk through the darkened streets of inner London, and he was soon clattering down the steps to a barred door.

'Identification,' said a voice. A pair of suspicious eyes glared out through a rectangle cut in the door.

Knight sighed. 'Come on, Charlie, you know who I am.'

The eyes narrowed. 'Identification,' said the voice again.

Knight grumbled, made a show of patting down his jacket, then pulled out his warrant card.

'Satisfied?' he asked, slipping the card back into a pocket.

'Very,' said the voice. There were several clanks as bolts were thrown, then the door opened, spilling out light and cigarette smoke. A hulking figure in dark trousers and a tight fitting skivvie confronted Knight. 'Sir,' Charlie said, touching his fingers to his temple.

'None of that nonsense now, Charlie,' Knight said, patting the man on the shoulder. 'We're off duty, after all.' He paused. 'Any Resistance members inside tonight?'

'If there are,' Charlie said, his face splitting into a smile. 'They've not announced themselves yet.'

'Good show.' Knight stepped inside. A corridor ran under the building. 'If you can see they don't raid the place tonight, that would be much appreciated. I need a drink, not a bomb down my pants.'

Charlie nodded, unsure how serious to take Knight's comment. After all, the Resistance were a known quantity. It wouldn't do to have an illegal nightclub, patronised exclusively by members of the security forces, bombed by the very people they had pledged to defeat.

Knight headed down the corridor. The weight of the building over-head pressed low. Legend had it that the nightclub pre-dated the Revolution, and had similarly catered for members of the military of that time. Knight smirked. The only thing that had changed, it seemed, was the uniform its guests wore.

Jazz music drifted towards him as he reached an open doorway. Jazz, of course, was illegal in the Republic. Knight had been young when the Africans residing in Britain had been rounded up and shipped to the Caribbean, but he could still remember some of the Leader's broadcast justifying the decision. Words like 'decadent' and 'filth' stood out. He didn't have any friends at the time who were black; in fact, didn't know anyone who was black. But he did know he would miss the music if the Party successfully suppressed it.

He nodded to the barman, a burly figure wearing a cloth cap.

'Harry,' Knight called above the music, which came from a stereo illegally imported from Imperial Japan. 'Scotch,' he said.

Harry nodded and moved away to get a glass.

'Something new on the player,' he said, as Harry slid the glass in front of him. Knight passed over a note.

Harry nodded. 'Got a parcel from a friend in Paris,' he said. Everyone knew Harry had contacts right across the Continent – half the liquor on display behind the bar was ordinarily banned from Britain, ostensibly to protect the local industry, but really to ensure that the Party maintained a control on the revenues from local production.

Knight raised his glass. 'Well, my thanks to your taste and contacts,' he said. Harry nodded again, then moved down the bar.

Knight closed his eyes for a moment, savouring the smoky flavour pouring down his throat. Then, he swung around and surveyed the room. There were about twenty people, men and women. Two couples swayed together to the music from the stereo, while several others lined the bar. There were more couples occupying the booths running along the back wall, their furtive activities rendered private by the dim lighting and the active disinterest of the other guests.

Calling this bolthole beneath an empty building a nightclub was perhaps too much of a stretch, Knight decided. What it did do was provide a welcome respite from the endless discipline of the Security Directorate and Alastair's moods. Knight enjoyed his work, more than enjoyed it, in fact. He revelled in the power that came with the uniform. But he was acutely aware that the column leader's personality was brittle, prone to lashing out. It wore at him. So, the cure was this place, somewhere he could be alone with a drink. And who knew, something better might offer itself if he waited long enough.

'Hello, sailor.'

Knight glanced to his left. A woman stood at the bar, looking at him. He hadn't noticed her arrive, but he certainly did now. A tight-fitting jacket over a white blouse, with a knee length skirt that hugged slim hips. He caught a scent of perfume, a sweet smell that did much to offset the cigarette smoke in the room.

'Security Directorate,' Knight said. 'Not the navy.'

'Really?' the woman said, looking him up and down. 'Didn't take you for one of the breakers.' She referred to the Directorate by one of its many nicknames.

'We come in all shapes and sizes,' Knight said. After a

moment, he smiled, and the woman gave him one in return. 'Benjamin Knight,' he said, setting down his drink and extending his hand.

She took it, and he felt the soft warmth of her skin. It was like an electric shock up his arm.

'Alice Winters,' she said.

'Service?'

'Women's Auxpol.'

'The Harpies?' Knight's smile widened.

Winters nodded.

'Most of them look like hard-faced harridans,' Knight said.

'And I don't?'

'Absolutely not.'

'Good to hear,' Winters said. Her smile deepened. 'Would you like a top up?'

'I would,' Knight decided, surprised at how quickly he had finished it. He turned to wave at Harry, but Winters placed a hand on his arm.

'Let me,' she said, signing to the barman.

Knight watched Harry hesitate, glancing between Winters and himself.

'Oh, don't worry about it, Harry,' Knight called out. 'What are they calling it now – that's right – Female Emancipation, or some nonsense. If she wants to order for me, she can pay for me as well.'

Harry nodded, and turned away to get them their drinks.

The two exchanged small talk, until Harry returned. They clinked their glasses together.

'Cheers,' Knight said, swallowing a mouthful. The Scotch burned pleasantly down his throat, and he felt the warmth spreading through his chest. He sighed and closed his eyes for a moment.

'Tough day?' Winters asked.

He opened his eyes, and found hers locked on him. In the half-light, they seemed bottomless.

'Aren't they all?' Knight said. He took another drink. The Scotch was really quite good, he decided.

'Amen,' Winters said. She watched him over her glass, and Knight found himself enjoying the attention.

'What?' he said.

'You've the look of a man who wanted to get something done tonight, but wasn't allowed. Am I right?'

'I'm not sure how comfortable I feel about people reading my mind,' Knight said, feeling a flush creep up his neck. 'But, yeah, you've hit the nail on the head.'

'The chain of command isn't all it's cracked up to be.' Winters swallowed a mouthful of her drink. They looked at each other for a moment, and then they both started laughing.

'Shall we go somewhere?' Winters asked Knight, though it wasn't really a question.

'Yes,' Knight heard himself say. He felt a little woozy now, and the heat in his chest had turned cold. He rubbed his cheek, and was surprised to find it numb. With fumbling fingers, he placed his glass back on the bar. Harry was there already, and scooped it up. He stepped back, watching Winters.

'Harry's taken a shine to you,' Knight said, chuckling.

He wasn't sure why he did that. Laughter didn't come with the job. He felt Winters' hand on his chin, turning his head towards her.

'Let's get you home,' Winters said, slipping an arm around his waist. 'Or would you prefer mine?' She glanced coyly up at him.

Knight laughed again, the sound distant and strange. The music sounded attenuated, the notes were even looser than before. The room seemed to elongate itself, and the floor tilted like a ship in a heavy swell.

'Have you... Have you drugged me?' Knight asked, his words barely a mumble.

'Come on now, big fella,' Winters said, helping Knight towards the corridor. A few of the patrons turned to look, some leering at Winters as she manhandled Knight towards the exit. Charlie opened the door and stepped aside, and then they were clambering up the steps.

'This isn't... This isn't right,' Knight said, but there was little he could do.

His thoughts, like his feet, kept stumbling in one direction, and now the numbness had extended into his chest and arms. The last thing he saw, as they emerged onto the street and the darkness swamped him, was a vehicle pulling up beside them. A door slid open, and then he was gone.

CHAPTER FOUR

LATER, WITH St Simeon's broken sobs still echoing in his mind, Alastair stood in a bathroom staring over the basin at his reflection in the mirror. Despite his glee at turning the tables on St Simeon, the taste of victory was like acid in his mouth. Despite his earlier resistance, St Simeon had crumbled too easily. The rage Alastair felt at the way he was treated at the party still bubbled in his chest and left him searching for an outlet.

He lifted his eyepatch, and focused in on the ruptured socket beneath. It was a constant source of irritation, of anger, that he couldn't even remember why and how he'd lost his eye. He'd asked James about it many a time, and his brother always, without fail, changed the subject. Except one time, when he was so annoyed by Alastair's incessant questioning, that James had told him to ask Father. And still, years later, he hadn't – couldn't. To even question Father would be to call into question the very idea of Alastair's loyalty. One day he would ask, one day he would find out.

It was just another mystery surrounding his childhood, the childhood he barely remembered. And for now, that served him well. It fuelled his anger. He shook his head, no longer willing to look at his sallow features. He replaced the eyepatch and turned away from the mirror. The green tiles rendered the quality of the light from the single bulb hanging overhead murky and strange. *Just like me*, Alastair thought, mordantly. Running the tap, he splashed his face with water before turning it off.

Reluctantly, he looked into the mirror again. St Simeon's face stared back. They would detain St Simeon for a few days, enough time for him to consider his fate should he break the rules again. Not to mention the effect on the boy's father. In Alastair's experience, any length of time spent in the cells beneath Leconfield House would be a lifelong lesson against dabbling with the democracy movement.

The door cracked open and a dark-haired section leader – Alastair couldn't remember her name – ducked her head in and snapped off a salute.

'Column Leader? Division Leader Pemberton wants to see you. Pronto.'

'Very good,' Alastair said, hiding his sudden anxiety by mopping his face with a piece of paper towel. Scrunching it into a ball, he tossed it into an overflowing bin. The door swung shut, and he glanced again at the mirror, hoping it would only reveal his face. To his relief, it did.

Straightening his uniform, Alastair exited the bathroom and made his way to Pemberton's office.

At this late hour, a skeleton staff kept the Leconfield House ticking over. Most of the building was in darkness. Even with the generators, it made sense to save fuel during the energy crisis gripping the nation. Winter had come early and savagely across the country. Alastair had read the reports of people dying in their homes due to hypothermia. Those same reports also recorded instances of rioting in some of the major cities, caused by extreme coal rationing, which were put down by the use of live rounds. *Firing into the mob is perfectly justified*, Alastair thought. *Nothing taught fear like fear itself.*

He entered the outer office. A section leader sat behind a desk, reading a report. The woman, a severe looking harridan who looked Alastair up and down reprovingly, buzzed Pemberton's intercom. There was a quick exchange of words, and then she indicated the inner door with a nod of her head.

Alastair stepped up to the door and knocked. There was a delay. A poster on the wall to his right caught his attention. UNITY IS STRENGTH it boasted, the words superimposed over the face of the Leader. He felt the eyes boring into him, had a half-remembered memory of a flickering image in a darkened room. Sweat broke out on his forehead. Hastily, Alastair wiped it away with the heel of his hand, then he heard a grunted summons on the other side of the door.

He opened it and entered.

'Shut it, please.'

Alastair swiftly closed the door. He took two steps forward, stopped, saluted, and then stood at attention, waiting.

A severe looking man sat behind the desk. Black hair carefully smoothed back from a high forehead, revealed a widow's peak pointing down to an intense pair of sunken eyes that stared intently at a report open before him. High cheekbones, thin lips and a generally disapproving air lent the final touch of austerity.

Alastair waited, gaze straight ahead. The office matched its master – Spartan to the point of bare. A portrait of the Leader hung on the wall opposite Alastair. It was a more recent image than the one outside - the Leader out of his traditional military uniform, instead wearing a suit, a white carnation in the lapel of a black, double-breasted jacket. There was still speculation within the Party as to the exact meaning behind the change.

'At ease, Lethbridge-Stewart.'

'Sir. You wanted to see me, Division Leader?'

'Tell me, Lethbridge-Stewart.'

'Sir?'

'I have a list of names in front of me. Revolutionaries, hoarders, democrats.' Pemberton almost spat out the last word. 'If you ask me, they're just fancy words for parasites. It's my job to determine their fate.' He looked up at Alastair for the first time. The skin beneath those sunken eyes was smudged black. Reputedly, Pemberton got by on less than three hours of sleep a night. 'What fate do you think is appropriate?'

'Execution,' Alastair said promptly.

Pemberton's lambent eyes bored into him. 'Very good, Lethbridge-Stewart. It's easier, executing them. A bullet, a burial, and then we can move on to better things.' The division leader looked down at the file and sighed. 'Sadly, labour shortages mean I can't follow your sterling advice, more's the pity. A good execution usually stiffens the spines of the men,' he said, unconsciously echoing Alastair's earlier thoughts.

He picked up a pen, ticked a box, and signed the bottom

of the page. He closed the folder and dropped it into a basket. Pemberton glanced up at Alastair and waved him towards a chair.

'Take a seat, Lethbridge-Stewart; you're cluttering up the place.'

Unsure whether to chuckle or not, Alastair covered up his discomfiture by dropping into the proffered chair. He straightened his jacket and looked up at Pemberton.

'How long have you been with the RSF?'

'Almost twenty years, sir.' It was an immediate response, and although he knew it was true, there was always a sense of a lie buried in there.

'Any duty overseas?'

Pemberton's voice brought him out of his musings.

'In the Middle East. That business at Aden…'

'Ah yes, the Expeditionary Force. Got a bit desperate, didn't it?'

'It did, sir. I led several punishment raids to suppress the local population. We came through in the end.'

'Punishment raids? Jolly good show. We could use a dose of that here at home.'

Alastair nodded in agreement. Pemberton picked up another file and opened it. Alastair wasn't surprised to see a black and white headshot of himself pinned to the front page.

'Ever since you came across to the Security Directorate, Lethbridge-Stewart, you've been a very good officer. Very good. Your advice has proved invaluable. And your willingness to get your hands dirty does you credit.' Pemberton thumbed through the report and shot a glance at Alastair. 'Very dirty, indeed.'

Pemberton rubbed his fingers and closed the report. 'I understand you've been angling for a promotion. You've taken the courses, passed with flying colours, really.' He paused, then smiled. 'I don't think you'd like to read the psych evaluation. No matter. Regardless of what a pointy-headed boffin might think, I need strong men like you. Still… that promotion. It can't be done… at this time.' Pemberton raised an index finger to forestall the protest hovering on Alastair's lips. 'My preference would be to agree to a promotion. But…' He shook his head, as if contemplating something he had tracked into his house on his boots. 'There are… sensitivities. I trust you'll understand. Your father's position in the Party and as Director of ExSec… At this moment, there are factions within the higher reaches that would look disapprovingly at any promotion for his son. With the Security Directorate being part of ExSec, Director Hipwood hates our existence. She thinks all the security organisations should be her exclusive domain.'

'That's unfair,' Alastair exploded, half rising from his seat.

'Life's unfair, Column Leader,' Pemberton shot back. 'Don't make a fool of yourself, boy.' The last word stung. 'Sit down.'

Breathing hard, Alastair did as he was told.

'You must practice patience, Lethbridge-Stewart.' Pemberton's sallow face assumed a sober look. 'For now, though, keep working, keep your head down, and the rewards will follow.'

Rewards? It was all Alastair could do not to scream in Pemberton's face. His damned father… Despite what Gordon Lethbridge-Stewart said, he continued to stand in Alastair's way. His Chosen Son! That's what James always called Alastair. He argued, said that Gordon Lethbridge-Stewart cared as much for James as he did Alastair. Each of them were tools to be used.

'Not you, Alastair. Ever since he first…'

James never finished that sentence. But in Alastair's mind it ended '…laid eyes on you'.

Alastair nodded, his mouth set in a grim line, all the better to keep the words safely inside. What else could he do? To even think of voicing his opinion would be a display of disloyalty that would cost him his life.

He would have to find another way to Eastchester. And he would. Even if that meant removing James himself.

Pemberton nodded. 'I want you in at ten-hundred tomorrow. I've more work for you and your team. Dismissed.'

Alastair stood. His face was carefully blank, but fury raged behind the mask. He saluted, turned on his heel and walked to the door.

'Alastair?' Pemberton called. Alastair paused and turned. 'The Republic faces some of its greatest threats since the

Revolution. It is up to men like you and me to safeguard it from those whose purity is less than it seems. Now is not the time to crack. Now is the time for strength, strength of unity and strength of purpose. Do you understand?'

'Perfectly, sir. Perfectly.' Alastair nodded, then left the room, closing the door softly behind him.

'I need a stiff drink,' he muttered.

The section leader looked up. 'Sir?'

'Eyes front, Section Leader,' Alastair barked. He swore inwardly, then marched through the outer door.

His need to be anywhere but there was urgent.

CHAPTER FIVE

A STROBING amber light, thick as treacle, briefly woke Knight from his slumber. Before the darkness pulled him back into its jealous grasp, he felt a choking pressure in his mouth and throat. He thrashed about, but a sticky, warm embrace, restricted his movements. The last thing he saw before darkness swallowed him was a grinning nightmare staring back at him with cataract-filmed eyes.

The next image was little better. The warm stickiness deafened him and numbed his sense of touch. It pressed on his eyeballs when his eyelids fluttered open, distorting his vision, enough to render the thing staring at him even more horrible. A face, denuded of skin; eyes staring starkly from bone white orbits; a hairless head and a grinning mouth with no lips. He struggled, but his limbs were slow and heavy. He sensed he was naked, but then his consciousness failed and he was dragged back into the dark.

The next time, the creature stared back at him. The striated musculature hid behind a pallid rind of skin, hairless and smooth. The eyes had colour and despite the lack of intellect within them, Knight sensed a kinship that sent a thrill of horror through him.

His hands lifted before his eyes, and it was then he realised he was floating in some sort of tank. He lashed out again in panic, and his fingers clawed futilely on the inside of a curved tube. A light blinked on and he felt the temperature of the fluid encasing him drop, taking all sensation with it.

Knight's eyes fluttered open an interminable time later. His eyesight had improved, and he could make out other canisters around his. In one, a familiar looking grotesquely fat figure of a man caught his attention. Before he could focus on it, he sensed a shape hovering just outside his eye line, but try as he might, he couldn't get his body to turn.

It was then he realised two things – that a harness held him upright, and that a tube, descending from above, was forced between his teeth and into his throat. Dimly, he thought he heard muffled sounds. The fuzziness of earlier seemed to be lifting, and with it, a heightened sense of where he was, or, more accurately, where he wasn't.

He looked around, and saw the other figure staring back at him. Like him, it was suspended in a tube filled with liquid. A black, organic looking tube emerged from its mouth, rising into the 'lid' topping the canister. This time, the eyes were filled with intelligence and watched him hungrily.

Again, a light blinked on, but just before the cold could drag him down, Knight realised with a horrifying shudder exactly who was looking at him.

Himself.

CHAPTER SIX

THERE WERE efforts early to create an ideology around which the Party could coalesce. Sympathetic writers from the Left, who joined the movement after Mosely's murder, found themselves co-opted into writing dry dissertations on the broken relationship between capital and labour. Other efforts were more ludicrous, including one pamphlet that argued for a grand bargain between the property owning and working classes, which would be achieved if only their representatives met to meditate at Stonehenge during the Winter Solstice.

All these attempts fell afoul of the grim reality of the Party's very nature. Unlike all the other political organisations in the world that embrace a name to indicate their intent, the Party is simply the Party. It does not exist to tilt at ideological windmills, nor does it fashion itself into a weapon to confront an equal and opposite menace. Indeed, with the death of Communism in its Russian cradle in 1921, there was no great beast of the Left for it to confront. No, the real reason the Party exists is this: to gain power, retain that power, and wield it in such a manner as to cow and break any resistance to it in society. The exercise of that power is there for all to see, should they be willing enough to do so. The labour camps that run the length of the Republic form a sort of archipelago containing the broken remnants of those who thought society could exist in a different, more just form.

From 'An Unpublishable Memoir' by [redacted]. Retained in the Security Directorate Archives.

Alastair left the office and walked down a flight of stairs. The concierge, a grey-haired old section leader, who claimed to have served in the Great War, dozed at his station. Given the approaches to Leconfield House were blanketed by security cameras festooned to the front of the building which were monitored night and day in a secure bunker below street level, Alastair was less than concerned. He considered ringing the bell on the desk out of spite, then decided it wasn't worth the effort. He exited into Curzon Street.

Buttoning his jacket against the cold, Alastair glanced up at the sky.

With most of London swathed in darkness, he had difficulty making out the indistinct bulk of barrage balloons, tethered by steel cables to concrete blocks. The three arrowed symbol of the Republic regime was dimly visible on the side of the nearest balloon. Alastair long ago convinced himself the balloons were a less than subtle reminder to the populace of the Party's dominance and rule. As above, so below. He shrugged mentally; it was of little concern to him how the regime maintained its control, only that it did.

His conversation with Pemberton unsettled him. Rationally, he understood his commanding officer's reasoning, but that didn't calm his anger. Once again, his father's needs came before his own.

It did mean he'd have to find another way to take command at Eastchester. Perhaps, if he could sabotage James' command, sabotage Operation: Mole-Bore itself, he could then push himself into that position. And why not? He knew all too well, opportunities were only there for those willing to take them. First, though, one had to *make* the opportunities available. He would give it more thought.

Going straight to his lonely flat and contemplating the frustration of his plans made Alastair feel ill. Adjusting his cap, he looked up and down the street. Posters were pasted every few yards, proclaiming the unity and strength of the Republic. A few people scurried along the opposite footpath; none thought it wise to be on the same side of the street as the oppressive entrance to the Security Directorate, especially with the thicket of cameras placed along its width. Alastair smiled, briefly, then decided he did indeed need a drink.

He left the unimpressive bulk of Leconfield House behind him and walked briskly toward Half Noon Street, which he turned down before exiting into Piccadilly. A pair of tottering old buses trundled past, belching fumes into the night. Waving his hand to clear the air, Alastair crossed New Constitution Hill to Spur Road. He saw *The Revolutionary Arms* up the road, still open, with twinkling lights in the windows.

Inside, lit candles stood on tables and shelves, providing warm, if not bright, lighting. The pleasant scent of wax hung thick in the air. The honey-coloured light added an old time feel to the space. Alastair silently commended the publican for his industry.

The Revolutionary Arms had a notorious reputation as an early hotbed of republican sentiment, when the idea of toppling the monarchy and democracy was considered by many to be a nonsense. Early meetings barely had a dozen men in attendance. As the economic circumstances of the '30s grew worse, though, attendance increased until it spilled out into the street. Fuelled by more than a few drinks, fights broke out between democrats and those who knew the nation cried out for a new direction. These brawls turned into running street battles through London, further undermining the government's claim to safeguarding its citizens. The meeting that proclaimed the Leader's ascension after Mosely's assassination occurred in the room Alastair had just entered.

Exchanging a nod with the barman, Alastair ordered a pint of bitter. A moment's work at the hand pump and the barman presented Alastair with his drink. Dropping a few coins on the bar, Alastair murmured his thanks. He took the glass and went over to an empty booth.

He noted a figure sitting in the next booth, obscured by shadows. Caught up in his frustration at Pemberton's decision, Alastair didn't think to look harder. Instead, he sank into the worn leather seat and stewed over what Pemberton had said about his prospects for a promotion.

'Nepotism,' Alastair thought. 'That's what Pemberton wanted to say but didn't.' He smiled humourlessly.

For all the fear that Pemberton generated, the division leader knew crossing Alastair's father with talk like that would see his own career ended.

Alastair turned the glass around and around, brooding. *It*

doesn't matter, he thought. *My time will come.* After all, he knew enough that if he went to his father with a complaint, his father would laugh in his face. And if he complained to Pemberton more forcefully, Alastair knew he'd be sent back to running a punishment labour camp, only this time on a remote rock like the Isle of Mull.

Grimacing, Alastair picked up his glass and took a sip. Despite his resentment, the beer was a balm against the anger he nursed. He felt the knot in his chest loosen a little. By nature not a strong drinker, he still appreciated the chance to unwind a little.

He stared into the fire. After the chill outside, he was glad for the warmth. He loosened his tie a little and took another sip. Setting down the glass, he glanced around the room.

This close to the New People's Parliament, Alastair wasn't surprised about the revolutionary regalia festooning the walls and ceiling. A black and white photograph of the burning of Westminster hung behind the bar. He could see the crowds at one end of the old Palace, watching as great columns of smoke rose into the air. He felt a vague thrill at the image – the cleansing of the stables, he remembered an old tutor saying. Other relics hung around the close confines – one wall was lined with framed images of Mosley from the 1930s, while banners and flags bearing the three-pointed arrow, the symbol of the State, hung from the rafters. There were newspaper posters behind glass frames, many proclaiming the party motto, fading black and white photographs of men in suits, meeting and shaking hands. There was even a photograph of the Leader in, what Alastair realised with a start, was this very pub, standing behind the bar and pulling a beer for a laughing apparatchik. Indeed, everyone around the Leader was laughing.

'Impressive, isn't it?' The voice startled Alastair.

He turned, craning his neck, and was surprised to see a woman seated by herself behind him.

'Pardon?'

'That photograph, above the bar.' She nodded in the direction of the picture of Westminster ablaze.

Alastair smelled a heady mix of cigarette smoke and perfume. It put him in mind of the party he had raided.

'It is,' he said, somewhat lamely. He returned to his drink, turning the glass around and around on the table.

He heard a rustle of clothing, then a shadow fell over him. Startled, he looked up, and saw a striking woman standing beside him, a glass in one hand and a cigarette in the other.

'May I?' she asked.

Alastair heard one of the nearby patron's snigger. He turned his head, trying to find the source, but no one looked at him. Glancing up at the woman, he coughed, and nodded.

'Yes,' he said. He sat straighter as she slid into the seat opposite him.

Her dark hair was short; cut in what Alastair understood was the modern trend. She wore a light green jacket with a matching skirt. No watch, or rings, or other adornments. Then her eyes lifted, and his breath caught in his throat.

Her eyes were dark, almost violet, the corners tilted to form an almond shape that made them strangely exotic. Her cheekbones were high, and she wore red lipstick that had to have come from overseas. It said something about her that she was prepared to pay over the odds due to the Party's high tariff wall.

'Who do you work for?' he asked, suspicious, yet intrigued.

'What a strange question,' she said. 'The government, of course.'

'Everyone works for the government,' Alastair pointed out.

She laughed, a high bright sound at odds with the mood of the pub. 'You are a funny one,' she said, tapping ash from the end of her cigarette into an ashtray. She leaned forward. 'I work as a liaison between several government research facilities and the Directorate of Energy.'

'Hush hush?' he asked, leaning forward.

She pursed her lips and tilted her head one way, then the other. 'Not really. I mean, I have security clearance, but I'm never near anything important. I'm just a research assistant. Really, I make coffee and file paperwork. All the interesting stuff is done downstairs. Underground.'

Alastair froze for a moment, his mind casting back decades. Something of his reaction must have registered on his face, since her eyes widened a little. Stabbing pain and flickering

41

images on a wall...

He rubbed his lips with a finger to distract himself, and then smiled.

'All that science nonsense,' he said. 'Unless it's designed to protect the homeland, what's its purpose?'

She looked at him in silence for a moment, then broke into a brilliant smile. 'That's exactly what I once said to Daddy,' she said, reaching out and grabbing his hand. It was warm and soft, Alastair realised.

'He works there?' Alastair said. He thought about removing his hand from under hers, but found that he couldn't. 'Your father, I mean.'

'Oh no. Daddy passed away some years ago. He was far too practical for what he called' – she waved her hand in the air – '"that airy-fairy stuff". No, he was a manager in the Directorate of Works. Shuffled people and paper around. Pretty impressive for a one-time valleys' boy.'

Alastair thought the girl a little empty headed, but found himself entranced by her. A warning bell went off in his head, but he ignored it.

'And you?' she said, nodding to his armband. 'Who do you work for?'

'Ahh,' Alastair said. He sat back, his hand slipping free of hers. While he took a sip from his glass, he toyed with the idea of lying to her. The Directorate wasn't a secret organisation, after all, but elements of it were. Still...

'I'm an officer in the Security Directorate,' he said. 'Alastair Lethbridge-Stewart. We're part of External Affairs.'

'External Affairs?' Her forehead crinkled. 'Your father isn't...?'

It was Alastair's turn to frown. 'He is,' he said, his tone closing off that part of the conversation.

The girl's eyes narrowed, then they widened.

'You're not a spy?'

Alastair surprised himself by laughing. 'Hardly,' he said. 'Think of me as an... odd job's man.'

'What, like a handyman?' She smiled. Then her forehead crinkled. 'I thought the Directorate of Internal Affairs handled that sort of thing. Don't you all end up stepping on each other's toes?'

Alastair nodded. The turf wars between the Internal Affairs and External Security were legendary. And bloody.

'It's a complicated dance,' he said. 'Let's leave it at that.'

The girl pouted, as if someone had taken away an especially nice toy from her. But then her face relaxed into a grin.

'Off duty, then?' she asked. 'Or are you chasing the Resistance tonight, Alastair?' Her voice was playful, though her eyes had become guarded. No surprise there, Alastair thought.

He turned the glass in his hands. 'One of my rare nights off.'

'Married to the job?' she said playfully.

Alastair smiled. 'All the responsibilities and none of the rewards.'

To his surprise, the girl laughed.

'I know how that feels,' she said. She ground her cigarette out in the ashtray. Slim flingers plucked another one from the packet in her purse.

A sudden thought occurred to him.

'Sorry,' he said, leaning forward over his drink. 'I didn't catch your name.'

'No,' she said, lighting the cigarette. Smoke wreathed her head. 'You didn't.' She inhaled deeply, her bewitching eyes focused on Alastair. 'Wright,' she said, smiling. Her teeth were very white. 'Sally Wright.'

Later, Alastair awoke to the distant sound of sirens. It sounded very much like screaming, the rise and fall of the damned wailing at their fate. Panic clawed at him and he felt himself tangled in the sheets. It was only when he felt a warm presence beside him that he realised where he was.

He settled back. His heart calmed and he closed his remaining eye. An unfamiliar feeling, a feeling that another person would instantly recognise, came over him. Contentment.

He slept.

Alastair awoke with a start. Light streamed through the bedroom window. He sensed a presence in the room and immediately reached for the bedside table closest to him. He heard a throaty chuckle and froze. Squinting, he saw a figure seated beside the window. She wasn't wearing anything.

'Sally?'

'I'm sure I'm not the doorman,' she said. She ran a hand over her stomach. 'Don't have the paunch, for starters,' she added, whispering conspiratorially.

Despite his embarrassment, Alastair couldn't help but laugh.

'You'll have to forgive me,' he said. 'This isn't something… I usually engage in.'

'Really?' Sally said. She stretched, arching her back provocatively. 'You could've fooled me.' The look in her eyes raised the hairs on the back of Alastair's neck.

'I… ah… I don't know what to say to that.'

'Don't say anything.'

Sally glanced out of the window at the early morning sunlight. Cars rumbled in the street and the distant chatter of pedestrians rose to the third floor flat.

When she turned back, Alastair was rubbing the skin around his ruined eye.

'You've not asked me about… this?' Alastair said, vaguely waving at his eyepatch.

'Did you want me to ask?' Sally asked.

'…No,' Alastair said, though it came out more as an uneasy question than a statement.

'Good then. Give it time, though, and I'm sure you'll tell me all about it.'

'Time? So, you want to see me again?' Alastair blushed.

Looking at him, Sally tilted her head. Alastair found himself lost in those dark eyes. 'Why wouldn't I?'

She didn't give Alastair time to respond. Instead, she rose from the chair and crossed over to the bed. Soon, answering her question was the last thing on Alastair's mind.

CHAPTER SEVEN

LATER, AFTER Sally had risen, dressed and left, Alastair laid in bed, his head and shoulders propped against the headboard. Before she slipped out of the door, Sally had agreed to a dinner date later in the week. Alastair replayed the events of the previous evening in his mind and smiled, briefly. Glancing across at the clock on the bedside table, he swore. He was late for his meeting at Leconfield House.

After a hasty shower and an even quicker coffee, Alastair let himself out of his Pimlico flat. He considered catching a bus, but a quick glance at the long queue at the nearby stop indicated they weren't running to schedule.

'Again,' he said. He noted a few uneasy glances in his direction. Nothing new, after all, he was in uniform. Then he remembered waking to the sound of sirens.

A feeling of excitement trickled through him. He turned smartly on his heel and began walking.

Inside Leconfield House, last night's quiet had been replaced by a whirlwind of activity. Lewisham was camped in Alastair's office. Of Knight, there was no sign. Lewisham held a manila folder, which she wordlessly handed to Alastair.

'Where's Knight?' he asked, settling behind his desk.

'He's not in,' Lewisham said. 'You need to read this.' She handed the folder to Alastair.

Something in her eyes made Alastair's spine tingle.

'What's happened?' he said, slapping the folder down on his desk.

'Terrorist attack. Last night.'

'Target?'

'The Revolutionary Arms.'

Alastair froze. He saw Lewisham's eyes narrow. To cover his reaction, he flicked open the folder and looked at the top page. Someone, likely Lewisham, had done some quick staff work. There were interviews with survivors, a provisional explosives report and a number of stark black and white photographs.

One showed the blown-out front of the pub. Little remained of the façade. Inside, the scene was much worse. Little more than torn clothing and splashes of blood remained of the patrons.

There was a brief knock at the door. They both looked up and saw Division Leader Pemberton standing in the doorway. They rose and snapped off salutes.

'You've been apprised?' he said, nodding to Alastair. Pemberton looked around. 'Where's Knight?'

'He's… on his way,' Lewisham lied.

Alastair thought Pemberton's stare could've drilled through steel.

'It's noble of you to cover for your partner's tardiness. I don't care whether he's been kidnapped by little green men or getting his leg over with his favourite barmaid. Find him. I want my best team on the case.'

Lewisham exchanged a glance with Alastair.

'Yes, sir,' he said. 'Consider him found already.'

'Good then. Roust him out of whatever bed you find him in and get down to the bombsite and see what you can learn. I've got orders from the DExSec – find these terrorists so we can string them up.' Pemberton sketched a salute then wheeled about and left the office.

'Where the hell is Knight?' Alastair said, rounding on Lewisham.

'You know as much as me, sir. I've sent a man around to his flat. He'll report back to me as soon as he knows something.'

Alastair chewed his bottom lip for a moment, then nodded curtly.

'All right, then.' He gathered up the report. 'You heard Pemberton,' he growled. 'Let's go.'

Passing through the staff room, which buzzed with activity, Alastair turned to look at Lewisham.

'Anything else come through on the wire last night?'

Lewisham nodded. 'Chatter about Resistance activities in the south and north west. There was a failed attack on an Auxpol barracks in Exeter. Four dead, none of them ours.' She hesitated.

'Out with it,' Alastair said. He held open a door that led into a concrete stairwell. He clattered after Lewisham as they descended into the parking garage.

'About Knight. There was some noise about Resistance activities in London. Do you think…?'

'I've known Ben a long time,' Alastair said, as they exited into the echoing garage. He strode towards a staff car parked beside a nearby pillar. 'If the Resistance has gone after him, I'm sure he can handle himself.'

'And if he can't?' Lewisham asked, as she climbed behind the wheel.

'Let's not complicate matters, Lewisham.' Alastair slammed his door closed. 'We've got a terrorist outrage on our hands and one officer missing. I know where my priorities rest. Do you?'

He saw her knuckles whiten as she gripped the steering wheel. After a long moment, she nodded.

'Good,' Alastair said. 'In the unlikely event he's dead; we'll hunt down those responsible and have ourselves a nice little hanging party. Until then, though, drive.'

The engine roared into life. Lewisham slammed through the gears with a teeth rattling crunch, and then the car burst out of the garage and onto the street. Lewisham spun the wheel and they roared down Curzon Street.

Glancing up from the report, Alastair saw people lining up outside the front of a supermarket. Something about their apathetic faces irritated him. With an effort, he dismissed them from his thoughts and turned his attention to the report open on his lap.

'What do we know so far?'

'At approximately nine forty-five last night a bomb exploded in *The Revolutionary Arms*. At this stage we've identified twelve dead, with three others assessed as critical in hospital.'

'Witnesses?' Alastair felt a tension in his chest.

47

He and Sally had left the pub only fifteen minutes before the explosion. If they'd waited any longer... The fact that he had escaped death by only a few minutes unsettled him.

'None capable of speech,' Lewisham said, taking the corner a little too tightly. The squeal of the tyres faded as she accelerated along the road.

'That bad?' Alastair said. He felt vaguely relieved.

'The three listed as critical aren't expected to live beyond today. We've got our people sitting with them, in case they awaken long enough to tell us something.'

'Who's in charge at the site?'

'Auxpol will be,' Lewisham said. '*The Revolutionary Arms* has long been something of a holy site for them. Not surprising, given its history. I'm sure the local police will be in attendance.'

'They may as well be mannequins, for all the authority the Auxpol will give them.'

Director Hipwood's Directorate of Internal Affairs managed the Auxpol militias, whose authority overrode the local constabulary.

'Anyone taken responsibility?' Alastair asked.

'None,' Lewisham said as she changed lanes. The staff car, a locally made model, wallowed a little as it built up speed. It didn't have the clean lines of the European vehicles that were banned from British roads. 'At least not yet. The Resistance will take responsibility; it's just a question of when.'

'I don't know what they hope to achieve,' Alastair said, glancing across at Lewisham.

She looked steadily ahead. 'I'm sure I don't, either.'

Alastair regarded her for another moment, then turned to face the road. Lewisham's... tolerance for certain things was known to him. She never went beyond skirting the boundaries of what was acceptable, but sometimes she sidled all the way up to the line.

A mixture of local constabulary and Auxiliary police held back small crowds at either end of the street. Lewisham parked a distance back, and the duo alighted. They came down the street from the north, picking their way through the crowd. Alastair sensed a tightness in the air, and the looks on the faces of the silent observers spoke of a barely restrained anger. But at who, he wondered.

Ahead of them, he saw a pair of Auxiliary police, their black shirts stark in the gloomy light, staring down an older woman. She was plainly dressed, with a headscarf over her greying hair. Tears streaked her face.

'My Jack is in there,' she said with a quavering voice. 'He said he was meeting a friend, but he hasn't come home.'

'ID card,' the taller of the two Auxpol said. A pair of uniformed police stood to one side, looking ill at ease.

'What do you want her card for?' someone, a man, called from the crowd.

'Because I asked for it,' snarled the taller Auxpol officer. In one hand he held a truncheon, a steel bar wrapped in rubber. He smacked it into an open hand. 'If you don't shut it, I'll ask for yours, and I won't do it politely.'

'Bloody Auxpol,' someone said, amid a general muttering of agreement.

'If I hear any more of that sort of talk, I'll have you all rounded up, do you hear.'

Alastair and Lewisham pushed through to the front of the crowd. They held out their ID cards, and the other Auxpol officer waved them through. This provoked even more muttering from the crowd.

'Here comes the cover up,' someone shouted. 'What will it be this time? Gas leak? Chip fryer got a bit too hot?' The muttering grew louder then, the tone shifting to anger.

'Let's get clear of this,' Alastair said, staring sidelong at the crowd.

'Bloody savages,' Lewisham said, shaking her head at the Auxpol officers.

Both had their truncheons out, and Alastair thought if the crowd grew restive, they would draw their pistols. It could get ugly quickly.

Hesitating a moment, Alastair surprised himself and reversed course. He walked back to the older woman.

'Do you have a picture of your son?' he asked. He ignored the glare of the nearest Auxpol officer. 'Or a description?'

Her hands shaking, the woman took a photograph from her purse. She handed it to Alastair. It was of a young man with a shock of dark curly hair, grinning impudently.

'His name is Jack Parsons,' the woman said.

Alastair looked at her, and she looked at him. An understanding passed between them. She knew her son was dead, and Alastair knew he would have to confirm it before the morning was out.

'I'll see what I can find out,' he said, slipping the photograph into his jacket pocket. 'You,' he said, pointing to the taller Auxpol. 'Get over here.'

Unwillingly, the Auxpol officer came over.

'If you want a riot on your hands, go ahead and start cracking heads,' Alastair snarled. 'If you do, you'll be on your own. If they haven't torn you limb from limb, I'll make sure you're brought up on charges. The last thing we need right now is more violence and more blood on the street.'

'Who the hell do you think you are?' The Auxpol officer's jowly face had gone red.

Alastair leaned in, a smile playing on his lips. 'Can't you read?' he said, waving his warrant card. 'Column Leader Alastair Lethbridge-Stewart. Of the Security Directorate. Would you like me to do some investigating into your background?'

The Auxpol officer screwed up his face, but kept silent. He offered a curt nod, then stepped back and turned to stare angrily at the crowd, which had grown quiet once more.

'Nice work, boss,' Lewisham said, nodding approvingly. 'What's got you in such a good mood?'

'When am I not in a good mood?' Alastair asked, flashing her a smile.

Lewisham almost stopped in her tracks. She looked at Alastair, then broke into a broad grin of understanding.

'Dear God,' she said, shaking her head. 'Will wonders never cease?'

The light mood drained away as they drew closer to *The Revolutionary Arms*. No photograph could do justice to the sheer havoc wreaked on the building. The upper two stories had collapsed into the gaping hole where the bar and booths had sat. The buildings on either side were badly damaged, and some of their structure had collapsed on top of the pub. A team of men poured over the ruins like ants on an upturned anthill.

A pair of men emerged from the ruins, carrying a covered body on a stretcher.

'Hold up,' Alastair said, walking over to the pair. He waved his ID card, which was enough to halt the men. 'Give me a moment.'

He flipped back the blanket, stared hard at what remained on the stretcher, then turned the blanket back. He shook his head.

'Where are you taking him?' he asked one of the stretcher bearers.

'Charing Cross Hospital.'

Alastair ran a hand over his chin. 'Wait here,' he said to Lewisham, and walked back to the crowd.

Lewisham watched Alastair approach the woman. She saw him hand over the photograph. He talked with the woman for a minute. She bowed her head, and her shoulders. Alastair awkwardly pat the woman on the back, then he turned and walked back to Lewisham.

'Come on,' he said, without looking at her. 'Let's see if we can find anything use—'

A roaring series of concussions split the world. Cataclysmic explosions filled the air. The ground shook and buildings on either side of the street swayed. Windows shattered, sending lethal shards spinning into the crowd. People screamed as they scattered, trampling each other in a mad rush to escape. The weak sunlight dimmed and a shadow fell across the street.

Ears ringing, Alastair tried to make sense of what had happened. Lewisham crouched nearby, her hands over her ears, but her eyes were wide, alert. There was a terrific grinding roar, and Alastair watched, open-mouthed, as a five-storey office building several streets away slowly toppled over like a felled tree. People leaped to their deaths from gaping windows, trailing streamers of dust like a comet. A massive rolling vibration sent people flying. Stone fragments cut down people. Clouds of dust filled the air, sifting down in a fine, choking rain. Through the dust, Alastair saw a police officer stagger into view, his face coated in dust. It made the blood spurting from his throat starker still. The police officer had his hands clasped over the wound in a vain attempt to stop

51

the pulsing ribbon of blood jetting from the ragged hole. The officer collapsed in front of Alastair. He laid there, eyes boring into Alastair, before life fled from them in the transition from one heartbeat to the next.

'Find shelter!' Alastair shouted, his voice tinny and blurred from the ringing in his ears.

A pillar of smoke, from the New People's Parliament, rose into the sky. One of Big Ben's clock faces had vanished, leaving a hole through which billowed smoke and fire. All around them, people fled in every direction. The enormity of the devastation rested on Alastair like a rock.

With Lewisham by his side, all he could do was bear witness to the catastrophe unfolding around him.

In a dozen locations across London, smoke rose into the sky, forming a rough ring around his location. Alastair couldn't see all the buildings that were affected. He knew in his gut, though, that the devastation was massive. He shuddered to think of the death toll. Alarms shrieked and whooped and clanged all across the city, triggered by the seismic tremors. To his right, he saw the remains of an apartment building, its central section simply blown to smithereens. Miraculously, there were survivors, all covered in a thick layer of dust staggering along the street, like escapees from Hell.

Not far wrong, Alastair thought, as a sundered gas main caught fire.

More smoke filled the air. Holding a handkerchief over his mouth and nose, Alastair acted on instinct. He grabbed an Auxpol militiaman, who had wandered aimlessly into his field of vision.

'Find as many of your men as you can,' he said, shouting into the man's face.

When he didn't react, Alastair slapped him twice across the face. The man started and his eyes went wide. He shook himself, as if waking from a bad dream.

'Get your men over there,' Alastair said, pointing to the shattered apartment building. 'Start digging. There has to be survivors.' The Auxpol officer nodded. He stumbled away, gathering a small group of people around him and disappeared into the roiling cloud of dust.

Alastair flinched as something brushed his face. A smouldering rectangle of paper, with words and images printed on it, fluttered to his feet. Paper began to rain down on them. Some of it burned, trailing banners of smoke darker than the white fog of dust choking the air. Alastair reached down and picked up the piece of paper.

DEMOCRACY NOW, it blared on one side. Turning it over, he read THE PARTY HATES YOU.

Looking around at the devastation, Alastair felt a surge of fury burst through him.

'How?' Alastair shouted so loudly it hurt his throat. 'How could this have happened?'

CHAPTER EIGHT

The night before.

'**ALL I'M** saying is I'm worried we're going too far. We risk losing the people.'

Shadowy figures shifted uneasily.

'The Pawn should know it is too late,' a woman said quietly, her voice a stone dropping into the silence that had spread at his words. 'We've come this far... To turn back now, it would be a betrayal.'

'The Rook should know it's never too late,' the Pawn said. He spread his hands, which were the only parts of him visible; they were thick and scarred, as if he had performed manual labour most of his life.

'We are talking about killing hundreds, if not thousands of people, in the next few hours. Men, women, children. Innocents.'

'That's the point, though,' said another woman. 'We have to bring the war to their front door. Else how will they understand?' There was a quaver to her voice, but that was only age, not a lack of resolve.

No one knew the identity of the other members of the cabal. Each led a cell and no cell had anything to do with any other cell. The effort at secrecy had seemed absurd, when they'd begun. But the original ring had been infiltrated and broken up, leaving only two survivors to escape and rebuild, while the rest died choking, dangling at the end of piano wire. It had stopped being absurd.

They had learned, as they continued to learn. Dead drops to share information, honey traps to turn agents within the security forces, encryption techniques cribbed from library books and surveillance, not only on members of the Party, but on each other. When the Party controlled all the levers of power, success only occurred in the shadows. Meetings like this were rare, and the precautions, onerous.

'Children will die, Bishop,' the Pawn said, turning in the direction of the older woman. 'Is that who we have become? Child killers?'

'As if we have a choice.' Scorn filled a third woman's voice. 'This is no time for scruples. The Party is corrupt, rotten to the core. The power cuts are more frequent, for longer. Food spoils. Hospital patients die. People freeze to death in their own homes. The Party has no answers to the problems the people face other than empty slogans. They cling to power for its own sake, battening like ghouls on the corpse that was Britain. The Party rules by fear, nothing more.'

Everyone went still at the sound of her voice. The cabal had no formal hierarchy. Decisions were reached by consensus. Nevertheless, she was one of the two survivors of the original group, someone who had been with the struggle from the beginning. Experience counted for something, after all.

'So if we win,' the Pawn said, his voice low and urgent. 'If we win, we will have blood on our hands. Blood from the murders we are agreeing to tonight, and if it works as you say it will, blood spilled from the rioting that will spread across the country. Is that how we end the Republic, by drowning it in blood, Queen?'

'I would rather it had been strangled in the cradle,' the Queen said. She sounded young, but the bitterness in her voice spoke of a long struggle against the regime. 'Give me a time machine, and I would do it.'

Subdued laughter cut the tension, a little.

A male voice sighed heavily. 'The Queen is right,' he said. He had a thick Yorkshire accent which sounded out of place with the richer southern tones, belying his pseudonym of the King. 'We will show the people that the Party cannot protect them. If we undermine their belief in that, we undermine their belief in everything the Party represents.'

A heavy silence settled over the participants as they contemplated their actions and the next few hours.

'Are we ready to move to the next phase?' the Queen said

at last.

The Rook replied. 'We are. The devices were placed in the last twenty-four hours. We have selected targets for their maximum impact, psychologically and in terms of infrastructure. Other operatives are ready to react once the explosives are detonated.'

'And our... suppliers? Are we prepared to pay their price?' The Pawn's voice grew strident. 'We risk replacing one puppet master for another.'

'If that should come to pass, the struggle will continue,' the Queen said, her voice steely. 'One way or another, Britain will be free again.' She clapped her hands, the sound loud in the large space. 'You all have your appointed tasks, as do I.' Her dim figure leaned forward. 'If we do this thing, the Party will be shaken to its very foundations.'

The group began to break up. Figures moved away through the shadows and into the night. The distant sounds of London's streets drifted along a slow breeze, reminding the Pawn uncomfortably of the victims of the coming carnage.

'You'd best be careful,' the Queen said. He could just make out her figure beside a concrete pillar. 'Some might think your loyalties lie... Elsewhere.'

'Some? You mean you?'

The Queen inclined her head. 'You've always been too cautious,' she said.

'Do you blame me?' he said. 'After what happened to the others...'

'They died. For the cause.' A pause. 'We lived. We lived so that their sacrifice had meaning.'

'How can you be so cold?'

'How can you not?' she asked, her voice flat. 'Everything we hope to achieve begins tonight. Britain was once a beacon of liberty across the world. Now that flame is almost dead. It is we few who dare rise up against the Party. It is we few who dare lift a hand against our oppressors so that Britain is free once again. I would risk everything for the chance to escape the Party's yoke. Everything. And anyone.'

Before the Pawn could reply, the woman turned and left. He watched her until she vanished into the night. He looked down at his hands, imagined them carmine with blood up to the elbows and shook his head.

He departed by a different way, aware that after tonight nothing would be the same again.

CHAPTER NINE

IT HAPPENED when Knight was unconscious. When he awoke, he saw that something terrible had happened to his counterpart. Terrible growths covered its upper body, distorting its face to the point where it collapsed in on itself. He blinked, slowly, and saw the other canisters were empty. Idly, he wondered what had caused his duplicate to fail so utterly.

He slid back into darkness.

Then light. And cold, bone aching cold. A terrible gushing sound and then Knight was sliding into open air. Something had made the outer shell of the canister slide open, thrusting him back into the world.

He sprawled, naked, on the concrete floor, the roughness of it a shock after the womb-like contents of the canister. He began to choke on the tube. With damp, wrinkled fingers, he clawed at it, trying to gain purchase.

Stars burst in his eyes as his oxygen-starved brain began to switch off. With a convulsive effort that split a softened fingernail, Knight wrenched the tube out. He flung it aside, where it lay like a dead snake amid the sticky fluid pooling on the floor.

On his hands and knees, panting, Knight vomited up more of that fluid, until his lungs and stomach were clear of it.

There were no klaxons, no strobing lights to announce his emergence. Only a sense of something gone wrong, of a switch turned at the wrong time, of a decision made without prior approval. The orderliness of the operation indicated his escape was a mistake.

Don't worry about what went wrong, he thought. *How do I get out?*

A forest of canisters stood around him. Some were filled with naked figures, men and women. He staggered up to one, which held a man with his eyes closed. Opposite stood another canister containing the man's duplicate. At the base of each canister was a display, with symbols in an unfamiliar language. It reminded him of medical equipment, providing data to those monitoring the people trapped inside.

'Who?' he wondered. Then a chill went through him when he turned to regard the duplicate staring at itself. 'Why?' Another chill ran through him. 'Which is which?' And that sent a nasty implication through him that his scattered thoughts weren't able to adequately process.

The sudden sound of a door opening sent Knight to his haunches. The hair on his arms rose and he tensed in readiness for action.

He saw a shaft of light at the far corner of the room and figures bulking in the doorway. Knight scuttled to his left, making for a nearby wall. He did so without being seen, a consequence of the chamber's dim lighting. Carefully, he made his way along the wall, a shadow within the shadows, conscious of the figures bobbing lazily in their canisters.

He heard voices, one a curious low buzzing sound that only gradually resolved into a language he could understand. It was like listening to words pressing through static, and it made his teeth hurt. Another was a slim figure, which to his shock, resolved into that of a woman. Her face was indistinct, but her command of English was perfect.

England, he thought. *Not spirited off by the Tsarists after all.*

The urge to linger and gather intelligence was hard to shake off. In the shadows of a canister, Knight paused, straining to hear.

'The process is going well?' the woman said. The curvature of a canister warped her features into an indistinct smear.

The buzzing formed itself into a one-word answer. 'Yezzzz'

Taller than the woman, the figure was clothed in a one piece overall. Its exposed skin looked odd. For a moment,

Knight thought the figure had been badly burned, leaving terrible scars. Then a chance reflection of light from the open door of a canister lit the creature in its full, horrific glory.

Knight pressed the knuckles of one hand to his mouth to suppress a cry of horrified disgust.

The figure, illuminated for one terrible moment, was bipedal, shovel shaped hands hanging dangling above its knees. Growths, like coral, made its shoulders and head bulbous and deformed. Filaments emerged from fissures among the growths, shivering and shuddering in time with the creature's breathing. Its eyes were shark black, drinking in the light. And of its mouth, Knight, hardened as he was to the grim realities of combat, had to turn away at the sight of a massive maw almost splitting the skull horizontally, with teeth like shards of glass glinting in that moment of light.

Mercifully, the dimness of the chamber thickened, and the creature once again moved in darkness.

Go, Knight silently urged himself. Never taking his eyes off the pair, he retreated along the wall. He heard them talking again; heard words from the woman that sounded like 'preparation' and 'plans', but the creature's replies were just blurred buzzing sounds.

His urge to flee grew stronger when they stopped beside his open canister. His pace quickened. He rounded the corner and made for the beckoning light. He heard a sudden shout.

Knight turned his head but didn't slow, as the woman began to run towards him, the creature lumbering in her wake. He saw she wielded a gun. *Civilians don't have weapons*, he thought as he raced for the door. The Party would never allow it.

By then he was in the doorway, transfixed by the impossibly bright light. He didn't stop to allow his eyes to acclimate; instead, he tore down the corridor, bouncing from wall to wall in his haste. Behind him, a shot rang out, and he ducked as a bullet shrieked past his head, clipping his ear and sending blood spraying across the wall.

With one hand clamped to the side of his head, Knight ran on, turning at the end of the corridor. At last, klaxons began to ring out and a door slid open. A figure, more grotesque in the light than the one chasing him, lumbered out and turned on Knight with all the implacability of a Dreadnought at sea. Buzzing filled the air and its monstrous arms reached for him...

CHAPTER TEN

THE UTTER disaster at Windscale, where a combination of hubris and haste led to the contamination of 500 square miles of the English coastline, put paid to the nuclear industry in the Republic. Even the Party, notorious for ignoring the feelings of the public, couldn't hide the extent of the devastation. According to reports, every single living thing downwind of the fires that consumed Reactors 1 and 2; man, woman, child and beast, died within two weeks. Most of the bodies remain where they fell, too contaminated to approach and bury. Not only was this an ecological catastrophe, it cruelled the chances of British energy independence. In turn, every crackpot scheme to provide energy to the expanding economy was entertained by a Party leadership wilfully ignorant of scientific learning, and eager to shortcut their way to energy independence. There will come a day when one of these endeavours creates a catastrophe far larger than Windscale...

From 'An Unpublishable Memoir' by [redacted]. Retained in the Security Directorate Archives.

'...again, we repeat, these were not attacks aimed at the people of London. For too long, we have been ruled by an elite, a power hungry, rapacious cult of personality, intent on keeping you down while they satisfy their bloated egos and thirst for power. Britain was never made to be a prison, and yet we are. Those who rule are nothing worse than parasites, stealing the fruits of your labour. While you starve in the darkness, they feast in the warmth of their country estates. While your children go without, theirs engage in a never-ending bacchanalia. It is time to rise up, time to tear down the Republic, time to free ourselves of those who spend every single minute of your lives stamping their boots in your fa—'

'Switch that damn thing off!' Director Gordon Lethbridge-Stewart ordered.

One of the Directors stood and turned the radio off, before sitting down.

The sombre mood in the Cabinet Room deepened. The curtains were drawn, to hide the steel shutters that had been lowered into place. Light came from three bronze chandeliers. Distantly, sirens wailed, as if mourning the thousands who had died.

'This is bad, this is very bad.' Arthur Fless, the Director of Information, sat with his head in his hands.

'Pull yourself together man, for heaven's sake,' Gordon said, feeling a sense of exasperation. He looked around the room, taking in the measure of those with him.

A dozen men and women, all veterans of the Revolution, sat around the table. All the chairs, bar one, were in use. The empty chair drew the attention of almost all the participants in the hastily arranged meeting. The glowering portrait of Walpole hanging on the wall put Gordon in mind of their absent Leader.

'He's not wrong, though, is he?' A fleshy looking man in a black suit looked around the table.

Freddie Frogmorton, Director of Energy. Froggie, to his enemies, which, given the seemingly never-ending blackouts, was most of Britain. Thinking like that made Gordon glance at Arthur. Now there was a dead man walking

The pirate broadcasts had started first on radio, breaking into the RBC afternoon programmes and then, shockingly, as the opening theme to the RBC Nine O'clock News on television began. Gordon had seen it himself. Robert Dougall's face had begun to fade in when a burst of static obliterated it. After a few seconds, a shadowy figure loomed out of the static and began reading a lengthy, prepared statement. That was when the messages ordering the Cabinet's attendance at Downing Street started going around.

'We've got vans circling London trying to pinpoint the source of it,' Arthur said, miserably. His eyes were red and

Gordon thought, with a pang of disgust, that the man might start weeping.

'Nothing?' Gordon said, enjoying the chance to twist the knife.

Arthur shook his head.

Gordon sat back in his chair and stared at the bullet holes that pockmarked the walls, relics of the last, bloody moments of the Revolution. He thought the details far too ostentatious, but who would gainsay the Leader, even at this late stage? He wondered if Arthur glanced at the bullet holes, would the man faint dead away?

An object lesson, he remembered the Leader saying one day, pointing at the holes as they'd shared a bottle of Scotch and made plans. How long ago had that been, Gordon wondered. Ten years? Fifteen? How quickly time had moved on. It was another reminder that if he didn't grasp it, his chance would flit by him like the years since the Revolution.

'Director? Gordon?'

Gordon narrowed his eyes and focused on the people around him.

'What is it, Felicity?'

The Director of Transport tilted her chin up. 'I asked, has the Directorate of External Security picked up any signals from the Continent? Are the Frogs stirring up trouble again?'

'Perhaps it's the Tsar's people,' Frogmorton said, leaning forward. 'Weaken us, and they claim our half of the Continent.'

'The French have been quiet since we shot De Gaulle and saved Algeria for them,' Gordon explained. 'I can't rule out elements of the 1789 Resistance movement, but I think we would be wise not to speculate. It would also be wise to wait for the Leader to attend before we share what we know. Best we don't hash out everything in his absence. We don't want to… worry him, now do we?'

The buzz of conversation subsided at Gordon's comment, and he allowed himself a moment of satisfaction. The Leader had lately grown irascible. Seeing conspiracies around every corner. More prone to lashing out at perceived threats and perceived disloyalty. Some at this table owed their position to those who had fallen from the Old Man's favour. It wouldn't look good to be seen to be discussing things behind the

Leader's back.

'I will say this, however,' Gordon said. He bared his teeth and looked around the table. 'Those responsible will be made to pay with their lives.'

His colleagues rapped their knuckles on the table in approval, the sound filling the room. It was at that moment the door leading into the Cabinet Room opened, and the Leader entered.

Gordon watched the heir to Mosley totter into the room, trying to contain his shock at his condition. In recent years, the Leader had taken to spending more and more time at his seaside villa in Bognor Regis. A modest affair, the Leader had once proudly announced, ignoring the two hundred men from Auxpol who guarded him day and night. He had spent the last two months sequestered there, pottering around his garden, some said. The change in his condition, from a relatively hale old man, to simply an old man, startled Gordon.

A long face, under a shock of white hair, wavered slightly on a thin necked creased with wattles of loose skin. The moustache needed trimming. The hands, marred by numerous liver spots, shook. But even with these physical signs of decline, Gordon sensed something of the Leader's old aura remained, an aura of a man who had taken up the bloody reins of the Movement after Mosley's assassination. Gordon had observed the Leader up close for almost twenty years. He knew, instinctively, within that wreck glittered an insatiable thirst for power and a rat cunning that could only be admired.

An aide assisted the Leader, discreetly holding his elbow and guiding him to the empty chair, the only one with arms. The others in the room shifted uncomfortably. The Leader's obvious infirmity spoke not just of advanced years, but the high chances of destabilisation within the Party as those with ambition began to jockey for power. Indeed, had begun jockeying for power.

The Leader waved away the aide and settled himself more comfortably into the chair. The aide stepped away, remaining within reach if needed.

'Celebrating something, were we?' the Leader said. His eyes, a faded blue, narrowed sharply as they swept up and down the room.

'Just our determination that those miserable traitors meet the fate they deserve,' Frogmorton said, pompously.

'Well, let's hope the lights are on long enough so the execution squad can see to shoot straight,' the Leader said.

A shocked silence filled the room. Gordon hid his smile behind his hand as Frogmorton descended into a choked silence.

'So,' the Leader said, turning away from the Director of Energy. 'What facts have we assembled? Paula?'

Paula Hipwood slipped her glasses on and opened a folder in front of her. The Director of Internal Affairs looked like a kindly matron, with soft curls framing a round face. Gordon knew different. They all knew different. Her many signal achievements included signing the execution warrants for the population – men, women and children – of the village of Edlington, when the workers at the Yorkshire Main Colliery went on strike demanding better conditions.

'Local police and elements of the Auxpol confirm that a dozen bombs were detonated in central London at 10.52am today. It's apparent each site was chosen specifically to inflict massive civilian casualties.'

'Hence the twin attacks in the Underground,' Gordon murmured.

'Exactly,' Hipwood said. She consulted the report in front of her. 'Two hundred and forty-three dead at Angel Station on the Northern Line and 162 at St James' Park on the District Line.'

'That close to Downing Street?' Gordon said. He looked at the Leader. 'There's a clear intention to send you a message, Leader.'

'I can assure you all that my department has been vigilant in ensuring the safety of the Cabinet,' Hipwood said.

'What about the attack at *The Revolutionary Arms*?' Gordon asked.

'What about it?' Hipwood stared over her glasses at him.

'Surely there is a link between what happened there the night before and the attacks today?'

'Possibly, Director. Possibly. But my attention is firmly on these monstrous attacks against our people.'

'We might be missing something if we don't investigate

it as thoroughly as these dozen attacks,' Gordon said, mildly.

'That's as maybe,' Hipwood said. She stabbed the file in front of her with an index finger. 'But there are larger fish to fry right here.'

'What does the Director of ExSec have to offer, other than investigating the destruction of a public house?' asked the Leader in a dry, wavering voice.

Gordon squared his shoulders. 'Nothing. As you all know, we have monitored democracy cells on the Continent. The authorities there, despite your efforts to stiffen their spines, Leader, are unfortunately lax in turning over those who seek to take Britain back to the days of degenerate royalty. I am confident, based on our sources, that these attacks were organised within the borders of the Republic.'

'So what should we do?' Frogmorton asked.

Hipwood shot him a look of withering contempt, the sort one might give to a child who had soiled their underwear in public.

'Round up the usual suspects, no doubt,' the Leader said, chuckling.

Hipwood's pained smile of agreement indicated she had been leaning towards something more. Gordon decided to oblige.

'Something appears to be troubling you, Paula.'

Hipwood's eyes were unreadable, but she nodded in response. 'Initial scientific testing on the explosive residue came back with a number of puzzling results.'

'Puzzling how?' Gordon asked. He had read the reports. He doubted the Leader had, and he knew for certain that the others around the table, especially Frogmorton, hadn't.

'Several of the compounds used were... unknown to the chemists on the team.' Hipwood sounded disturbed.

Gordon was intrigued. 'Has the evidence been tainted in some way?'

Hipwood shook her head. 'All the usual protocols were followed. They know the stakes involved and the punishments that can be meted out for breaking the rules.'

I'm sure they do, Gordon thought.

'So the compounds involved don't appear on any boffins chart. Big deal,' Frogmorton said. 'Isn't the important thing to discover who set the explosives?'

'I'm sure Paula would say that both may be linked,' Gordon said.

Director Hipwood nodded.

'Assuming these compounds are home grown,' the Director of Transport said,' do we have the resources available to determine their origin?'

'We do,' Hipwood said promptly. Here she was on firmer ground, and eager to ensure that her department had carriage of the matter. 'Internal Affairs has a facility in Northumberland that specialises in these sorts of matters. I've directed the compounds to be delivered there.'

'The Vault?' Gordon said, rubbing his chin. He was thinking furiously. 'You've no military scientists there, do you?'

'No. I'm sure Don would have kittens if I asked him to send a detachment. Isn't that right, Don?'

The Director of War nodded. 'I prefer to train the armies' guns externally, rather than internally. I'll leave that sort of behaviour up to your Auxpol thugs, Paula.'

'But someone with military experience would be useful, don't you think?' Gordon said. 'Someone with exposure to military grade explosives in the field.'

'No doubt you have someone in mind, Gordon,' Hipwood said. 'Really, Leader, I must protest. This is a serious investigation, not a chance for Gordon to promote his chosen son.'

'Protest away, Paula,' Gordon said, eyes narrowed. He looked at the Leader. 'My son has been in the military for years. He is reliable, steady, a good soldier for the Republic. Whatever you… *I* ask of him, he will achieve.'

'And a devoted son to you, Gordon, no doubt,' the Leader said. That reptile gaze was back on Gordon. He shifted uncomfortably in his seat.

'If you're thinking of asking me to allow your son free rein in my facilities, I think we'll have to part company there, Gordon,' Hipwood said.

'Leader,' Gordon said. 'This should be a situation where the relevant Directorates come together to fight a common cause.'

Gordon's appeal to the Leader was a calculated one.

'At this time of national emergency... and if I hear any of you use language like that outside this room, I'll have you shot... it makes sense for the public to see that the Party is working together to resolve the crisis.' The Leader nodded, despite Hipwood's protestations. 'I understand your concerns, Paula, but there are bigger things at stake than looking after your patch.'

The Leader looked around the room. 'More than ever, the Republic needs its finest sons and daughters to rise to the occasion, to ensure that the next generation has the experience to take up the reins when the time comes.'

He looked at Gordon, a brief smile playing on his lips.

'Which is why I'll be monitoring young Lethbridge-Stewart's progress. And his father's, of course.'

Gordon could only nod in agreement.

The Leader slapped the table. 'Good then,' he said. 'Paula, you make sure your people start rounding up the usual suspects. I want the riot division of Auxpol out on the streets of every major city in the country. They are authorised to use live rounds if the crowds do not disperse. If there is one thing I have learned in the last forty years, it's that suppressing fire will always beat the ideals and complaints of those who do not know their place.'

There were murmurs of approval.

'Don, I want the reserves called up for a three day turn out. Have them muster in their local counties. Get them parading by Great War memorials, that sort of thing. It's good to remind the people of the sacrifices that were made for them.' He paused, his eyes narrowing. 'Where's Arthur?'

There was a sudden grinding noise as a chair jerked back. Arthur stood, swaying, his face like chalk.

'There's my Director of Information,' the Leader said, a tiny smile playing on his lips. 'How goes our pirate broadcasters, eh? Caught them yet?'

'We're doing all we can to detect the source of the signals and I'm sure that in time we will have found it and eliminated it as soon as possible it really would be a marvellous thing if I could have additional time to see the thing through—'

Arthur lurched to a stop. Gordon looked away,

embarrassed by the man's dribble.

'You're looking tired, Arthur,' the Leader said into the awful silence. 'So very, very tired. I think it might be time for you to have that rest you've always been talking about. I tell you what, come see me in my office afterwards. I think we might have a governorship in West Africa that's suddenly opened up.'

The Leader steepled his fingers and rested his chin on them. 'Paula,' he said, after a moment's thought. 'Now that Arthur has other concerns, get some of your people over to the RBC and cut together a piece for the television and radio. Something that condemns the attacks, and lays the blame at those blasted Irish Nationalists. They may as well be of some use in diverting attention away from the real attackers.' He paused, thinking. 'Yes, that should do it,' he murmured. 'I seem to recall we ran a live broadcast in 1966 when we hung the Cumbria Six. Make sure you add that into the television footage. I want the people to get our message loud and clear, that we are in charge, and that those responsible will face the punishment they deserve.

'And, Gordon, I want you to send out a message to our embassies abroad. This isn't a moment for anyone to be presuming the Republic is weak, or incapable of dealing with a few recalcitrants who know how to build a bomb. Make sure the message sounds like the warning I want it to be.'

Gordon nodded.

'Excellent. This is nothing more than a nine-day wonder.' The Leader waved his hand, and the aide stepped forward. 'Be a good fellow, Jessop, and help me out of this chair. Damn things too heavy to move.'

With some difficulty, Jessop helped the Leader to his feet. Together, they shuffled to the door, which Jessop opened with his free hand. On the threshold, the Leader paused, and turned.

'Arthur, be a good fellow. We'll have that meeting now, yes?'

The Leader turned and left the room.

Like a condemned man arriving in sight of the scaffold, Arthur made his slow way around the Cabinet table. He, like the Leader, paused on the threshold, and looked over his shoulder. None but Gordon and Paula would meet his gaze.

Arthur seemed to shrink under the weight of what he saw. He shuffled out.

That was the sign for the meeting to break up. Gordon and Paula lingered.

'When did we start to rely on people as soft as Frogmorton?' Hipwood asked.

'Time doesn't stand still, even for the heroes of the Revolution,' Gordon said.

Hipwood snorted.

'You know what Freddie did during the Revolution? He was in his daddy's villa in Spain. The only thing he did of any value was haul down the local British consulate's Union Jack and run the Party flag up the pole. Somehow he's managed to parley that into a place at the heart of government.'

'The wheel turns, Paula,' Gordon said, softly. 'Nothing lasts forever. Even the great and good get ground under.'

'Really? Are you going to mouth clichés at me?' Paula glared contemptuously at Gordon. 'I expected better.'

'Does this pass muster for the truth, then, Paula? The old man won't be around for much longer. He tries to hide it, but he's lost more than a step. And when he goes...'

'When he goes,' Paula said, smiling genuinely for the first time that night,' it'll be you and me climbing the greasy pole to see who reaches the top first.' Her smile broadened. 'I look forward to it.' She turned and walked out, leaving Gordon to ponder the empty room.

He glanced up at the portrait of Walpole.

'So do I,' he murmured. 'So do I.'

CHAPTER ELEVEN

'**APOLOGIES FOR** rousting you out of bed so early,' Pemberton told Alastair. The frostiness in his voice belied the words. Outside, it was still dark. 'New orders,' Pemberton said, handing Alastair an envelope.

Ripping it open, Alastair eagerly scanned the page. His face fell.

'What's this?' he said, crumpling the paper. 'Northumberland! I want to be hunting terrorists, not playing nursemaid to a bunch of scientists.'

Pemberton shrugged. 'I'd rather be out in the field shooting revolutionaries, Lethbridge-Stewart, but they have me behind this damned desk. In a way, like water, we find our own level. Was there anything else?'

Alastair quietly seethed, but shook his head.

'Good then. Make sure you file progressive reports, in the usual timely manner. Dismissed.'

Alastair snapped off a salute, wheeled about and exited Pemberton's office. In the outer office, Lewisham waited for him. She looked worried.

'I don't like that look,' Alastair said. 'What is it?'

'I've heard back about Knight,' Lewisham said. She spread her hands. 'Or rather, I've heard nothing. He's definitely missing.'

'The police have been through his place?'

Lewisham nodded. 'Checked with his neighbour, as well. I've put in a call to the nursing home where his mother is, but she's sunk so far into dementia she doesn't recognise herself.'

'Damn it,' Alastair said. 'Well, we can't do much about it now. Keep your contacts on the hunt. There's too much going on, otherwise I'd be on his trail myself.' He hesitated. 'I'm sorry, Lewisham, there's nothing else I can do.'

Lewisham nodded. She tried to hide it, but beneath the professional façade, Alastair could sense her anxiety. He had long suspected Lewisham and Knight were more than just partners. She nodded to the papers in Alastair's hand.

'What's the job?'

'They want us to go up to the Vault in the Cheviot Hills. Something about checking chemical compounds. Madness,' he said, lowering his voice.

The section leader at the desk seemed to be listening.

'Needs must,' Lewisham said, shrugging her shoulders.

'Yes,' Alastair said. 'Needs bloody must.'

'My God,' Lewisham called out above the loud drone of the Beagle's twin engines. 'Look down there.'

After leaving Pemberton's office, Alastair had made a call to the RAAF, requesting a Beagle B.206 light aircraft.

'Might as well make the most of it,' he had grumbled, as they were driven to the nearest military airfield on the northern outskirts of London. They boarded the Beagle with the dawn breaking over a tense capital.

Alastair took one look at what Lewisham had pointed to and tapped the side of his headset.

'Can you get us down closer for a look?' he asked the pilot, through the Beagle's communications system.

'Can do, sir,' the pilot said. The plane bucked a little as he pulled the stick to the right, before smoothing out. 'Will a thousand feet do it?'

'Should,' Alastair said, as the plane began its spiralling descent. He looked through the window next to him and swore. 'Where's that?' He jabbed a thumb towards the glass.

The pilot checked his readouts. 'Gateshead.'

'Gateshead is burning,' Lewisham said, mordantly.

Flames leaped from the quays on the River Tyne up the slope towards the Mosely Hospital which sat on the hill that dominated the area. Silence descended over the Beagle's occupants as it levelled at a thousand feet and soared across the city.

Though sunlight had begun to fringe the horizon, most

of the city remained swathed in darkness, which, given the scheduled power cuts, was no surprise. What stunned everyone into silence were the fires burning in the centre of Gateshead.

Flames shot from the curved upper deck of the Trinity Square car park, a brutal concrete structure. Alastair saw figures milling in the streets around it, and fancied he recognised, despite the chancy light, the dark uniforms of the Auxpol. The violent struggle in the streets was clearly evident. Clumps of people moved back and forth like waves on a beach, first one side plunging into the centre of the other, before retreating. He imagined the bloodshed on the streets, and despite his experience, winced at the thought of the carnage.

'I'm going in lower,' the pilot announced, without prompting.

The Beagle tilted to the left, and the plane descended, following the Tyne. Bridges began flashing beneath them, leading to Newcastle on the northern bank.

'There's fighting on the bridges,' Lewisham said, her voice shocked at the scale of the violence.

Flashes of images seared themselves into Alastair's memory – burning vehicles blocking the centre span of a bridge; figures throwing bricks and Molotov cocktails against a bloc of black uniformed figures on another; civilians streaming south as gun wielding Auxpol fired indiscriminately at their retreating backs; and people leaping into the Tyne, aflame, as some in the Auxpol deployed flamethrowers.

'Can you dial into the command frequency?' Alastair said.

The pilot nodded. He flicked a switch and the low static hum in their headphones squalled for a moment before a frantic voice broke through.

'...this is Column Leader Campbell. Your orders are to shoot anyone remaining on the street south of the town centre. I repeat, your orders are to shoot to kill...'

The static burned through, then another voice emerged from the fog. '...we can't kill women and children.' Even with the effects of the static, the shock and disbelief in the voice was evident.

'...any officer who damn... orders will be shot themse...

74

clear those streets!'

'Higher,' Alastair ordered, as bullets began pinging off the Beagle's hull. One of the windows cracked with a sharp report. The pilot pulled back on the stick and the Beagle's nose rose sharply. The engines throbbed as the plane ascended, before they quietened when the plane levelled off and headed northwest.

The Beagle flew on, the interior cabin quiet as they digested what they'd heard on the radio.

'Report back to base on the secure channel,' Alastair ordered the pilot. 'Tell them there's uncontrolled rioting in Gateshead and the Auxpol have yet to establish control.'

'Are you going to tell them those Auxpol thugs are killing children?' muttered Lewisham.

Alastair kept his counsel. Now wasn't the time for a clash over Lewisham's sentimentality.

Forty minutes later and the Beagle descended through low clouds towards an airstrip set at the rear of the grounds that comprised the Vault. The sun had risen, and light streamed across the compound, shadows long and stark in the bright light. A jeep waited for them, exhaust fumes visible in the chill air. While the pilot taxied the Beagle to a nearby hangar to refuel, Alastair and Lewisham clambered into the jeep, which drove off with a crunch of gears.

Suspicious guards went over their identity documents at two checkpoints between the airstrip and the entrance to the Vault's upper level. Passing inside, steel doors slid shut behind them, blocking the sounds of the outside world. A hush descended over them. From a central reception area, polished concrete floors radiated out like spokes in a wheel. Coloured lines painted on the floor indicated the way to different areas.

'Here comes the welcoming committee,' Lewisham said, nodding towards two people, a man and a woman, who marched towards them.

Alastair watched them with interest. The man was taller, and older, his beard tinged with grey. Intelligent eyes watching warily from behind black-rimmed glasses. He chewed his lip as he approached. Alastair dismissed him as someone who was keen to get along. The woman, on the other hand…

Tall, slim, with short black hair. And given the look in her eyes, there was no hiding her disdain for her visitors.

'Column Leader Alastair Lethbridge-Stewart,' Alastair said, introducing himself. He indicated his companions. 'Platoon Under Leader Frieda Lewisham.'

'Why is it, Column Leader,' the woman began, 'that my time is being wasted acting as nursemaid to you two?'

'Anne!' the older man said, stepping forward. 'Please forgive my… please forgive her,' he said, clearly discomfited. He glanced quickly between Alastair and Anne, who exchanged a long, frosty glare.

'He means his daughter,' Anne said, breaking contact with Alastair long enough to lash her father with her gaze.

'I hardly think providing information to the Security Directorate to enable us to hunt down the murderers behind yesterday's terrorist attacks is acting the nursemaid,' Alastair said. 'You may want to consider that.'

'I've got better things to do than coddle two Directorate officers from London,' Anne said. 'My investigation is of paramount importance.'

'Your investigation?' Alastair said. 'I think you'll find that this is very much my investigation. You answer to me, no one else.'

The atmosphere plunged. Anne looked ready to explode.

'All we are after is information,' Lewisham said, trying to calm matters.

'And information is what you'll receive, Column Leader,' Anne's father said, placatingly. He glanced warningly at his daughter. She ignored him. He offered his hand, which Alastair shook. 'I'm Professor Edward Travers, facility director. Pleased to meet you.' He shook Lewisham's hand.

'Doctor Anne Travers, head of research,' Anne said. Her right hand stayed resolutely by her side.

'Well, it must've been a tiring journey,' Professor Travers said. He glanced anxiously between Alastair and Lewisham. Half-turning, he indicated the corridor. 'My office is a better place to continue this discussion. I think you'll find we have information that will prove useful to your efforts to secure the perpetrators.'

76

'The journey wasn't without its… issues,' Alastair conceded.

'You mean evidence of rioting,' Anne said. There was no mistaking the look on her face. 'Reports have reached us, even in this remote redoubt. I assume the authorities are exercising maximum force?'

'Oh,' Alastair said. 'The security forces have orders from the very top to ensure dissident elements are put down with extreme prejudice.'

'Excellent,' Anne said, an icy look of triumph crossing her face. She gave Alastair an appraising look, and some of her ire faded. She turned to her father. 'That means they're shooting to kill, father.' She glanced at Alastair. 'Unity is Strength.'

'Indeed,' Alastair said. 'Unity is Strength.'

Professor Travers, to Alastair's mingled amusement and disgust, looked embarrassed at mention of the Party's motto.

'Well then,' Travers said, rubbing his hands as if to warm them. 'My office, shall we? I've laid on refreshments. After, we can deal with the matter at hand.'

'What sort of research do you do here?' Lewisham asked as they followed a green line down the corridor.

'As you know, we're a part of the Department of Energy. Though with that boor Frogmorton at the top, there's precious little energy or direction,' Anne said.

To Alastair's amusement, Professor Travers gave a strangled cough.

'We're quite happy with the leadership provided by Director Frogmorton,' Professor Travers said, turning a corner.

A door presented itself at the end of the corridor. Travers made a beeline for it like a drowning man struggling towards a lifeboat.

He ushered them inside his office and closed the door. A table had been set up on one side of the large room, with coffee and tea and two plates of sandwiches laid out.

'Please,' Professor Travers said, indicating the refreshments. 'I'm sure there was little opportunity for breakfast on the flight here.'

Alastair poured himself a coffee and added two spoonfuls of sugar. He stepped back, allowing the others room.

'Miss Travers,' he said, watching her over the rim of his cup. 'You were talking about the research you conduct here.'

'I was,' she said, looking at him. The frankness of her gaze seemed to be a direct challenge to Alastair. After his encounter with Sally, he was beginning to think the world had suddenly filled with provocative women.

'What Anne means is that we are primarily interested in the field of energy. Energy development, mainly.'

'Mainly?' Alastair said.

'Oh, there's all sorts of offshoots that come with the research,' Anne said. 'Energy independence and dominance, dare I say it, will be the marker of the Republic's greatness. We have several areas within the facility looking at all energy options.'

'Even nuclear?' Lewisham said, genuinely curious.

'I think after the debacle at Windscale, nuclear is completely off the table,' Professor Travers said, somewhat piously. 'Everyone in Seascale dead and the entire village entombed under a concrete dome put paid to that option. The fools didn't listen to me.'

'Quite,' Anne said, cutting her father off and looking sidelong at him before returning her attention to Alastair. 'We have other areas of research we are exploring. We're hopeful of discovering new forms of energy generation.'

'Any breakthroughs?' Alastair asked. 'I'm sure you understand the Party is quite eager to resolve the situation across the country as soon as possible.'

'Which situation is that, Column Leader? Do you mean the energy situation or the escalation in Resistance activity?'

Professor Travers looked stricken. He opened his mouth to respond, but Alastair gestured him to silence.

'Your concern for your daughter does you credit, Professor.' He looked around the room. 'We are all friends here, yes? Good. Ordinarily, I would have to report Miss Travers' comments, but I think we face a graver crisis than a frank expression of opinions.'

The look of relief on the older man's face was almost pathetic.

'The answer to your question, Miss Travers, is both. Fix the energy situation, and the unrest in the community dies away. Yours isn't the only facility interested in tapping the energy potential around us, or so I hear.'

He switched his attention to Professor Travers. 'And no matter how interesting that all is, the reason we are here today is to discuss your findings regarding the chemical traces found at the bomb sites from yesterday's outrages. You have something to report, Professor?'

Travers nodded, though he looked hesitant. 'The short answer, Column Leader, is that we don't know.'

'Really?' said Alastair, his voice flat. 'What's the long answer?'

'The long answer,' Anne said, cutting in, 'is that the compounds retrieved from the devices planted in London are characterised by a series of elements whose atomic structure isn't present on this planet.'

'Anne…' Professor Travers shook his head.

'What do you mean, "isn't present on this planet"?' Alastair glanced at Lewisham, who shrugged her shoulders.

'Exactly that,' Anne said, ignoring her father. 'Not. Of. This. Planet.'

'That's patently ridiculous,' Alastair said, setting aside his coffee cup. 'If you expect me to believe that the source of these bombs are little green aliens, I'll have you sent down to the nearest labour camp where you can break large rocks into smaller ones for the next ten years!'

'The military mind,' Anne said, lifting her chin and staring down at Alastair. 'Has it always been this vacuous?'

'I would remind you, Miss Travers, that my patience isn't infinite.'

'It should be, Column Leader,' Anne said. She glanced at her father, who shook his head. Annoyance crossed her face. 'Whether you like it or not, Column Leader, there is clear evidence of events in the last decade that lend themselves to an interpretation that alien forces have become entangled in affairs, here, on Earth.'

Lewisham barely suppressed a snorted laugh. Anne's glare could've frozen the sun.

'That's one interpretation,' Professor Travers said. Ignoring his daughter, he pressed on. 'It seems likely that our findings relating to the compounds are a consequence of the intense heat and pressure the explosive chemicals underwent when detonated. What Anne is interpreting as... err... alien, is merely the effects of an extreme chemical reaction.'

The look of betrayal on Anne's face was stark. Alastair thought the woman was a fool. Her father was attempting to save her career, even as she cut her own throat with this nonsense. Alastair didn't really care. He had come for answers.

'That's not to say, though, that the materials originally weren't exotic in origin,' Professor Travers said, hurriedly.

'Exotic?' Alastair asked. He was beginning to lose his patience with these fools.

'It's probably best I don't bore you with the technicalities, though I'm sure I could go on at length.' Travers saw the look on Alastair's face and hurried on. 'For health and public safety reasons, a register is maintained of the stocks of chemicals created and shipped within the Republic. In essence, we know who makes what, what goes into each product, and where it is shipped.' He paused, and adjusted his glasses. 'Based on my research, the chemicals found at the bomb sites were not manufactured in the Republic.'

'Who did, then?' Alastair said. 'I assume other nations keep similar registers.'

Professor Travers nodded. 'We have other information that seems to confirm my hypothesis.' He hesitated, then turned to his daughter. 'I think this is where you should take over.'

Anne, who had withdrawn into herself while her father spoke, looked up from some internal reverie. Alastair thought she looked deflated.

'What sort of information?' He was tired and felt the edges of his temper beginning to fray. 'I trust this doesn't involve transmissions from Mars?'

'Quite,' Anne said, but with none of her earlier urgency. It seemed she thought she had rolled the dice and lost. She pointed to an inner door. 'You'd best come with me.'

Sharing a glance with Lewisham, Alastair followed Professor Travers and Anne through the door into a smaller room.

On a table had been set a large audio playback device, into

which a tape had been threaded.

'Close the door,' Anne said.

Lewisham did as instructed. The thick carpeting and close confines created a funereal hush. Alastair felt a prickle run down his spine.

'As I said earlier, the Vault investigates a wide range of matters related to energy production and transmission. We have done some investigation into the feasibility, indeed, the possibility of wireless transmission of energy.'

'Is that possible?' Lewisham asked, ignoring Alastair's glare.

'We are testing the hypotheses,' Professor Travers said. He shrugged his shoulders. 'As with most of what we do, it will likely not work out as we hoped.'

Alastair cleared his throat.

'Well,' Professor Travers said, hastily returning to the topic at hand. 'We were conducting some tests in the last few days and came across a set of transmissions. They are... unique.'

'Out with it, man,' Alastair growled.

Professor Travers' insistence on distracting himself from the main thrust of his conversation was maddening.

'They are unique in the sense that they were made on a frequency that has never before been used for communications. As you know, the Party is rigorous in maintaining its control of transmission devices. I'm sure you, Column Leader, of all people, would understand the ramifications of that sort of hidden communication.'

Alastair nodded, slightly mollified by the man's understanding of Party policy.

Travers raised his hand to forestall his daughter, who had begun to speak. 'No, Anne. We've already discussed this, and we won't be doing so again.'

Anne subsided, but her look of frustration spoke volumes.

Professor Travers sighed. 'You'd better listen to the recording. One of our technicians came to us with it. If advice hadn't come from London that you two were flying up here, we would've couriered them down on the double. Anyway, this is what was recorded.'

Pressing a switch, Travers took a step back, as if there

were something dangerous about the recording. There was a clank, then the tape began to turn. A crackling hiss filled the air, rising and falling like a heartbeat.

'…are you sure this can't be traced…'

'Tell your Quee… highly unlikely your technology allows these transmissions to be detected. Our scram… ensures…' Here the signal warbled, rising and falling like the babbling of schoolchildren in the playground.

Alastair listened, his face intent.

'…our plans and yours coincide… the synchron… of activities will ensure maxim… ffect…'

'…and the trigg… mechani… are foolproof…'

Again the signal collapsed into a distortion of howling static and psychedelic moans before re-establishing itself.

'…they are sufficient to… your purposes. The co-ordinated attacks you… planning on your capital will… sufficie… to cause upris… and divert attention from our plans. We will be waiting…'

The player stopped, the tape spool spinning on for a few seconds before coming to rest, the tape flapping in the air like the tail of an eager dog. There was silence in the room for a few seconds more.

'It's the reference to the Queen that proves its veracity,' Alastair murmured, rubbing his jaw.

'What do you mean?' Travers said.

'That's classified information,' Alastair snapped, aware he had spoken out of turn. He nodded to Lewisham and indicated the tape with a jerk of his thumb.

Lewisham responded by stepping up to the player and removed the spool.

'What are you doing?' Anne asked, stepping forward and putting her hand on Lewisham's arm.

Lewisham looked down at her hand then up at Anne's face. Anne stepped back, her hand balled into a fist.

'We're taking that back to London,' Alastair said. 'That's evidence relating to the bombings.'

'Evidence?' Anne said. 'It's my proof…'

'Anne!' Professor Travers said, moving to stand beside his daughter. Together like that, the family resemblance was unmistakable, as were the looks of unhappiness on each of their faces.

'There are bigger things going on than your stupid investigation,' Anne said. A blush crept up her neck and into her face. She quivered, like a taut bowstring. Alastair thought she might leap at him, and relished the idea of knocking her down.

'Your... aliens?' he said, the corner of his mouth quirking. 'I think, Professor Travers, that your head of research needs a long holiday. Perhaps... Cromer? I hear it is quite relaxing at this time of year. Certainly, my great uncle thought so when he was executed there.' Alastair smiled; he was enjoying himself. 'No aliens, last I heard.'

'You bloody fool,' Anne said, almost hissing. 'You're so caught up in your ignorance you refuse to see what's in front of your face. The chemical traces are not of this Earth. That... thing on the recording even refers to London as "your capital". Who speaks like that?'

'Oh, I don't doubt there are aliens involved, *Miss* Travers,' Alastair said, as he paused by the door. 'Foreign agents, of course. Not to worry. We'll catch them, try them, then execute them. You've done us a great service, with this recording. You will maintain a watch, to see if there are more transmissions. Good. Unity is Strength.'

He promptly left the room with Lewisham in tow.

'What did you think of all that?' Alastair said to Lewisham. 'All this talk of aliens.'

'She appears to be a woman of conviction, sir. But convictions can take you down a blind alley.'

'They can.' Alastair nodded. 'She's been cooped up in this burrow for too long. Place like this, it can queer your mind.'

Lewisham nodded. They turned the corner at the top of the corridor, when an approaching figure forced Alastair to a halt. His jaw dropped.

'Sally? My God, what are you doing here?'

The slim figure of Sally, holding a folder and wearing a grey pencil skirt and a pale pink blouse, stopped just in front of him. Her eyes widened in surprise, before a warm smile flooded her face.

'My goodness, Alastair. Of all places.'

Alastair was intimately aware that Lewisham had stopped when he did. He turned his head and saw her smirking. Straightening his shoulders, Alastair managed a smile.

'What are you doing here?'

'It's like I said when we met. I work in various facilities. This is one of them. We're a touch shorthanded. But it's nice to be needed, don't you think?'

Alastair heard a cut off giggle behind him. He saw Sally's eyes narrow a little, and had the image of Lewisham clamping a hand over her mouth to stifle more noises. Aware that his face had grown flushed, Alastair forged on as best he could.

'We're part of the investigation into the London bombings. We're picking up the results of the chemical tests.' He nodded to Lewisham. 'We might have the plotters recorded on tape.'

'Well done, you,' Sally exclaimed, reaching out to grip his arm. She leaned forward, as if to make their conversation more intimate. He smelled her perfume; the heady scent of lilacs brought back memories of their night together. 'Are they linked to the bombing of *The Revolutionary Arms*?'

'Too early to say,' Alastair said. 'One thing though. These people... They're absolutely brazen.' He shook his head. Sally nodded sympathetically. 'Once we catch them, it'll be down into the cells they go.' Sally shuddered. Alastair felt a queer sensation at her reaction. 'This tape may provide us with a chance to roll up the entire network of Resistance cells in London.'

'And you're the man for the job,' Sally said. She looked at him with those dark eyes and leaned in. 'How about supper? Tonight?'

'Tonight?' Alastair was surprised. He felt off balance. 'We're aah... We're flying back now. Did you want to...?'

'Oh no. I have to sort a few things out here. But don't worry, I'll be back in London this evening. I'll make a booking for St Kilda's, around the corner from the Adelphi. I know it's awfully European to eat so late, but how does nine-thirty sound?'

'Wonderful,' Alastair said, suddenly awkward. 'We have to be going. I... Ah... I'll see you tonight, then?'

'Oh yes.' Sally's smile was wide and inviting. 'You certainly will.'

With that, she tipped Alastair a wink, nodded primly to Lewisham, and walked passed towards Professor Travers' office.

'Not a word,' Alastair warned, glaring at Lewisham. His eye drifted, focusing for a moment on Sally, before returning to his platoon under leader. 'Not one bloody word.'

'Sir,' Lewisham said.

Alastair chose to ignore the amusement in her eyes. They walked on, heading for the exit and the waiting plane.

CHAPTER TWELVE

POWER, OF course, is a drug. The more you use it, the more you want it. The thing that those with power fear most, is losing it. Hence, after the Revolution, the establishment of the security state became the Party's number one priority. People's Courts were set up the length and breadth of the nation. Leading members of the dissolved political parties, military, the judiciary, the universities, the church, civil servants and academia were the first to be hauled in and judged. Many of these 'trials' were recorded, and played as newsreels in the cinemas. The verdicts were pre-ordained and the executions wildly applauded by baying crowds in their Sunday best.

But the decapitation of the collective memory of the pre-Revolutionary state wasn't enough. Isolated instances of resistance were made to be worst by the Directorate of Information. The Revolution hovered on the edge of ruin, or so said the voice on the radio. So, gradually, with the public aim of protecting the Revolution in the name of the people, but the private reality of ensuring the retention, in the Party's hands, of power so bloodily won, the security state was born. The Directorate of Internal Affairs became the main guardian of the Republic. Granted summary powers, it arrested, interrogated, punished and executed without answering to anyone, bar the Leader. It enforced its will through the Auxpol militia, a breeding ground of eager thugs.

The notion of a private state, where someone could safely contemplate their own thoughts and needs and desires, became anathema. The school curriculum mimicked the Party line. Internal Affairs recruited an army of snoops. The radio, in between hours of martial music, became filled with nothing more than pap and propaganda. The television, once the Party grasped its ability to influence the people, became the central means of disseminating information.

And, in time, the work of Internal Affairs became easier. While External Security occasionally encroached on its patch, Internal Affairs reigned supreme. After all, if the mere idea that Auxpol goons could come smashing through your front door in the dead of night and haul you into a darkened cell where you would be condemned to a violent death on the say so of a disgruntled neighbour, then of course you would be glad, at every opportunity, to be seen echoing whatever was spoon-fed to you by the Party.

From 'An Unpublishable Memoir' by [redacted]. Retained in the Security Directorate Archives.

Gordon Lethbridge-Stewart sat at his desk in his offices in Whitehall. Thick checked carpets swallowed the noise of the scratching of his pen as he read an intelligence report. The Tsarists were up to their old tricks in Afghanistan. Gordon was determining whether a diplomatic salvo would do the job, or something launched from thirty thousand feet was more in order.

A door between a set of floor-to-ceiling bookshelves led to his outer office, where a team of assistants sought to tame the flow of departmental paperwork, giving Gordon the space to plot and scheme and manipulate. The Department of External Security's remit began at the water's edge, but Gordon had long determined to know what happened at home as well as abroad. Some in the Cabinet called him the Spider behind his back, but he didn't care. If they knew what he knew about them...

A bottle of Scotch sat open on his desk, and he'd already refilled the glass twice. Gordon lived for his work, and spent most of his days and evenings in the office he had fought hard to gain. His flat was a place where he slept and bathed; his country estate more a museum than a home. It was here, in this office, seated at the centre of a globe-spanning web of intelligence and influence that Gordon felt most comfortable. The Republic of Britain held its Empire still. Someone had to make sure it remained that way.

A chill breeze wafted through an open bulletproof window. It exasperated his security detail, which gave Gordon some comfort. It meant they weren't simply going through the motions of protecting him.

'Just making life a little bit interesting, Charles,' Gordon had once said to his head of security.

Charles, a bullet-headed man with shoulders that would shame a gorilla, merely nodded. He knew better than to chance his master's good humour.

There came a tap at the inner door. Looking up, Gordon pinched the bridge of his nose, sighed, then tossed aside his pen. His man in St Petersburg clearly thought he was writing a thriller, not reporting on the inner machinations of the government of Alexander VI, Tsar of Russia, King of Poland and Grand Prince of Finland. He was glad to be spared it, even for a moment.

'Come.' He settled back in his chair, savouring the chill breeze from the window, and the sounds of the city at repose.

As Director of External Security, Gordon had a large staff. He had been Director over a decade, an accomplishment in an era where departmental heads came and went, often at the Leader's increasingly capricious whims. Gordon firmly believed he wouldn't have survived as long, even with his remarkable skills at political infighting, without a cadre of committed loyalists. The woman who opened the door, Irene Carson, ostensibly one of his secretary's, was much more than that. A grim-faced woman, she stood sentinel as he went about his duties, screening his calls and visitors, ensuring his schedule remained on the straight and narrow. Her devotion to him, he was firmly convinced, extended to taking a bullet for him should the need arise.

Carson came in, an irritated look on her face.

'Director Frogmorton is here to see you, Director.'

Before Gordon could respond, the familiar, bulky figure of Frogmorton appeared in the doorway. He brushed passed Carson, who shot him a venomous look, before returning her gaze to Gordon.

'It's fine, Irene,' Gordon said, rising from his seat and rounding the desk. 'Director Frogmorton is always welcome to visit, aren't you, Freddie?' He waved Frogmorton towards an overstuffed chair, into which the Director gratefully sank.

'Can you get the Eastern European file ready for me, Irene? I'll want to look it over before I leave.'

Irene nodded, and scuttled from the office, closing the door behind her.

Frogmorton chortled. 'Trouble with the Slavs, Gordon?' he asked, shaking his head. His jowls quivered. 'Russia is a problem we should've dealt with decades ago.'

Gordon was a little surprised by Frogmorton's comment. The man usually interested himself in his vices – food, women, flogging his servants – and less with issues affecting the defence of the Republic.

'Nothing ExSec can't handle. And if all goes well with Operation: Mole-Bore, we'll be in an even better position to deal with the Slavs.'

'Ah yes, your son's little pet project. Terrible name for it.'

Gordon raised an eyebrow. 'Indeed. Considering the inferno that will ensure if it succeeds... Well, perhaps a new name will be considered later. Now...' He looked at Frogmorton for a moment. The man's eyes looked black. He wondered what drugs the man had taken. 'Would you like a drink?'

'Absolutely,' Frogmorton said. 'There's never not a good time for a drink, eh?'

Gordon nodded noncommittally, and poured Frogmorton a stiff drink of Scotch into a fresh glass. He handed it to him, retrieved his own glass, and sat in the chair opposite Frogmorton.

'So, what can I do for you, Freddie? It's rather late for you, isn't it?'

Frogmorton's gaze turned sly. 'That's rather cheeky of you to say, Gordon. I take my responsibilities in the Department of Energy very seriously. After all, how can one hold a good debauch when the lights are out?' He laughed at his own joke, then noisily swallowed a mouthful of Scotch. 'Lovely to see you have the good stuff on tap.' Frogmorton held up his glass and looked at the contents appreciatively.

Gordon watched the performance with a furrowed brow. He knew the man was a pig, but even for him, this was a little too much.

'Freddie, why are you here?'

'I'm worried about the succession,' Frogmorton blurted out.

Gordon froze. Openly talking about what might occur in the days after the Leader's death was verboten. He knew of at least one Director whose unexpected death was linked to asking a similar question in jest, a decade ago.

'The Leader's health is not in question,' Gordon said, automatically.

He felt as if he was being observed from all parts of his office. Frogmorton grinned beatifically at him, as if engaged in a burlesque routine.

'Oh, come on, Gordon,' he said, drinking another mouthful of Scotch.

The man's ability to put away alcohol was legendary, but his behaviour tonight was something new.

'No one lives forever, no matter how many guards one has between you and the common folk.'

'I'm not sure what you want from me,' Gordon said, setting aside his drink. 'But I don't appreciate your tone or the direction of this conversation.'

'Oh, relax, you stuffed shirt,' Frogmorton said. Gordon's face stiffened in shock. Frogmorton had never before dared speak to him like that. 'I'm not one of your sons, you know. The youngest especially. You've whipped him like a dog, haven't you? Scared of his own shadow, or so I've heard. Don't get me wrong, he deserves his rank, but you've cruelled his character. You're not right to lead, did you know that, Gordon? Not after what you did to your boy.'

It took Gordon a moment to realise that Frogmorton had effectively declared war on his ambitions for the role of Leader. It stunned him, stunned him so much that when Frogmorton clambered to his feet, it was all Gordon could do but stare at him, his mouth open in shock.

'Consider this a friendly warning, Gordon,' Frogmorton said. 'I have ambitions of my own. Just because you and Paula think the top job is yours to fight over once the Old Man is dead, doesn't make it true.' He leaned forward. Gordon smelled Scotch on his breath, and something else, a smell like jasmine.

'The day will come when we're all standing around looking at the Leader stretched out in his tomb. And then the gloves will come off.'

Without further word, Frogmorton lumbered around the chair and over to the inner door. Opening it, he paused on the threshold and turned to Gordon.

'Have a good night's sleep, old chap. I fear you'll need it.'

The door shut with a soft whisper, leaving Gordon alone.

Dumbfounded, Gordon rose from his chair and circled back to his desk. The sheer gall of the man, he thought, pensively staring out of the window. The city was as silent as the grave, matching his mood. Frogmorton's unexpected announcement of his intention to bid for the Leadership had thrown him.

A few minutes later, there came a scratch at the door.

'What now?' said Gordon angrily. He hated feeling at the whim of events, and not their master.

Carson came in, ashen faced. Gordon immediately felt adrenaline begin its icy surge through his veins.

'Is it the Leader?' he asked, half expecting the news.

Irene shook her head.

'It's Frogmorton,' she said. While her face was white, her voice was as steady as a rock. 'He's dead. Members of the Auxpol found his body an hour ago.'

CHAPTER THIRTEEN

KNIGHT BOUNCED off the creature's side and slammed into the wall. Winded, he still managed to duck under its outstretched arms. A smell, like jasmine, lingered in the air. Up close, the filaments embedded in the fissures running over its body trembled ecstatically.

The creature groaned, the sound like glass breaking. All this came in a flash of sensations as Knight somehow kept his feet and ran along the corridor.

He stopped at a junction, looked left, then charged to the right. The blaring of the klaxon drowned out his panting breaths. He saw an open door, ducked through and slammed it shut.

The room was unlit. Shapes swam into view, impressions of solidity. Benches and shelves and cabinets. All normal, all prosaic.

There are monsters chasing me, Knight thought desperately. Gathering his scattered thoughts, he saw several overalls the creature wore sitting on a bench.

Aware of the feeling of vulnerability his nakedness instilled in him, Knight crossed to the bench and pulled an overall from the pile. He spent a few seconds struggling with the sleeves and legs, but he managed it in the end. All this focused his attention. He heard the klaxons, heard distant sounds of pursuit and shouting. Instinctively, he knew if he was captured they would kill him.

'Don't get caught then,' he said.

He cast around, looking for something, anything, to arm himself. Inside a cabinet, he saw several metal rods sitting in clamps. Each had a claw-shaped tool at one end, and a recessed stud at the other. After puzzling out the release mechanism, Knight extracted one of the rods. Despite its thickness, it felt light in his hands. Knight pressed the stud and electricity sizzled and sparked from the claw. Actinic light lit the room. The clean scent of ozone filled the air, banishing the ever-present scent of jasmine clogging his nostrils.

Knight smiled. Now he could fight back.

He stood at the door, listening carefully. Through the crack between the door and the frame, he saw a looming figure. Stepping to one side, Knight pressed his back to the wall. The door opened and light streamed in.

The figure moved through the gap. Knight jabbed the claw into the junction between the creature's neck and massive shoulders and pressed the stud.

The figure's mouth yawned open in agony. Smoke erupted from the contact point, a poisonous reek that made Knight's eyes water. The creature lumbered around, staring at Knight with those black, dead eyes. It reached for him.

Knight danced away from its grasping hands, then moved in, digging the claw into the creature's flesh. Pressing the stud, he felt power flow into the creature. It gave a bubbling shriek, then staggered backwards, crashed into a bench and toppled to the ground.

It lay there, motionless.

Knight waited, listening keenly for any reaction from outside. Nothing. The klaxons continued their wild howling.

Affecting a confidence he didn't feel, Knight eased the door open. He checked and saw the corridor was empty. Stepping outside, he began hunting for an exit.

CHAPTER FOURTEEN

ALASTAIR WASN'T long back from the trip to Northumberland. He had farewelled Lewisham at the airfield, sending her off with orders to check on the status of the search for Knight. As for himself, Alastair spent the afternoon reviewing files, looking for known Resistance members with training in chemicals. The search had borne no fruit, leaving him feeling testy. He checked over the daily report that had been dropped on his desk by a harried looking section leader half an hour before.

All quiet at the borders, the report said. An enormous amount of chatter detected among known Resistance sympathisers. The rioting had mostly levelled off, with Auxpol conducting summary executions amidst the ruins of the centre of Gateshead. Investigators had been able to shut down the pirate broadcasts, tracing them to an abandoned flat in the Shoreditch area of London. There, they had found a recording, playing and rewinding, playing and rewinding. The Department of Information had a new Director, the report said.

Sitting at his desk, Alastair checked the time. Just after 7pm. His mood lifted a little at the thought of supper with Sally. He poured himself a Scotch, glanced over the test results one more time, then fell to brooding.

After a few minutes, he shifted his gaze warily to the reel sitting on his desk, as if it were a cobra ready to strike.

The test results were gobbledygook to him; a technocrat's babble of jargon designed to ring-fence their conclusions from any outside contradiction. But while Alastair had a suspicion about the scientists, he wasn't so arrogant he could confidently dispute the science. After all, the scientists knew what the consequences were if there was any inkling of subterfuge or subversion. A bullet, if you were lucky, or a labour camp if you weren't.

Alastair turned back to the report. Clearly, Anne Travers was highly strung. Based on her file, which he'd accessed on his return, she was devoted to the Republic. Perhaps too devoted. Her understandable suspicion and fear of internal subversion had seemingly morphed into a paranoid belief in actual extra-terrestrial interference on Earth.

Professor Travers, though, was too steady for his conclusions to be dismissed outright about the likely source of the chemicals. That, and his family's connection to the Revolution. Alastair had given a low whistle when he'd read the report that the man's uncle had been one of the first through the gates at Buckingham Palace on that glorious day in 1943. Travers had been overseas, in the East, when the Revolution upended centuries of neglect and corruption, but he had returned, according to the reports, to assist the national struggle to rebuild Britain along Republican lines.

'Unity is Strength,' Alastair said, a little dryly, toasting his empty office.

He felt a surge of guilt then, at his flippancy, and looked hard in the corners of the room. Sighing, he swallowed a mouthful of Scotch, and then abruptly wondered what Sally was doing at that moment.

Frustrated, he set his glass down with a thump, bumping the reel.

He picked it up and turned it over in his hands, remembering the crackle of static and the voices whispering to each other. He imagined them; the Resistance traitor and their supplier, bent over their transmitters, sending their treason through the air. His grip tightened on the reel until he heard it creak under his fingers.

His hand jerked open, and the reel clattered onto the desk. Leaning to one side, Alastair pulled open his drawer and took out a small reel-to-reel player. Occasionally, he would sit at his desk late at night listening to interrogations. Placing it on the desk, he expertly threaded the tape until it was ready.

He reached for the PLAY button. Gripped by a sudden

urge, Alastair flicked off his desk lamp, plunging the room into near darkness. He hesitated a moment, unsure, then, annoyed with himself, pressed the button. Closing his eye as the tape turned, Alastair leaned closer to the player.

Static filled the air, the insistent hiss crowding out his thoughts as it insinuated itself into him. He thought for a moment he heard a voice lost in the static, then discounted it as a fancy brought on by the dark. The hissing grew louder and louder, stretching out until Alastair thought something had gone wrong with the tape. Then, the static fell away, and the voices began their conversation.

The warbling on the tape seemed stronger than before, a siren call from the depths of space. Alastair felt himself lost in an unfamiliar sensation of calm. The words were an annoyance, their interruption unwelcome as he sought out the silence within the warp and weft of the frequencies tangling and untangling on the recording. He thought of Sally, her smile, the unexpected pleasure of meeting her in the Vault. All these were unfamiliar sensations, after a lifetime of struggle and pressure from within and without.

'We will be waiting…'

Alastair's phone rang, the noise like an explosion. His eye fluttered open and he saw for a moment the shadows seething in the corners of the room. Panicked, he slapped at the switch on the lamp. Light banished the shadows and left him pinned to his chair. With his other hand, he fumbled the telephone receiver to his ear.

'Alastair.' The voice made his heart flutter.

'Father.'

There was a moment of silence, as if his father was mulling over a response.

'I need… I need your assistance.'

'What's wrong with James? Can't a brigade leader be of better service?'

As soon as he said it, Alastair was shocked. But his father didn't respond to the bitterness. Of course, he still resented his father's standing in his way, that willingly or not, his father was preventing him from getting the promotion he deserved. But to voice such dissatisfaction…

'I need you.'

For a moment, Alastair couldn't place the discordant note in his father's voice. Then, with dawning shock, he recognised it. Fear.

'What's wrong?' he asked, suddenly glad his father had come to him, not to James. If he played this right, perhaps he could usurp James from Eastchester after all. With his father's blessing. 'What sort of help?'

'I need you in my office. Tonight. Now.'

'Why?'

Alastair thought of Sally, and knowing he might miss supper angered him.

'Damn it, boy. Do as you're told!'

'I'm not your dog, Father,' Alastair snapped back, unable to contain his own anger. Yes, he wanted the promotion and would do what was necessary, but he wouldn't be treated like this either. 'I will not be commanded about with the offer of a treat and a pat on the head. Why?'

There was a long pause, broken at the end by his father's sigh.

'Because the Republic needs you.' A longer pause. 'Because I need you.'

Precisely twelve minutes later, Irene Carson let Alastair into his father's office. Seated behind his massive desk, Alastair thought his father looked like some sort of eastern potentate. It was all Alastair could do to resist saluting.

'You came.'

'You asked,' Alastair said. He looked closely at his father. Beneath the reserve, he sensed a mind in turmoil.

'Close the door, Irene,' Gordon said. Carson nodded and left them alone.

'A good woman in a crisis,' Gordon murmured, glancing down at his hands splayed on his desk. He looked up, and for a moment, Alastair thought he saw the mask slip.

'You should find yourself a wife, Alastair.'

Alastair thought about Sally. He desperately needed to see her.

'One day, Father,' Alastair said, dutifully. 'The Party is a jealous mistress.'

'She is,' Gordon said.

'One question. Why not call on James? He has the higher rank, he essentially put the RSF together.'

'Yes, but he's...' Gordon blinked. 'His loyalty is not as certain. He thinks I do not know, but I keep a close tab on both my sons. You, Alastair... You are the right man for this job.'

He stood abruptly, the action sending his chair banging into the wall behind him. Alastair took an involuntary step back. Unleashed, his father's temper rivalled his own. But his father wasn't angry, not this time. Another emotion commanded him.

'I don't understand what happened, but not twenty minutes ago, Director Frogmorton was in my office, sitting over there, drinking my Scotch and talking nonsense.'

'I understand the Director is a gregarious fellow, Father. He likes his drink... As do we all.' Alastair treaded carefully. His father's emotions were like a minefield.

'Gregarious?' Gordon shook his head. 'You don't know the half of it, boy.' He turned and walked over to the window, looking out over the city with his back to his son.

Alastair waited, feeling the tension in the air grow worse.

'Time is of the essence,' his father said at last. 'Despite what I saw, despite what Ms Carson saw, the Director of Energy has been found dead...' Gordon waved his hand to silence Alastair. 'Don't interrupt. He was in this very room, seated not ten feet from you, when by all accounts he was dead. Killed in an accident involving a vehicle, with two others.' He stopped and shook his head. 'Do you understand what I'm saying, boy?' His voice rose an octave. 'I was speaking with a dead man!'

'What proof do you have Frogmorton is actually dead, and died before you saw him here?' Alastair asked.

Gordon flipped open a folder, to reveal a number of grainy black and white photos. 'I had an Auxpol commander telex these pictures to my office. These were taken in the last hour.'

The images were poor, but the content clear enough. A van, its nose a crumpled wreck, lay upside down. Another picture, taken through a shattered side window, showed two broken bodies piled up against the broken dashboard. Another shot, from the rear of the van looking into the back, showed a corpulent body lying on its back, arms and legs lashed together.

And a final shot, a close up of a bloodied face. Slack mouth, tongue protruding obscenely through torn lips. A black hole at the temple, where the skull had been staved in. The eyes wide open and glassy and very, very dead.

'Proof enough?' Gordon said. He'd freshened his glass of Scotch and had already drank half of it.

'There must be something wrong with your timing,' Alastair said. 'A man cannot be in two places at once, especially someone who is dead.'

Gordon frowned, as if an unpleasant memory had just surfaced. 'You might be surprised... No, this is different.'

A thought occurred to Alastair, and he turned away, frowning.

'What are you thinking, boy? Out with it.'

'It's insane,' Alastair began, before faltering to a stop.

'I spoke with a dead man. How's that for insane?'

'When I visited the Vault to discuss their analysis of the chemicals used in the bombings, I met their head of research. She was adamant that based on the test results, the chemicals were alien in origin. I laughed it off, but...' He looked up. 'I was also provided with a recording of a transmission between a member of the Resistance and someone who supplied the explosives. The Vault's claim is the frequency used to communicate is previously unknown to them. It makes for interesting listening.'

'This is madness,' Gordon fumed. He retreated to his chair and sat down, the glass of Scotch within easy reach. He looked at Alastair. 'You'll have to investigate this for me.'

'Now hang on,' Alastair said. 'The Security Directorate is ExSec's eyes and ears on internal resistance, not ordinary criminal cases.'

'Don't tell me what the Directorate does and doesn't do,' Gordon stormed. With an effort, he calmed himself. 'What could be more disruptive than the death of a Director?'

'I'm already investigating the bombings.'

'Not anymore,' Gordon said. 'I've already informed Pemberton you will report directly to me, for the foreseeable future. This is important. I can't believe Frogmorton was in two places at once, but if I doubt the evidence of my own eyes, I have to start questioning my sanity. I need to understand what is happening.'

'The local authorities will be difficult,' Alastair said.

Gordon smiled, the first since Alastair arrived. 'I've intervened to put our people in charge of the scene.'

'Really.'

'Yes, really. External Security can't do its job if we don't know what's happening on the home front. We have our eyes and ears, loyal men and women, informing for us. The safety of the Republic is my paramount concern.'

'Save the oration for the Leader's funeral, father,' Alastair said, shocking himself with his directness.

'The boy has grown a spine,' Gordon said coolly, looking at Alastair with a calculating glare.

'But that's what you've always wanted, isn't it?' Alastair said, taking another step closer to the abyss. 'If not you, then a mirror image, someone to carry on your dreams of power.'

His father's nostrils flared in anger. 'A mirror image. How apt. Ah, the things you don't know.'

'I know enough, Father.'

'No, you don't. And I don't appreciate being questioned in my office about my motives, Alastair.'

This time, Alastair knew he had gone too far. His father rarely said his name, and then only in anger. But then Alastair thought of Sally, and the bold manner she looked at him.

'I've have aspirations too, Father,' Alastair said, hotly. 'I can't just be your shadow, following you wherever you go, doing whatever you want. And, frankly, it should be at Eastchester.'

Gordon's gaze swept over Alastair, who set his jaw against it. Gordon nodded. A smile flitted across his face. 'Perhaps your aspirations and mine go hand in hand. We live in a world where the strong do as they must, do you understand?'

'I understand Father, but you must let me stand on my own two feet.'

Gordon turned and stared pensively out the open window. The sound of booted feet marching rose to them, a distant echo.

'The Auxpol are out tonight,' Gordon said, turning briefly

100

to look at Alastair.

'Breaking heads, no doubt.' Alastair had passed a column of the black uniformed Auxpol marching towards Trafalgar Square. The look on the faces of some of the men was a prophecy of violence.

'Do you have a problem with that?' Gordon said. He turned to look again at Alastair. 'The boy I raised never had an issue with harsh measures.'

'Did I have a choice?' Alastair said, quietly.

'No. I had grand plans for you, boy. Still do. And look where my guidance has got you,' Gordon said. The curtain billowed before collapsing.

'Up a blind alley,' Alastair said, leaning on the other side of the desk. 'I have followed your dictates, done all you've asked of me. And I've washed up here, as a column leader, where they're ten a penny across the Republic.'

Gordon walked around the desk until he stood inches from his son.

'You are where you are because of my will and your decisions. Without me, you'd be nothing but one of the proles, cowering in their homes while the Party ensures we retain control. The Republic is on a knife's edge, boy. You have a ringside seat, but only if you grasp your chances.'

'Chances? More like the scattering of bread crumbs.'

Gordon smiled. It wasn't a nice thing to see. 'Play your hand correctly now, and perhaps you will get that post in Eastchester you crave so much.'

'You said you needed my assistance,' Alastair said. 'What do you need me for?'

'You say you want to stand on your own two feet? Very well, then. Prove it. Freddie Frogmorton is dead. And yet he was alive, here, at the same time as the vehicle he was travelling in crashed. How is that possible? If true, what does it mean?'

Alastair frowned. 'Is there any hint of suspicion regarding the accident?'

'At this stage, no. But there could be… If you find it.'

Alastair's mind raced. 'You're looking for leverage, aren't you? Against… Director Hipwood?'

Gordon nodded, his face relaxing into a genuine smile at

Alastair's deduction.

'Good, my boy. Very good. Responsibility for the safety of all members of Cabinet lies in the hands of the Director of Internal Affairs. If it can be shown she has been lax...'

'Lax? That's a little too transparent, isn't it? There will be many, let alone Hipwood, who will suspect you used Frogmorton's death for your benefit.'

Gordon nodded. 'Suspicions I can handle. Being brazen has its advantages. People will think that in the existing surveillance state, no one could possibly get away with anything so obvious. In any event, they'll be too busy scrambling for advantage. And while they do that...'

'You'll tighten your position as the obvious successor to the Leader,' Alastair said. Damn the man, but he knew what he was doing.

Gordon nodded, a look of approval in his eyes. 'Very good. You've learned something, after all. Director Hipwood is my only possible rival – the others are placeholders or non-entities. Do this for me.'

'And my reward?'

'That long hoped for promotion, replacing James, and a chance to be your own man.'

Alastair stared at his father for long seconds. Hope flared in his chest. A familiar craving for approval, for reward for his suffering and hard work, coursed through him. But then his hand drifted up to his eye patch, and an equally familiar sense of despair, long coiled in him, made itself known.

'We'll see,' he said. 'But what of this duplicate Frogmorton? If there is... alien activity about, we can't have a duplicate director on the Cabinet.

'One step at a time, boy,' Gordon said. He rubbed his jaw. 'Determine if Frogmorton is actually dead. Then report back to me. In the meantime, I'll deal with this supposed duplicate.'

Alastair nodded, not quite believing the discussion. Aliens...

'All right,' he said, after a few moments. 'Give me an hour or two, then I'll call back.

'I'm relying on you,' Gordon said, as Alastair turned to leave. 'Be my eyes and ears, do you understand? This may be the most important thing you ever do.'

CHAPTER FIFTEEN

ALASTAIR PULLED up in a side street near the London docks. He took a long barrelled torch from the glove compartment and slipped it into his coat. The road gleamed after a recent shower. It was quiet, a reflection of the curfew and the generally rundown state of the area. Alastair stepped out, nostrils flaring at the smell of the Thames. He glimpsed the running lights of a lone barge. The long, mournful blast of its horn echoed over the landscape, before dwindling into the night.

The accident was around the corner. The van had lost control, possibly on the slick road and crashed down an embankment. A lone figure stood at the top, almost hidden by the shadows. Alastair saw a familiar flash of metal held at hip-level, and lifted his hands away from his body to show he wasn't armed.

'Easy,' Alastair said.

The figure stepped forward, revealing Du Plessis.

'So, it's you my father sent,' Alastair said.

'Got a call, boss.' Du Plessis flashed him a grin. 'Can't say no to the top man.'

'I take Klaasen is down there?' Alastair nodded at the embankment.

'That's right,' Du Plessis said. 'It's not pretty down there.'

'Anyone been past?'

Du Plessis nodded. 'Local police car went by about fifteen minutes ago, boss. One, maybe two figures inside.'

'You think they were looking for the van?'

'Yes,' Du Plessis said. 'They didn't stop.'

'Not the police then? A stolen vehicle with fake officers

inside, looking for the van?'

'It's what I'd do. Posing as the police is the best way to get around during the curfew.'

Alastair considered it for a moment, then nodded. 'If the Resistance have got their hands on police issue equipment and uniforms, it makes our jobs harder.'

'In or out of uniform, men die the same, boss,' Du Plessis said, grinning crookedly. He glanced at the embankment. 'Frogmorton is in the van.'

'So, it's definitely him down there?'

'Why wouldn't it be? Saw him with my own eyes.'

'Right,' Alastair said, aware he had to tread carefully. 'I'd best get down and see what's what.'

Du Plessis nodded, and reached for his walkie-talkie to announce Alastair to Klaasen.

The recent rain made it difficult, but Alastair scrambled down the weed-choked embankment with most of his dignity intact. Klaasen emerged from the other side of the upturned van.

'Boss,' he said, nodding as Alastair rose to his feet.

'Let's have a look, shall we?' Alastair said.

The van had left a trail of broken weeds and bracken down the length of the slope. Judging by the extensive damage to the bodywork, the van had rolled several times before coming to rest on its roof. One of the rear doors stood open.

Switching on the torch, Alastair crouched by the passenger window and played the light into the cabin. He winced at the two battered and broken bodies slumped against the dashboard. Broken glass dusted the corpses, which twinkled under the light.

His nostrils flared again. Under the tidal reek of the nearby Thames, he smelled something… fragrant.

'Jasmine?' he murmured.

'What was that, boss?' Klassen's boots crunched towards him.

'Nothing important,' Alastair said. 'Do these two have any identification on them?'

'I've been through their clothing, and the van. Nothing.'

'There will be a record of them, somewhere.' Alastair looked up at Klaasen. 'Radio Du Plessis and arrange transport to come here from Leconfield House. One man only, someone you can trust to keep his mouth shut. I want these bodies moved onto Security Directorate property. Make sure there's space in the morgue, as well. And get Henderson in. I want an autopsy done before dawn.'

Klaasen stepped away and began speaking into his walkie-talkie.

Alastair rose to his feet, wiping his hands on his trousers. He went around to the upturned rear of the van and looked inside.

Alastair had met Frogmorton once, at a party his father held several years ago. The Director of Energy's appetites were well known – food, drink, women. Gross in every sense of the word, the man had repelled Alastair even as he had forced himself to shake his hand and exchange pleasantries.

Now that hand was bound to the other by a rope which cut deep into the engorged wrists. As in the photographs, Frogmorton's corpse lay on its back. An eye, clouded like a marble in death, stared at Alastair. The tongue protruded from the mouth. Alastair also saw a bulge in the neck where the forces unleashed by the tumbling van had shattered Frogmorton's spine.

Alastair stood there for a long while, taking in the enormity of the situation. If the Party had sanctified the Leader as God, then His Directors were angels flanking His throne. The death of a Director could only mean trouble and dissension in the highest ranks of the Party.

How in holy hell did they kidnap him? Alastair thought. He went around to the front of the van again and looked at the two dead men. Again, that sweet smell of jasmine wafted towards him. It was stronger on the driver's side of the van.

'Klaasen, do you know what I reckon?' Alastair said, musing as much to himself as the mercenary.

'No, boss.'

'I think these two worked for Frogmorton. Either his personal staff or bodyguards. There will be two men missing from his household, mark my words.' He glanced up at Klaasen, whose broad face looked troubled. 'It doesn't look good, that's for sure,' Alastair said, levering himself upright. 'The idea that a director's bodyguard would be implicated in his death…' Alastair shook his head.

'Won't be good for Director Hipwood,' Klaasen said, looking carefully at Alastair.

Alastair shrugged his shoulders noncommittally. 'I'm just a soldier. What do good soldiers do, Klaasen?'

'Look straight ahead and do what they're told.'

'Exactly.' Alastair went up to Klaasen and tapped him on the shoulder. 'And see that you do,' he said to him.

Klaasen's eyes remained fixed ahead, but he managed a tight nod.

Alastair sighed. 'Don't worry, Klaasen. If your head is ever on the chopping block, it's because mine was there first. Your loyalty to the Party is appreciated, even if we have to pay for it.'

'Unity is Strength,' Klaasen said, with only a hint of irony in his thick accent.

'Unity is Strength,' Alastair echoed, gravely. He glanced at the embankment and sighed again. 'I'll see you back at HQ.' He sketched a salute, which Klaasen returned.

Alastair began the laborious process of climbing the embankment. At the top, he saw Du Plessis approaching.

'You better take this, boss,' he said, handing his walkie-talkie over to Alastair.

'Who is it?' he said, dreading the answer.

'It's Lewisham.'

The soft crackle of static grew louder as Alastair placed the walkie-talkie against an ear.

'Lewisham? What's happening?'

There was a long silence there, a pregnant pause that made Alastair uneasy and angry at the same time.

'It's Benjamin,' Lewisham said. Was that a sob Alastair heard? 'His apartment block was levelled in the explosions. They've dragged five survivors from the rubble. Not him.'

Alastair felt his heart skip a beat. 'Are you sure?'

Du Plessis had turned his head to look away. His team was tight.

'His name isn't on the list of survivors they've dug out.'

Closing his eye for a moment, Alastair let out a long sigh. 'There's nothing we can do for him, then. We wait for the final accounting. If he's dead, we mourn him after we round up those bastards and execute them. Do you understand, Frieda? We remain focused on the investigation.'

'Understood.' Even through the static, Alastair heard the hate in her voice.

He handed the walkie-talkie back to Du Plessis.

'Bad business, boss,' Du Plessis said as he clipped the walkie-talkie back into place on his hip.

'They'll pay,' Alastair muttered. He rubbed at his temple. 'Once the corpses are gone, call for a surveillance team. If the Resistance is looking for the van, I want to know. They'll be agitated enough to risk looking for their own.'

'They're risking a lot if they get caught.'

'It would be a measure of their desperation. It's clear they were looking for the van, which means it's late to an agreed destination. Detain anyone on foot. Follow anyone travelling by vehicle. There's a slim chance we could break up a Resistance cell.'

The prospect lifted Du Plessis' mood. He cracked his knuckles in anticipation. Alastair poured cold water on his hopes.

'They've moved boldly tonight,' he said. 'The accident was pure chance. Lady Luck won't smile on us twice.' He looked at his watch and winced.

'Dinner date?' Klaasen said.

'As a matter of fact, yes,' Alastair said. 'I'll be back at Leconfield House before midnight. See that Henderson has started before I get there.'

With that, Alastair marched into the night, his boots echoing in the empty streets. His thoughts turned unwillingly to Knight. He shook his head, trying to come to grips with the news. To his unease, he found he couldn't. He gritted his teeth and thrust thoughts of Knight from his mind.

'Home first,' he said, looking down at his muddy boots and trousers.

Despite his father's task, despite Knight's apparent death, he wasn't going to miss seeing Sally. All the pressure, all the sense that something bad was coming... He needed to see her. To talk with her. To do something... normal.

Before he met Sally, the idea he would shirk his duty to attend to his barren private life would've filled him with horror. Now, though…

Alastair parked his car and walked up the steps and entered the restaurant. He paused for a moment with the *maître de*.

Showing his Directorate card, Alastair leaned in. 'There may be a call. Make sure I'm informed.'

The *maître de*, a slight fellow whose stature was at odds with his elevated hauteur, nodded.

Sally had already taken her seat. Her work with the Vault provided her with the appropriate clearance to be out on the streets during the curfew. In fact, Alastair thought, looking around the crowded restaurant, it seemed that half of London had similar clearance. When he made the point to Sally, she leaned back and laughed gaily.

'Alastair,' she said, reaching over and placing her hand on top of his. Its soft warmth made him shiver. 'The curfew is for other people, not those of us in the Party. The same goes for the power cuts. Surely you know that?' She winked at him.

'I know that without discipline, all that we've achieved could fall away. Decadence like this…' – he waved his hand around the restaurant – '…is the sort of thing you see on the Continent.'

'Oh, Alastair,' she said, laughing. That drew the attention of the diners around them. 'The Party isn't going anywhere. Aren't we entitled to enjoy ourselves?'

'Maybe,' Alastair conceded. 'But the price to be paid.' He looked aside for a moment, pensive.

'What's happened?' Sally said. Her grip on his hand tightened. 'Has someone you know…'

'Died?' Alastair nodded. 'At least, we think he has.'

'Was he a friend?'

He opened his mouth to answer, then paused. 'I think he might've been,' he said. 'In this job, it's hard to get close to anyone because…'

'Because they might die right in front of you?'

He nodded.

'You can't live your life like that, you do know that?' Sally said. 'Live for the moment, Alastair.'

'There's plenty of that thinking on display here,' he said, looking around at the smiling diners. 'Is that what we're doing right now?'

'Living for the moment? I hope so.'

'Still,' Alastair said, glancing again at the other diners. 'There's a lack of sacrifice amongst this lot.'

'Oh, I wouldn't say that. I mean, yes, they're willing to sacrifice others for their pleasure, of that I have no doubt.' She stopped, suddenly looking uncertain.

Alastair chuckled, and felt the tension in his chest begin to loosen.

'Of that I'm certain,' he said. 'It's galling though, that in the aftermath of these attacks, I think there should be much more...'

'Unity *and* Strength?' Sally looked serious now. 'The Party has done great things for Britain. That trash they swept out of the old Palace for starters.' She leaned forward. 'Did I tell you my parents were one of the first to storm the place, back in '43?'

'Really?' he said.

'Really truly,' Sally said, smiling. 'My dad never talked about it. Except when he had a few drinks on Victory Day. "That stuttering fool deserved what he got," was one thing I distinctly remember.' She lowered her voice. 'He did say he felt bad about the girls, though.'

'It's not a crime to show some human kindness,' Alastair said, a little primly. 'Is your father still alive?'

Sally shook her head. 'He died five years ago. His heart,' she said, faltering a little. She turned her head aside, blinked several times, then looked back at Alastair. 'Mother is still with us, happily. She's retired to the coast. A little village by the sea. I visit as often as I can, but work is work.'

A waiter interrupted them, took their drinks order, then swept away.

'What about your father?' Sally asked, a little tentatively. She looked up at Alastair from beneath her eyelashes.

'No need to be shy, Sally. You worked out who he was the last time we met.'

'What's he like?' She asked, as the drink's waiter arrived with a clinking tray.

After he left, Alastair swallowed a mouthful of Scotch, considering his response.

'It's complicated,' he said at last. He glanced at Sally, wary about her reaction. She stared at him with a look of genuine interest.

'Parents are always complicated,' she said, taking a sip from her wine glass. 'Mum and Dad fought all the time. I think the things they did in the '40s and afterwards, to secure the gains of the Party, deeply affected them. They were proud of their efforts, don't get me wrong, but it took a toll. And, of course, Dad often bemoaned not having a son.'

Alastair nodded. 'Father is more than complicated. After this...' His hand strayed up to his face, briefly touching the scar on his cheek.

'Go on,' Sally said. The warmth of her hand melted some of his reserve.

'After this, he was very protective,' Alastair said, looking down and to one side.

'How did it happen?'

'It's the strangest thing,' Alastair said, his eye looking into the middle distance. 'Father always said it was some sort of accident, but I can never remember. He said that I underwent treatment to help it heal. He would never tell me what sort, and I can't remember. Perhaps the trauma of it affected my recollection.' He frowned, and found himself picking at a nagging memory.

If he could just reach it... James knew, of that Alastair was sure. But, of course, his brother wouldn't tell. There were limits to even his courage.

'The best parents are protective of their children,' Sally said, patting Alastair on the arm.

He found the gesture oddly patronising, but let it go.

'That's the thing,' he mused, then swallowed another mouthful of Scotch. 'He was protective for a while, then afterwards he became driven. To be honest, Father is a terrible parent.' Alastair paused, shocked at what he had said.

Sally looked at him carefully, as if aware she had walked into a minefield.

'I'm sure he's not,' she said.

'He is. He's driven, meticulous, and very paranoid. He's plotted and planned every move he's ever made, even down to directing the lives of my brother and I. Mine, especially.'

Alastair realised he had raised his voice, and saw nearby diners glancing nervously at him. He lowered his head, balled his hand into a fist, and willed the anger away. 'He knows what he wants, that's all I'm saying.'

'I'm sure you do too, Alastair. You've reached a position of power and influence yourself, from what I can see. Anyone who has climbed the Directorate's greasy pole so high must be doing something right.'

'I must, mustn't I? Still, it haunts me,' he said, surprising himself again. Before he could explain further, he saw a waiter approaching purposefully to their table. 'Yes?' he said, sounding testy at being interrupted.

'Message for you, sir,' the waiter said.

Alastair managed a pained smile for Sally.

'If you'll pardon me,' he said.

Sally nodded, watching him stand and walk to the front desk. He picked up the receiver.

'This had better be good,' he growled, glancing at Sally as he spoke.

She lifted the wine glass to her lips and observed him over the rim.

'It is,' said a familiar voice.

'Dr Henderson?'

'Apologies for cutting into your supper, Column Leader, but I'm ready to make a preliminary report.

Alastair closed his eye, briefly. He sighed. Sally looked directly at him, a smile playing on her lips. He managed a strained smile in return.

'All right,' he said. 'I'll be there in fifteen minutes. This information had better be useful.'

Alastair crossed back to the table. 'I really am sorry,' he said, offering an apologetic smile. 'I've been called away to attend to something important. Perhaps we can do this again another night?' He saw Sally's smile slip, then she brightened.

'Your work is never done,' she said, rising and kissing him soundly on the lips.

Feeling an unfamiliar burning in his cheeks, Alastair stammered a reply. She reached into her handbag and pulled out a slip of paper and a pen. Jotting down a number, she handed it to him.

'Call me when you're free,' she said. 'We can go somewhere more private, with far less interruptions.'

'Thank you,' Alastair said, feeling slightly embarrassed by how forward she was. He tucked the paper into the inner pocket of his jacket. 'I certainly will.'

He nodded to her and left the restaurant. Outside, he looked through the broad window and saw Sally sitting alone at their table. Her head was slightly turned, and he saw a pensive look on her face. He thought about the kiss, smiled to himself, and then made his way back to his car.

CHAPTER SIXTEEN

FLASHING HIS card at the officer manning the entrance booth, Alastair drove down to the basement level, parking in a corner near the entrance to the stairs. After the loudness of the restaurant, the quiet of the parking garage was a balm. He walked across the concrete to an interior door, then began his descent to the morgue.

With each step, the atmosphere became colder and danker. The walls gleamed with condensation, and the lighting fizzed and jumped. Exiting into a corridor, the door behind him slammed shut, sending echoes booming around him. Suppressing a yawn, Alastair followed the corridor to a set of double doors. Pushing one open, he entered the morgue.

Gleaming metal drawers studded the wall on his right. The thrum of the generators came through the floor, evidence that despite the power outages, there was sufficient coverage to keep the contents fresh. In the centre of the room stood a line of gleaming metal tables. The corpses from the van were laid out on two, beside the table containing Frogmorton's gross corpse.

A figure wearing a bloodstained apron over a black suit turned at the sound of his entrance.

'Column Leader Lethbridge-Stewart,' the man said.

'Dr Henderson. Good to see you again.'

He had socialised with Henderson several times, and knew the man well enough to respect his capabilities.

'Likewise,' Henderson said. He turned and nodded at the naked corpse lying on the nearest slab. 'I'd like to thank you.'

'For what?' Alastair said.

Blood didn't bother him, but what Henderson had done to

the bodies made him wince. Y cuts had been made to the torso of each, and the skin and muscle pulled back, revealing the skeleton and organs beneath. Henderson had gone one better with Frogmorton – not just the incisions to the torso, but he had also removed the top of the director's skull, exposing the bulging brain.

In death, Frogmorton was just as gross as he had been alive. Waxen, heavy skin hung in thick folds. Through slack lips protruded a purpling tongue. The bared teeth made it look as if Frogmorton was grimacing. Under the smell of refrigerant in the air, Alastair was suddenly aware of the taint of death.

'Was that necessary?' he asked, pointing at the exposed brain.

Much of its natural pinkness had been replaced by a curdled grey. Alastair felt acid roil in his stomach.

'One must practise one's skills, Column Leader,' Henderson said, with a look of ghoulish delight. He straightened under Alastair's glare. 'I wanted to check if there were any contusions to the brain prior to death. It would indicate if he had been struck before he was kidnapped.'

'And was he?'

Henderson nodded. 'While the body was knocked around during the accident, it is clear that the original injury occurred prior to death. Cause of death was a crushing impact to the C2 and C3 vertebrae here,' he said, pointing to the base of the skull. 'But he was very likely knocked unconscious beforehand.'

'So, whoever kidnapped him was able to get close enough to knock him out,' Alastair said. When he saw Henderson quirk an eyebrow, Alastair shook his head. 'Just testing a theory. What about the others?'

'This is where it gets… disturbing.' Henderson nodded to a corpse. 'We've identified this fellow. James Pickney. Has links to convicted Resistance members but, until now, we never knew for sure that he was involved. He died from damage caused to his heart when he slammed into the dashboard during the accident. It's the sort of standard road trauma we see when people don't wear their seatbelts. As for his friend…'

'Out with it, man,' Alastair said.

Henderson glanced between Alastair and the corpse, weighing his thoughts. At last, he answered.

'He's not human.'

'He… What?'

'My examination revealed that he isn't human.'

'Not human?'

Even after the confrontation with Anne Travers at the Vault, Alastair still found it difficult to countenance the idea of alien infiltration.

'You're mistaken, Dr Henderson. Or you've been drinking.'

Henderson bridled at the comment. 'With respect, I reject the insinuation.' He pressed his lips together, regaining control. 'Look, I'm a doctor, Column Leader. I evaluate the evidence, weigh it against my experience and come up with a diagnosis.'

'And what's your diagnosis in this case?'

'This one is undoubtedly human,' Henderson said, pointing to Frogmorton. He paused. His entire posture was one of unwilling acceptance at the evidence in front of him. 'But these two… The muscular-skeletal frame is human, or as close enough as damn it.' He beckoned Alastair closer. 'Take a look at this,' he said, picking up a probe from a tray and turning back to the nearest corpse.

Alastair looked into the chest cavity. Where the heart and lungs should've been, he saw a sort of curdled soup, almost like minced meat, packed into the space. From it came that scent of jasmine he had smelled earlier. Henderson jabbed the mass with the probe and was rewarded when it seethed like seafoam on a beach. It roiled back and forth, but the movement was weak.

'Whatever this thing is, it is undeniably dead. Or as close to dead as we're ever going to be able to detect.' Henderson's face was a mixture of shock, doubt and elation. 'It's an alien life form, Column Leader. It's a soup of chemicals bonded together in a manner I've never seen before.'

'How is that possible?' Alastair asked.

'It's possible because it is,' Henderson said. He looked carefully at Alastair. 'I'm not sure what the Party's line is regarding the odd and unexplained, Column Leader, but this is as good an example as I've ever read about.'

'The Party has no fixed view on the odd or the unexplained, Dr Henderson. Only that they bend to the Party's will on all things.'

'As should we all.' Henderson returned his attention to the corpse. 'There's something else you should be worried about. I assume these were the director's bodyguards? In which case, not only are they not human, but judging by their features, they were duplicates of his bodyguards.'

Alastair looked at the corpses, stony faced.

'You understand the ramifications of what—?'

'Of course I do,' Henderson snapped. 'There must be an investigation.'

'Don't tell me how to do my job, Doctor.'

'I wouldn't dare. But this is—'

'Something the Directorate will handle.'

Henderson opened his mouth to reply, but closed it when he saw the look Alastair gave him. Henderson changed tack.

'I look forward to discussing my discovery with the Republican Society. There is data here that has huge implications for a number of fields.'

Alastair froze. 'Are you sure that's wise?'

'Wise? This is a major scientific discovery. There are possible applications here that could revolutionise our understanding of biology. Medicines, treatments, even the possibility of gene therapy for a wide range of diseases.'

'It might be better to defer discussion for a while.'

Henderson drew himself up to his full height. 'You were right to advise me not to step into the Directorate's purview, Column Leader. I would expect the same from you with regards to my area of expertise.'

The two men stared at each other for a long moment. In the end, Alastair nodded.

'Very well. Summarise your findings for me as soon as possible. I'll need it to make a report.'

'Can it wait until the morning?' Henderson asked.

Alastair nodded. 'Have it ready by oh-nine-hundred.'

'Will do.' Henderson turned his back on Alastair to ponder the gutted corpse. He bent over the incision, digging in with the probe's tip.

Alastair's eye narrowed. Unwillingly, he allowed mental

gears to click and click and click, then set themselves on a new course.

He turned and left the morgue.

Later, after he had obtained the address from Directorate files, Alastair drove out to a development housing a broad mixture of mid-level Party members. Clean streets, well-tended gardens, all with a uniformity which the Party appreciated above all else. He parked around the corner and sat, listening to the ticking of the engine as it cooled. Clouds scudded low overhead and an occasional shower swept through the suburb. Finally, Alastair reached into a bag sitting on the passenger seat, took out an implement, then exited the car.

Given the power cuts, the homes lining the streets were dark. With the curfew, no one went about after the mandated time. He saw a cat streaking across the footpath, pausing in the middle of the street to stare at him. The ambient light picked up its intense green eyes, which drilled into him. Then the cat fled away in a blur, disappearing into a garden.

He found the address with little trouble. He hesitated for a moment, wondering if it would be better, easier, if he slipped down the lane beside the house and entered through the rear. But that would take longer, and he was impatient to tie off this particular loose end.

He walked up to the front door, screwing the silencer on to the end of his pistol before tucking it into his belt and smoothing his jacket down to hide it. He pressed the buzzer and stepped back. He glanced up, and tracked a satellite passing serenely overhead, the silver dot impossibly distant from the events on the ground. For a moment, he yearned to be in orbit with it.

The chain rattled and the door opened a crack. Henderson peered blearily at him. He rubbed his face, and his eyes came into focus, widening in surprise when he recognised Alastair.

'Column Leader, what are you–?'

'I'm here for the report.'

'Can't it wait until tomorrow?'

Alastair heard another voice farther in the house, and ground his teeth together. Complications.

'It's fine, dear. Go back to bed. No, it's work. Go back to

bed.' Henderson turned back. 'All right,' he said, staring at Alastair with a strange look on his face. 'Come in.'

Opening the door wider, Henderson ushered Alastair inside. Stairs led up, while a corridor ran into the rear of the house. Henderson walked into a side room, his office, judging by the desk and filing cabinet sitting beside it.

'It's all here. I stayed up to make sure it was ready for you. Really, I could've handed it to you—'

There was a suppressed click, soft and lethal. Henderson staggered back, a hand clutching his chest. Alastair deftly moved forward, grabbing Henderson with his free hand. Gently, he guided Henderson to the ground. Henderson opened his mouth to say something, his bloodstained teeth glinting in the moonlight coming through the window. But Alastair put a gloved hand over his mouth and pressed hard.

In a minute, Henderson was dead. Alastair folded the file and stuffed it into his coat. He looked around, satisfied the desk was bare. Closing the office door behind him, he crossed to the stairs and began to climb.

Henderson's wife didn't prove to be a problem. He found her sitting on the other side of the bed, her back to him, obviously waiting for her husband. She did turn, at his tread, but Alastair was ready. He shot her, twice, once in the upper back, then when she slumped to the ground with a thud, he shot her in the back of the head. He stared at her for a moment, unfathomably glad he couldn't see her face.

He left the bedroom and stepped into the corridor. The slim shape of a boy, rubbing at sleepy eyes, stood at the other end of the corridor.

By chance, shadow striped the boy's face, covering one eye and leaving the other wide in a pale face. Alastair, standing in darkness himself, could only aim his pistol at the boy, unable to pull the trigger.

Do it, a voice urged in his head, a voice that sounded frighteningly like his father's. *What's another one to the tally?*

He knew the voice spoke the truth, that it was his duty to ensure that no one knew what had happened tonight. But he couldn't. Try as he might, his finger wouldn't tighten on the trigger. For an awful, vertiginous moment, staring at the boy, whose face was half-blinded by shadow, Alastair was looking at himself.

'Go to bed, son,' he said.

'Where's Mummy?'

'She's asleep,' Alastair said, and felt a wave of nausea sweep through him. There was a knot in his throat. 'Please,' he said, almost begging. 'Go back to bed.'

There were a few agonising moments where it looked as if the boy were about to protest. Then, yawning deeply, he turned and went back into his bedroom.

Alastair let out a shuddering rush of breath and felt the corridor yaw and pitch. After grabbing the doorframe to steady himself, he managed to stagger down the stairs without falling. He opened the front door and exited. Sixty seconds later, he was in his car. Another sixty seconds, he pulled over, opened the driver's door, leaned out, and vomited onto the asphalt.

Wiping his mouth, he glared at his image in the rear-view mirror until the shaking in his hands stopped.

Irene Carson let him in, her eyes watchful. Alastair, feeling exhaustion press on him from all sides, was annoyed to see his father bristling with energy upon entering his office. Gordon lept to his feet and came around the desk, rubbing his hands together.

'Busy night, boy. Busy night. Tell me, what did you learn?'

Alastair took out Henderson's report and laid it on his father's desk. He gave a dry recitation of his investigation – the examination of the scene of the accident, Henderson's report in the morgue, even the executions he had committed to cover up the evidence. Everything but his supper with Sally. He'd decided in the car he wouldn't surrender that piece of himself.

'You did the right thing with Henderson,' Gordon said. 'The survival of the Party is paramount. Henderson was a fool. Without us, the Republic would fall apart.' His eyes were alight with fervour.

'Unity is Strength,' Alastair said. He uttered the ritual phrase with none of his father's fanaticism, but Gordon didn't notice.

'So, it's all true, then?'

'It's true,' Alastair said, simply.

'All of it?'

'All of it,' Alastair said.

'Remarkable,' Gordon said. He went over to the window and looked out. Alastair, feeling a wave of exhaustion, sank into the nearest chair. He held his head in his hands and felt the pulse in his temples thudding like a bell of doom. He looked up at his father.

'What are we going to do?'

When Gordon looked back at his son, Alastair could see the light kindled in his eyes leap to new heights. 'You sit there as if this is the end of the world, boy, instead of the greatest opportunity to fall into our lap.'

'Opportunity? Are you listening to yourself? I'm having trouble believing it, but I've seen the evidence myself. I saw Frogmorton's corpse. He's as dead as a door nail. Killed by what he thought were his bodyguards, but turned out to be alien copies.' Alastair shook his head, still in denial that the impossible was somehow, insanely, true. 'You saw his duplicate, in this room, when the real one was dead. If not for a stroke of luck, we'd never have known that Frogmorton had been replaced.'

'This is not without precedent. I have heard stories, rumours, of encounters with an alien intelligence, of... other things. Not least the events that brought you to...'

Gordon blinked. For a moment it looked like he was going to tell Alastair his biggest secret, but the moment was gone and once again the fervour filled Gordon's eyes. He paced back and forth in front of his desk, his hands cutting through the air like knives as he made his points.

'Don't you see? There is a conspiracy aimed at the very heart of the Party to overthrow it. It's likely that key members of the Party have been replaced. Who are our friends and who are our enemies, eh? It is clear to me that members of the Resistance are in league with forces alien to our world. We can use this to break the Resistance once and for all, and...' There he trailed off, caught up in the possibilities unfolding before him.

'And make you the hero of the hour, when you have exposed their machinations,' Alastair said, finishing his father's sentence. 'You will be the Leader's designated heir, the man who saved the Party and the Republic from traitors, both internal and external.'

'Exactly,' Gordon said. He looked younger, the excitement of what had been presented to him stripping years of care from his face. 'You and me, boy; what we could achieve together!'

'And James?'

'Your brother has made his position clear enough many times. His priorities have shifted, ever since he met Rachel Jensen. Ever since...'

'He became a father himself?'

'Exactly. For now, James isn't an issue. He is content at Eastchester. In time, though...' Gordon smiled. 'Well, the day will come when it comes. Until then...'

Alastair was silent. But the promise Gordon made was clear; James would be removed when he no longer served any purpose.

'You have to be able to carry it off, though,' Alastair said. He enjoyed seeing the flash of uncertainty cross his father's face. It was so unusual Alastair actually smiled.

'You've grown bold,' Gordon said. He looked at his son as if seeing him for the first time. 'What's brought that on, I wonder?'

Aware of his vulnerability, even with his father, Alastair changed tack. 'If we are to pull this off, we will need to be careful. Frogmorton's duplicate will be a problem; as will discovering the Resistance cell that has cooked up this plan.'

'Don't worry about Frogmorton,' Gordon said. 'I've the men and the means to keep an eye on him for the moment. What about the Resistance? They're up to their necks in this.'

'I have my team.' Alastair rubbed his jaw. He hesitated, thinking about Knight's disappearance. He clamped down on that thought, and continued. 'It's beyond doubt that there are a number of factors coalescing together to force the Party from power. The recent bombings, designed to undermine our hold on the people. The recording I have from the Vault is a discussion about implementing that phase of their programme. The alien duplicates must be the other phase. It's damned audacious.'

'Can you handle your end of things?'

121

Alastair nodded. 'A plan of this size would be too big to hide, even with the threat of death for disclosing any details. Someone, somewhere, must know something. The Directorate has its hooks into a few low-level informers, people we've used in the past. We can start turning over some rocks, see what scuttles out.'

'It seems unreal,' Gordon said. He had returned to his place behind the desk, staring through the window across the slumbering city. The dark silhouettes of buildings marched into the darkness, hulks lost in the sea of the night. 'Aliens, in London.' He turned to look at Alastair, his face saturnine in the gloom. 'You know there have been reports before, about unusual activity? There are reams of them in the archives. In Scotland, around Loch Ness. Tales of shaggy ghosts in the Underground. Talk of the Devil in a Bronze Age burial mound. There's even rumours coming from Stahlmann's facility in Eastchester...'

'Let's keep our focus on the prize hanging before us, Father,' Alastair warned. He would discover the truth behind Stahlmann's Operation: Mole-Bore in due course. He checked his watch, and swore under his breath. 'Maintain a watch on Frogmorton; see what he does, who he meets. I'll start on my Resistance sources. Let's meet again in twenty-four hours – that should be enough time to shake loose some information.'

Gordon sketched a mock salute when Alastair finished, but nodded in agreement all the same.

'This may be the making of you, boy,' Gordon said, watching Alastair walk to the door.

'Oh, it will.' Alastair paused for a moment. 'And I'll make sure you don't shirk giving me what I'm owed.'

CHAPTER SEVENTEEN

WHEN ALASTAIR arrived at his flat, all he wanted to do was sleep. Thoughts of his father's ambitions, notions of alien interference in the affairs of the Republic, even Sally, exhausted him. He had spent the better part of his life ruthlessly regulating his every thought and action, not simply because the Party demanded it, but because he demanded it of himself. But now, after a seemingly endless chase from one end of Britain to the other, his body cried out for rest.

It wouldn't receive it.

Even before Alastair inserted the key into the lock of his flat, he felt uneasy. He paused, the key half-in and half-out. A voice in his head urged him to open the door, to shuck off his clothes and fall into bed. Another told him he'd best draw his pistol and make sure he wasn't framed in the doorway by the moonlight. Alastair lived a cautious life; he wasn't about to change now.

The door drifting open of its own accord forced his hand. He held the pistol by his side, its weight reassuring his jangled nerves.

Come out, come out, wherever you are, Alastair thought. He glanced into the gap then pulled back. Nothing. He entered and closed the door with a soft click.

In short order, he checked the bathroom first, pulling aside the shower curtain in a smooth movement. It, like his bedroom, was empty. The living area beckoned, just beyond a stippled glass door.

Alastair thought about going downstairs and calling in Du Plessis and Klaasen, then cursed himself for being a coward. He hadn't lived this long, risen so far, in a dangerous world, by relying on other people. Using them, of course, but relying on them... That was weakness. His pride told him to move forward, to deal with whatever might be on the other side of the glass.

He rested his hand on the door handle and contemplated the warped view through the glass for a moment.

With his pistol held at chest level, Alastair turned the handle and thrust open the door. In an explosive move, he rolled forward, minimising his profile for crucial seconds, before returning to his feet, the pistol aimed at the heart of a figure sitting on his couch.

'Took your bloody time, Alastair,' Benjamin Knight said. 'Don't stand there gawping – rumours of my death have been greatly exaggerated.'

'Your apartment block was flattened,' Alastair said. 'Lewisham told me you were dead.'

Knight held a steaming mug of coffee. He'd had a chance to shower and put on some clothes, taken from Alastair's wardrobe. He sat at the kitchen table, his eyes darting from the door to the curtained window and back to Alastair. For all his bravado, Alastair noted, there was no mistaking Knight was very nervous.

'She did, did she? And yet here I am, as much alive as you are. More than you, to be honest. You look like hell, Alastair.'

'I've got my own cross to bear,' Alastair said. He had managed to grab an hour of sleep in his own bed, with Knight crashing onto the couch. A chair placed under the handle of the front door was the best security that Alastair could muster, after Knight refused to countenance any security from the Directorate.

'Don't we all,' Knight said. He looked away for a moment, his eyes haunted.

'What happened to you?' Alastair said. 'We thought you were dead.'

'My memory is a mess,' Knight said, taking a sip from his mug and wincing at the coffee's hot bitterness. Still, it put a bit more colour into his face, which until then had looked like a waxen mask. 'All I know is I never made it back to my flat. I went out for a drink, met a girl and then...' He pinched the bridge of his nose, as if trying to force the memories into a coherent order.

'How many?'

'There were… two? Three people. A woman, definitely. I can't remember her face; it's all a blur. She drugged my drink, I reckon.'

'And then spirited you away to this facility? In London.'

'Yes,' Knight said. 'Don't ask me where. I only made it here on pure instinct. The place was filled with glass canisters. Row after row of bodies. Duplicates, Alastair. Duplicates of people.'

'Duplicates?' A familiar feeling of dread flooded his veins. 'Are you certain?'

'As certain as I am that you and I are sitting in this room,' Knight said.

Alastair rubbed his chin with his thumb, then looked at Knight. Suspicion filled him.

'How do I know you're who you say you are?'

Knight looked stunned. 'Are you serious?' he asked, his voice rising in anger.

'Yes.' Alastair aimed his pistol at Knight. His thoughts turned to meeting Henderson in the morgue. 'There might be a way to confirm if you're real or not.'

'Of course I'm bloody real!' Knight stormed. 'The duplicate they made of me, it was covered in growths. It was dead!'

'Come into the kitchen and sit at the table,' Alastair ordered. His eye was cold, like a chip of ice. 'I've seen enough in the last few days. I'm going to need more evidence than just your word.'

He backed into the kitchen. By feel and memory, he rummaged through a draw and pulled out a large bread knife.

'Show me your hand,' he ordered, beckoning with the knife as Knight settled into the chair. 'Palm up. Good.'

'What are you doing?'

'A test,' Alastair said. He sat opposite Knight, still training the pistol on him. 'Both of us have seen evidence of human duplication. It's insane, but nothing about the last few days feels right. This will hurt, but if you pass, you live.'

Without waiting for Knight's reply, Alastair leaned forward and ran the knife across his open palm. As Knight stared at Alastair in shock, blood pooled then spilled from the wound.

'You've gone stark raving mad.'

At the sight of blood, Alastair relaxed. Red and thick, it was nothing like the oily black fluid inside the corpses in the morgue. He holstered his pistol and grabbed a dishcloth from its hook. He tossed it to Knight, who wrapped it around his hand.

'You'll live,' Alastair said. 'You might not believe this, but I've just proved you're human.'

'Thanks,' Knight said, not seeking to hide his sarcasm. 'You had better tell me what the hell is going on.'

Alastair spent five minutes bringing Knight up to speed. He could tell his oldest friend, indeed, possibly his only friend, was finding it hard to believe.

'It's insane,' Knight said, when Alastair finished.

'You escaped from a secret facility duplicating members of the Party, apparently operated by aliens collaborating with the Resistance. You know better than anyone else how true it is.'

Knight looked at Alastair, a queer expression on his face. 'How do I know you're human?'

Alastair opened his mouth to reply, then let it close. In a growing panic, his mind unwound his recent memories like a film strip, trying to find a disconnect in them, an inflection point where he might've been taken and copied.

'No,' he said, shaking his head. The socket of his ruined eye itched, and he felt an old, familiar panic scrabbling in his chest. 'I know who I am.'

'Prove it,' Knight said, nodding meaningfully at the bread knife.

Looking down at it, Alastair saw his distorted reflection in the blade. His vision swam and he wiped at his beaded forehead. Unwillingly, but compelled by an almost suicidal desire to know, he passed the blade handle first to Knight, then held out his hand.

'Slide your pistol over, Alastair.'

The two men stared at each other for a long moment, Knight's face quietly determined, while Alastair's was unreadable except for a twitching of the flesh under his remaining eye. Finally, he pulled his pistol free, and pushed it across the table towards Knight.

'You've nothing to worry about, old chap,' Alastair said, his voice strained but calm.

'We'll see, shall we? Just know that if you bleed anything but claret, I'll shoot you dead.'

'Would I even know I was a duplicate?' Alastair wondered, staring in fascination as Knight readied the knife over his hand. 'Would you?'

'I know who I am,' Knight said, swiftly running the blade across Alastair's palm.

Blood seeped from the shallow cut. Both men looked at each other.

'And now I know who you are,' Knight added, sitting back and sighing with relief.

Alastair remained silent as he took a dishcloth from a drawer. When he returned, the pistol was on his side of the table. A little clumsily, he re-holstered it with his left hand, then settled back into his chair.

'What do we do now?' Knight asked.

'What do we do? You're coming into the Security Directorate with me. We'll have to debrief you and—'

The telephone rang. The shrill bell stopped the conversation stone dead. A chill swept through Alastair. Uneasy, he stood and walked over to the stand. Picking up the receiver, he answered.

'Hello?' His brow furrowed. 'Who? That's… No, no, don't send her away.'

He did little to hide the excitement in his voice.

'Escort her to my office and lock her inside. I don't want anyone talking to her or otherwise interacting with her, do you understand? If I find that anyone has spoken with her before I arrive, I'll have you shot, Bell. Do you understand?'

Alastair hung up the receiver. He stared down at the telephone for a moment, then turned back to look at Knight.

'I think we'll hold off on the debrief,' he said. He unfurled the dishcloth from his hand and inspected the wound. 'Let's get these bandaged properly and we'll head into HQ.'

'What's going on?' Knight asked, as Alastair went in search of sticking plasters.

'I think we've got a line on a high-level Resistance meeting,' Alastair said. He looked over his shoulder at Knight. 'We're finally going to nail them.'

Alastair unlocked his office door and opened it. Anne Travers looked up at him from her seat at his desk. A black briefcase sat at her feet. Alastair swept in, with Knight closing the door and moving to stand in the corner to Travers' right.

Alastair sat down. 'Well,' he said, leaning forward. 'Do you have it?'

Anne nodded. Alastair noted the earlier arrogance she had exhibited in the Vault was absent. *Good*, he thought. Leconfield House's reputation was justly earned.

'You must understand I'm here of my own volition,' she said. 'I do it purely out of loyalty to the Party.'

'Oh yes,' Alastair said, glancing at Knight and quirking an eyebrow. 'Definitely loyalty.'

'Don't mock me, Column Leader,' Anne said, pausing as she sat the briefcase in her lap. 'I've listened to this tape. There are… participants on it whose voices I recognise. The Party and the Republic are in grave danger.'

'Hand it over,' Alastair said, flatly.

He waited impatiently while Anne fussed with the locks. Staring at her, Alastair thought she might've been pretty, without the habitual scowl. The woman's loyalty to the Party was stamped all over her face.

At length, Anne pulled out a white, plastic reel. Almost gingerly, she handed it to Alastair. He pulled open the bottom drawer of his desk and took out the small reel-to-reel player. Deftly, he threaded the tape into the machine, before glancing at Anne and Knight.

'You were in the room when this was recorded?'

Anne nodded.

'How many were in the room with you?' Alastair asked, his voice deadly quiet.

'Just the technician and I,' she said. She swallowed. 'Father ordered his dispatch to a labour camp. He won't be heard from again.'

'You seem confident of your own continued employment,' Knight said.

Anne almost jumped at the sound of his voice.

'Don't worry about my friend,' Alastair said.

He was enjoying seeing the fear creep onto Anne's face. Idly, he wondered what Sally would look like with the same emotion gripping her. He would like to find out, he decided, then felt a little ill.

'I worry about everything,' Anne said, turning back. 'You. That tape. You won't do anything to me,' she said, unconvincingly. 'My father has friends.'

'That's funny,' Alastair said, leaning back in his chair. 'My father has friends, as well.'

Knight snorted with laughter. Anne began to look frightened.

'I jest, Miss Travers,' Alastair said. 'You've done well to report directly to me with this tape. Let's see what you've uncovered.'

The hiss and crackle of the recording was loud in the room.

'Atmospheric disturbance,' Anne pointed out.

Alastair, his face a mask of concentration, waved her comment away.

'This is Queen. Are you receiving?'

There was a long pause. Softly hissing static filled the gap. Finally:

'Receiving,' a male voice said.

Alastair went pale. That voice…

'Are you in place?' Queen asked.

The hiss and crackle of static distorted the words, rendering the voice robotic.

'I am in place,' Frogmorton said. There was none of the fat man's jovial bonhomie, or eagerness to please. In its place was a plastic facsimile, shorn of emotion and humanity. It chilled Alastair.

'Report.'

'I have made contact with the Director of External Security. There was no sign of any suspicion. A Cabinet meeting is scheduled for tomorrow. Everything is as planned.'

'Good. You should know that the original Frogmorton has gone missing. We believe that his kidnappers were being followed while attempting to dispose of his body and have gone to ground. At this time, we are unaware of their whereabouts. Regardless, the raid will go ahead tonight, as planned. But we have brought forward the timetable for the other matter. Signal your understanding.'

'Confirmed,' Frogmorton said. 'The timing of the Italian Job has changed.' There was a moment of silence. 'Is that wise?'

At the reference to what was clearly some sort of code name, Alastair glanced at Knight, who shrugged his shoulders.

'Your place isn't to worry about what is wise and what isn't,' Queen said.

'Understood.'

There was another long pause, the static rising and falling, threaded through with the crackling of the empty spaces of the universe.

'It is imperative you follow your instructions,' the Queen said, at last. 'There are many plans in motion, all designed to cause maximum mayhem, before we launch our decisive stroke. Battersea is one of those plans.'

Static rose until it was a roaring shriek. At a nod from Anne, Alastair switched off the reel-to-reel player. The three of them sat in the office as, outside, the day to day activity of Leconfield House whirred into life. Here, in this little room on the third floor, Alastair held the future of the Republic in his hands. He felt his heart surge. He would prove his worth to his father, now, with this information.

'This was recorded last night?'

Anne nodded. 'I drove down myself with the recording.' She looked at him with curiosity. 'What will you do?'

'What will I do?'

Anne recoiled at Alastair's shark-like smile, all teeth and no humanity.

'Hunt them, corner them, kill them. It's time the Resistance learned what fury the Party can rain down on their heads.'

Alastair stepped into his father's office. Knight was downstairs in the staff car, waiting. Outside, the sun had already set and the planned power cuts were in full swing, swathing London, for the most part, in darkness. At a heliport to the north, on Alastair's orders, two helicopters were being fuelled in readiness for an assault on Battersea Power Station.

'Father,' Alastair said.

Gordon looked up. He blinked, focusing on his son. 'Well. What have you to report?'

Direct, as always, Alastair thought. 'It's worse than we understood,' he said, walking towards the desk.

His father didn't offer him a seat and Alastair didn't ask. He wanted to be gone as soon as possible. He had the thrill of the chase in his nostrils, and not even his father's sarcasm and bullying could diminish his coming enjoyment.

'Really?' Gordon said, leaning forward. 'Frogmorton is a manageable problem. I have my people watching him. What else is there to worry about?'

'Battersea,' Alastair said. 'The Resistance is planning an attack. Tonight.'

'Damnation,' Gordon said, shaking his head. He rose from his chair and leaned forward with his fists supporting him on his desk. His jaw stuck out. 'They must be stopped. Battersea is the key to the power supply for Greater London. If they knock it out…'

'It's back to the Stone Age. I've got two teams ready to swing into action.'

'Pincer movement,' Gordon said, nodding his approval.

'Whichever way they run, we've got them cornered.'

'Rats in a trap.' Gordon straightened, then went to the window which, as always, was open. 'Make sure you stop them,' he said. 'But… make sure you make as big a splash as you can, too.'

'Why would I…?' Alastair stopped, realising what his father was saying. 'You want there to be some… collateral damage, is that it? But if it doesn't work, you're asking me to jeopardise the Party's hold on power.'

'Don't be such a sanctimonious bore,' Gordon snapped.

The tension between the two men was palpable. Alastair's ruined eye socket throbbed beneath the leather patch, and an old ache in his upper arm returned. *Memories,* he thought, then savagely clamped down on them.

'You want the turbines at Battersea to be damaged,' Alastair said, close to shouting. Only the thick walls and electronic security measures he knew his father employed allowed him the freedom to express himself so candidly, and loudly.

'One,' Gordon said, his face flushed. 'One of the turbines. I'm not a damned fool. Let the Resistance damage one of the turbines. We'll still have power. And I'll kill two birds with one stone. Hipwood will fall from favour. After all, she's in charge of security at Battersea.'

'You're asking me to storm Battersea Power Station. There's a risk I'll have to kill our people. That's a hard ask.'

'Nothing in this life is easy, boy,' Gordon said. 'Where necessary, you will shoot to kill. It will make the Resistance look even worse, killing mere civilians doing their jobs. You will ensure that the Resistance plan is partially successful. And you will take as many prisoners alive as possible. One of them will crack. One always does. And then we will have the Resistance in the palm of our hands. And with Hipwood discredited, I will be the Leader's unquestioned heir.'

'She won't go easily.'

'I wouldn't expect anything less. Hipwood may think she is on the march, but there are currents running against her in Cabinet, and especially in the Party. If it's seen that my son is putting the squeeze on the Resistance, then it's all to the good.'

'For you,' Alastair said.

'I wouldn't be so grubby as to own up to that, my boy.' Gordon winked at Alastair. 'But yes. The association won't hurt. The Lethbridge-Stewart family has long represented the Armed Forces of this nation when it was a degenerate playground for debauched aristos and democrats.'

'Save the speech for your inauguration,' Alastair said, feeling a little ill at his father's politicking.

'Oh, I will, my boy, I will.' He watched Alastair move towards the door. 'Happy hunting, Alastair.'

Outside, Knight was slumped in his seat. Grey smudges marked the skin under his eyes.

'Good chat?' he asked, summoning a smile with an effort.

'Like chewing nails,' Alastair said, slamming the door shut and savagely twisting the keys in the ignition. 'I very much want to shoot someone,' he said, then drove off with a crash of gears.

CHAPTER EIGHTEEN

WITH THE Auxpol manning roadblocks across the city in the aftermath of the bombings, Alastair had sought to minimise any more delays by calling up two Chinooks to ferry his teams above the tense city. The silent whap whap whap of the rotors was more a pressure on the ears than an actual sound. Frigid air whipped through the helicopter's cabin as Alastair leaned out over the skids to get a good look at the surroundings through his Starlight goggles.

The world lit up in eerie shades of green and black. Two hundred yards from him, another helicopter, a twin to the one he rode in, hunted through the night like a black hawk. Below, he saw the city of London laid out like a set of children's toys strewn across a blanket.

After the bombings, Auxpol were persecuting the curfew with brutal force. Plugged into the local command channel via his headset, Alastair had heard Auxpol officers ordering about their forces. The chatter of machine gun fire had twice come through as rioters descended on the roadblocks en masse, armed with Molotov cocktails and insane bravery, hoping to take advantage of the general disorder spreading across the country.

Spot fires appeared as blazing balls of light in the goggles as rioters fought running battles with the Auxpol. Already a dozen were visible, and several more sprung up as Alastair watched. He felt a tension in his gut, a desire to be down there, fighting toe to toe with the enemy. He saw the Thames snake through the city like a slick of oil, gleaming in the twinkling of the stars and the moon's wan light.

Despite the energy shortages, the New People's

Parliament was lit up like a Christmas tree. The great shrine to the people's victory over the decadents could never be swathed in darkness, Alastair thought moodily. In the goggles, the building looked like a vast mausoleum.

'Cyclops One in position,' he said, keying his microphone, as the helicopter began to swoop towards the ground.

Some of the technology Tech Ops had stolen from the Americans was amazing on the one hand, and humbling on the other. British pride in the genius of the lone inventor increasingly counted for little against the American drive for innovation through massive investment of money and people. Uneasy allies in a cold war for global influence, from their capital in Richmond the Americans warily watched the British. Trade was two way, but the Americans almost never gave up the fruits of their extensive investment in technology without a fight. Tech Ops had won a rare victory and had enabled the British understanding of communications technology to leap ahead at least a decade.

'Trap One in position,' responded Klaasen, his voice buzzing amid a wash of static.

Alastair glanced at the other helicopter. He could just make out Klaasen's bulky shadow, his legs hanging over the edge of the doorframe.

'Watch you don't beat the chopper to the ground, Trap One,' Alastair said gruffly.

Klaasen's roar of laughter made Alastair wince and smile at the same time.

'We'll be at the target in sixty seconds,' Alastair said, above the howling of the frigid wind.

'Good thing too, boss,' Klaasen responded with his trademark drawl. 'The boys are eager to bite.' Klaasen keyed his headset off and Alastair watched the helicopter plunge towards the rear of their target.

The Chelsea Embankment swung into view, and to the south, the dark bulk of Battersea Power Station. Like Klaasen, Alastair chafed at the delay. He turned around to look inside the cabin.

Lewisham had given Knight a fierce hug when they were reunited on the tarmac. With the Chinooks powering up, there had been little opportunity for words, but Alastair could see the relief stamped all over her face.

Now, Knight hunkered in his seat, his haunted eyes looking inwards. He had exchanged Alastair's clothes for a dark jumper and jeans. Lewisham sat beside him, her head next to his, saying something to him. Du Plessis was a colossus in black, his bulk spread over two seats. Several other heavily armed members of the Security Directorate rounded out the team.

Alastair's headset buzzed.

'Brace for landing,' the pilot said, his voice awash in static.

Alastair felt his stomach lurch as the helicopter began a tight, spiralling descent. London smeared itself across Alastair's vision, then they were down beside the Thames with a thump.

'Everyone out!' Alastair ordered.

The team boiled out the cabin, Du Plessis inevitably the first, his Uzi held in front of him. Alastair brought up the rear, keeping low beneath the whirling rotors. The helicopter's backwash sent up a flurry of dirt and then it was in the air, turning to port before disappearing silently behind one of the power station's massive chimney stacks.

'Team Alpha is down and safe,' Alastair said into his microphone.

'Team Beta approaching the rear entrance,' Klaasen said. 'Good hunting, Cyclops One.'

Over the hiss of static, Alastair heard Klaasen order his team forward. Switching off his headset, Alastair turned to his people.

'The cordon is in place, the staff reduced to a skeleton crew.'

'Couldn't we have ambushed the Resistance fighters before they entered the facility?' Knight said.

Alastair shook his head. 'We've a higher chance of capturing more of them corralled into one place. Otherwise, they'd scatter like cockroaches.'

The helicopter had deposited them on a grass slope leading down to the Thames. Water slapped against the embankment. The London skyline stood stark against the night sky, lit here and there by burning buildings. While Du Plessis formed up the team, Alastair went over the plan one more time. Even now, Klaasen and his squad raced towards the power station's rear entrance. Once inside, they would make for Building 'B' and commence a floor-by-floor sweep. To maintain the ruse, the on duty staff had strict orders to remain at their stations and to surrender immediately if they encountered the Resistance.

Alastair glanced at De Plessis' hulking figure and was unsurprised to see an almost boyish grin on the South African's face. A cold wind ruffled his blond hair, turning it into a blazing banner under the moonlight. For a moment, Alastair imagined Du Plessis as a Viking reaver, ready to lay waste to all before him with a berserker's fury.

'They're ready, boss,' Du Plessis said, almost hopping from one foot to the other in excitement.

'Klaasen reports they've breached the exterior,' Knight said, listening intently to the chatter in his right ear. As he did, he raised his pair of Starlight night vision goggles up to his face, sweeping the area for signs of movement.

'Good,' Alastair said. To the right, he saw the lights of a train moving through the railyards beside Building 'A', the staccato reverberations of its passage across multiple points echoing distantly.

'Column Leader!' Knight loomed into view. He pointed to an object thrusting into the air towards Building 'B'.

'What is it?' Alastair asked, his hand dropping to his holstered pistol.

'That's the conveyor belt from the coal repository,' Knight said. 'It was crawling with people ten seconds ago.'

'That's how they're gaining access,' Alastair said, almost admiring their bravado. 'Is it all quiet up there now?'

'Yes. Should I take some people and follow them in?'

Alastair almost agreed, then shook his head.

'There's not enough of us for the main task if I send a couple with you.' He thought for a moment, considering Knight's rough shape. Knight would argue against it, but it was up to Alastair to determine the best use of available resources.

'I need you up there protecting my flank. Make sure no one is waiting behind.' He raised his hand to forestall Knight's protest. 'Despite all you've been through, I trust you to do the job.'

A moment's relief crossed Knight's face, and he nodded. Without another word, he dashed away into the night

There was a moment of silence as the others waited on Alastair. He glanced up at the vast, squat bulk of the Battersea Power Station. The lights from the fires spotting London cast it in satanic glow. Alastair checked his watch.

'All right. We're the Resistance for one night only.' He heard chuckles in response. 'Spread out and make for the entrance. Section Leader Du Plessis, lead the way.'

His team raced for the steps leading to the main entrance. Drawing his pistol, Alastair moved up to Du Plessis' shoulder. The nearest chimney stacks pointed accusatory fingers to the heavens. Birds circled at their summits, their pale forms flitting in and out of the smoke trailing into the sky. Everything about the brick buildings spoke of gigantism, an urge to dominate and conquer. They crouched on the waterline, glowering at the city across the Thames. With the energy crisis in full swing, Alastair knew that keeping the station functioning was the thin red line holding the nation and capital together. And his father had asked him to put it into hazard.

The memory of the look of rapture on his father's face attracted and chilled Alastair as they raced across the plaza towards the entrance. The Party had been built on strength – strength of body, and strength of will. The old kingdom had been on its knees in the '30s, slave to bankers and a rotting architecture of democracy. Only Mosely, and his successors, had seen what was coming – continue on the same road, and Britain would become an irrelevance, picked off by the rising powers in Asia and North America. But take a new path, and a nation renewed by the Party's rile would rise once again to power and glory. And so it had been.

With Du Plessis in the lead, the team stormed the reception area. Their boots echoed loudly around the marble clad floors and walls. Several shocked guards scrambled to their feet. Du Plessis poured fire from his Uzi. The lead guard's chest blew out in a crimson burst and he fell to the ground. Another guard let off several panicked rounds, which careered around the stainless steel interior, before Lewisham shot him twice in the chest. The remaining guard tried to flee, but Alastair shot him in the back. The guard sprawled headlong on the ground, dead.

A balding man in a bad suit cowered behind the horseshoe shaped front desk as the echoes of the gunfire faded. Behind him, a massive art deco installation hung from the wall – a naked figure in bronze wrestling with the sun. Alastair hesitated a moment, then marched up to the desk, his pistol stretched in front of him.

'Buzz them through,' he grated, his voice a menacing growl.

With his head turned to one side, the concierge stabbed blindly at a panel of buttons. Through some combination of muscle memory and blind luck, he struck the right sequence and an interior door opened on silent hinges. Alastair vaulted the counter, clubbed the man behind the ear with the butt of his pistol, then followed his team into the interior of the complex.

The atmosphere was humid, tinged with the smell of sulphur and burning metal. Gantries arced over a vast, airy space, and several galleries skirted the perimeter of the interior on several levels. Below, the turbine rumbled, a chained monster being fed a supply of coal that had become more tenuous over the years. Incongruous looking wrought iron staircases led up into the shadows overlooking the turbine room.

'Welcome to Building "A",' Alastair said.

He gathered his team around him.

'Lewisham, take three and check through levels four to six. Du Plessis, you and the remainder are with me.' He looked at each of them. 'I know this isn't easy, but these are my orders, so they're yours, too. Rough up the staff and round up as many Resistance members as you can pick off. I want them alive, but not at the risk of your lives, do you understand? Dead heroes aren't of any use to me. Now go.'

The team split in half, and Alastair led Du Plessis and the others on their search. They climbed a spiralling staircase, gaining height and a better look across the vast empty space. Alastair peered into the cavern below and saw the huge, steel encased turbine. Distantly, he saw several white clad technicians checking readouts, their attention elsewhere.

'We'll start on three and move down,' Alastair said.

The atmosphere in the central chamber was eerie. To his discomfort, Alastair found his heartbeat began to match that of the turbine's throb. He imagined the furnaces into which the tonnes of coal were fed by the conveyer belts as raging infernos, a diabolical mechanism fuelling the ever-hungry power needs of the capital.

They reached the third level and spread out. Control room after control room presented themselves, banks of dials and readouts marching into the white tiled distance. The constant thrum of power was an ever present background pressure on the body and mind that spoke of a barely contained power ready to burst its chains and send itself ravening across the landscape.

Alastair's headset came to life in a burst of static.

'Cyclops One,' he said.

'Knight reporting. I've blocked the entrance up here. The last of the Resistance members have crossed into Building "B". Klaasen should have contact any moment now.'

'Good. Follow them in, but keep your distance. Render assistance as you see fit.'

'Roger,' Knight said.

Alastair thumbed his headset off. He signalled to Du Plessis. 'This area is clear. Come on, we'll head to—'

A distant explosion shook the control room. The lighting dimmed and dust sifted down from the ceiling. Dozens of dials flashed red, dipping the room in crimson. The turbine's throb faltered, before it raced like an overheating dynamo. The shriek of it was enormous, filling the world as Alastair and his team clamped their hands over their ears. The sound died as suddenly as it appeared, and the turbine calmed a little, the former throbbing replaced by a ragged vibration that indicated it had sustained damage.

'Where did that come from?' Alastair shouted.

The others looked around in confusion, until his headset crackled into life.

'Beta team here,' came a ragged voice. 'Is anyone responding? This is Klaasen.'

Alastair heard the splash of water over the sound of alarms.

'Cyclops One,' he called, his voice clipped after his moment of panic.

'They've set off a bomb on the second level,' Klaasen called. 'One of the conveyer belts has been blown away. I've got coolant water coming out like you wouldn't believe.'

'How many of Beta team are down?'

Alastair and his team rushed towards an exit.

'Two,' Klaasen said. 'Samuels and Everard. Part of a wall has collapsed on them. I can't get them.'

'Leave them.' Alastair was calm now, seemingly afloat.

'Leave them?' Klaasen yelled. 'They may not be dead.'

'I don't care,' Alastair said. 'The mission is what is important.' He was aware the others were looking askance at him, but their opinions didn't matter. He was in charge. That was all that mattered. 'Form a perimeter defence. If they attack, hold them off. We'll be there in a few minutes.'

He led the charge along a gantry over the dizzying gap above the turbine in Building 'A'. Beneath, he saw technicians attending the turbine like nurses around a patient. Smoke belched from several rents in the turbine's metal carapace, flurries of sparks flew from where metal rubbed against metal. Steaming water pooled around the turbine. It was like looking into the depths of a foundry in Hell.

Immediately, shots began to spark left and right as they were peppered by bullets. One of his team went down, crashing against a railing then toppling slowly over the edge. A terrible thud cut short a despairing wail as the body landed atop the turbine and then slid into a bubbling pool of water. The body left an ugly crimson streak on the metal, like a child's rough daubing of paint on a canvas.

Alastair saw a shadow lurking in a gap and fired twice. The first shot missed, sparking against the metal doorframe, but the second catapulted the figure backwards. More shots rained down, before the roaring clatter of Du Plessis' Uzi opened up. Resistance figures scrambled to escape, fleeing along gantries. Some were hit and pitched into the gap, while others flung themselves through open doorways and the dubious refuge of narrow passages. Du Plessis stopped firing as the surviving members made it across the gantry and took up defensive positions.

Another explosion rocked the building. This one was closer. The rivets holding a gantry on the sixth level popped out one by one with sounds like gunfire, sending the metal walkway plunging into the gap. It struck the railing several feet from Alastair with a massive boom, tearing the metal away and leaving only a dozen yard section of the walkway jutting into the air. The echoes of its collapse reverberated around the vast empty space.

Back pressed against the wall beside a door, Alastair turned at the sound of someone approaching. It was Knight.

'Are you all right?' Alastair yelled, above the sound of more gunfire.

Knight nodded. He looked shattered.

'Good. Cover me.'

White faced but steady, Knight moved into position as Alastair ducked low and edged to the doorframe.

Dodging forward, he glanced through the doorway. Satisfied it was empty, Alastair rose to his full height and entered the gap. Stepping over a corpse, he moved down the corridor. With its flickering lights and crawling shadows, its narrow confines were daunting. With Knight at his shoulder, and the others following, Alastair went ahead.

Checking side passages, they moved through the level with urgency. They entered a control room, a space filled along one wall with monitoring equipment. The dials and output meters were in a frenzy as the surging power tripped relays and threatened to overwhelm the overflow gates.

'We need a damn technician,' Du Plessis said, yelling above the klaxons and looking helplessly at the equipment. 'We've no idea if this place is going to blow sky high or not.'

'Not yet, I reckon,' Alastair shouted.

He moved to another control station, then froze. A device had been clamped to a panel, the squat black thing exuding menace. A lit readout read 180.

And then began to descend.

'Bomb!' Alastair shouted, immediately regretting the panic that overwhelmed him.

He balled his fist, feeling his nails bite into his flesh. The pain settled him and his pulse eased. He looked around and snapped his fingers at one of the team.

'Benton, get over here.' A henchman with dark hair hurried forward, unfurling a leather satchel.

'Can it be disarmed?' Alastair asked. He looked around. 'I don't think we can afford to lose this control room.'

The readout passed 155.

'Two minutes should do it,' Benton said, as he swiftly checked around the metal device. 'Assuming it's not booby-trapped,' he added, his fingers freezing into place.

Resisting the urge to step away, Alastair crouched beside Benton. 'It won't matter if you don't disarm it. If this control room goes, I'll hazard the turbine will go up with it. And dead or not, if we lose the turbine, London will be without power for weeks.'

Benton nodded and began removing screws from the casing. The screwdriver twirled in his hand and, within twenty seconds, he had the casing free, exposing the bomb's innards.

Alastair rose to his feet. 'Du Plessis, you lead the rest of the team out. Begin the sweep of the next floor.'

He waved away Du Plessis' protest, just as shots rang out. A black clad figure emerged from a door at the far end of the room and fired again. Du Plessis' Uzi opened up, brass casing spilling onto the floor in a tinkling rain. The resistance fighter screamed and flung himself back through the gap.

Du Plessis gave chase, with the remainder of Team Alpha in close pursuit.

Alastair looked down and saw Benton rooting among the inner workings of the bomb.

'Crude but powerful.'

Wires were wrapped around a black core of solid metal. Looking closely, Alastair saw silver traces moving in ever expanding swirls through the metal. The hypnotic pattern was like nothing Alastair had seen before. As the readout descended, the swirls grew more agitated.

Alien, he thought. He shuddered.

'Here goes nothing,' Benton said. He had tinsnips in one hand and in the other, a pair of metal alligator clips. His hands hesitated a moment and Alastair saw him glance at the readout as it swept passed 30.

'Hurry man,' Alastair said, fighting the urge to run.

Benton nodded. He clamped a bypass clip on an exposed

strip of copper wiring, then proceeded to cut a series of wires. The movement within the orb grew more frantic and intense, until a sickly green light lit up Benton's face like a corpse.

6 5 4 the readout read, when Anderson made his final adjustment. Without fanfare, the readout froze at 3. The light bled away, leaving Benton's sweat drenched face frozen in shock. Alastair clapped him on the shoulder.

'Well done,' Alastair said. He wiped his upper lip. 'Secure those explosive materials,' he ordered, waiting patiently while Benton extracted the metal orb from its nest of wires and stowed it into his pack.

'We need to catch up with the others,' Alastair said.

They hurried to the door and emerged into a corridor, as another explosion shook the facility. This time, the lighting died completely, before amber emergency lights came online. The situation was beginning to spiral out of control.

At a dead run, Alastair headed for the nearest stairs. Heedless, Alastair and Benton plunged down the wrought iron steps, the clanging of their boots deafening in the confined space. Alastair pushed through the access doors on the level below. They boomed extravagantly, announcing his arrival in the midst of a firefight.

A group of Resistance fighters had Team Alpha pinned down. In one quick glance, Alastair estimated there were a dozen enemy combatants, all in black fatigues, all wielding a variety of firearms. Ducking behind a desk, he came up short as bullets pinged around him. Quickly, he became aware of a body lying next to him. He glanced down, expecting it to be one of his men, when he saw Lewisham. His breath caught in his throat and the sounds of gunfire drained away. Lewisham, eyes open but clearly dead, stared blankly at him. The arch of her skull was punctuated by a missing chunk of bone. Blood and brains dribbled down her face.

In that brief bubble of time, Alastair's world collapsed to just him and Lewisham. The woman had infuriated him more times than he could remember. Of her abilities, of her calm under pressure, of her excellent investigative instincts, he had no doubt. And now she was dead, a pathetic rag doll lolling against a wall. The need for violence boiled up within and exploded.

The sounds of the fight erupted like a rocket overhead. Bullets screamed through the air and guns roared. Alastair saw a black clad figure appear to his right and he opened fire at it, gunning it down.

Turning, he advanced towards the line of Resistance fighters, pouring gunfire into their midst as bullets pinged around him. The knot of fighters wavered, then broke as he came relentlessly forward. They scattered towards the rear exit. A sudden silence enveloped the room.

'Secure that door,' Alastair barked, and as one his team went to the exit.

Turning, Alastair staggered for a moment as the surge of adrenaline abated. He straightened with an effort, and saw Knight move into view.

'Have you seen Lewisham?' he asked. 'She was near the doors when we got sep—'

He stopped when Alastair shook his head. Knight closed his eyes, briefly. When he opened them, they glittered with tears and rage.

Du Plessis joined them. The big South African bled from a nick in his left ear, but otherwise looked fine.

'They've cleared off,' he said and grinned, his big square teeth gleaming. 'But we've captured one of them. Tried to blow her bloody brains out, but we disarmed her.'

'Show me,' Alastair ordered, feeling that familiar trickle of ice through his veins.

Du Plessis led Alastair out of the exit and onto the gallery outside. There, trussed up with cabling, sat a woman wearing black. Blood trickled from her temple, but otherwise she looked unhurt. The look of defiance she gave to Alastair could've stripped paint. He smiled, bleakly.

'You've killed some of my people.' He knelt beside her. 'You're going to pay for that, but not before I've dragged every last secret out of you.'

'Do your worst, you dog.'

Alastair opened his mouth to respond, but the crackle of his headset interrupted him.

'Column Leader?' It was Klaasen.

'Yes,' Alastair said, clamping the walkie talkie to the side of his head.

'They're on the run.' There was a note of triumph in Klaasen's voice. 'They've broken out and are heading south east. Should we follow?'

'Negative,' Alastair said. 'Let the Auxpol patrols deal with them. We've got what we came for. Assemble at the staging point. See you in ten minutes.'

Klaasen signalled his understanding, and broke the connection.

Alastair nudged the woman with his boot. 'Get this traitor up and moving. Radio ahead. I want one of the interrogation cells at Leconfield House ready by the time we arrive.'

Distant booming sounds echoed through the air around them. Alastair braced for impact, then realised the explosions weren't within the Battersea structure.

'That'll be substations going up because of power surges,' Knight said, staring at the skyline through a shattered window.

'There'll be rioting in the streets if the power outage lasts into the day,' Du Plessis said, quietly. 'Auxpol will be cracking heads for as long as they want.'

'That's not our problem,' Alastair snapped.

He looked around at the wreckage in the turbine chamber. The massive piece of machinery was largely intact, though its output had fallen away dramatically.

'Let's get out of here,' he said. A great weariness had settled on him.

He had accomplished what his father had asked; victory, but only partial. Still, given what he knew about his father, it would be enough to achieve his goals.

And Lewisham is dead because of those goals, a cold, dry voice said in Alastair's head.

He didn't like the feeling of sorrow that lanced through him when he thought of Lewisham. It smacked of weakness. Glancing at the Resistance fighter, Alastair's thoughts darkened.

'Bring her,' he said. 'And don't be too gentle about it.'

CHAPTER NINETEEN

THE CABINET meeting was less organised and more harried than the last, and that had been bad enough, Gordon decided. He affected a look of calm and composure, while offering comments that attested to his growing alarm. Director Hipwood sat in her usual seat, several places down from him. When she did deign to look at him while they waited for the meeting to come to order, it was with utter loathing, her basilisk gaze horrible to witness.

Only Freddie Frogmorton seemed to be enjoying himself. He had been one of the first in the room when Gordon entered; a jolly fat man sitting in a groaning chair. Gordon nodded to him when he came in, and Freddie had rewarded him with a huge grin. He looked ready to eat everyone at the table, Gordon decided with a shudder.

His hand strayed to the bulge hidden under his well-tailored jacket. Weapons were never allowed in the Leader's presence, unless they were his bodyguards. But the meeting had been hastily called and none of the guards were present when Gordon arrived.

The cross talk around the table was accusatory and infected with panic. While the Resistance attack on Battersea had been beaten back, the damage to the turbines was such that even with the enforced power cuts, essential services were badly affected. Reports had arrived that patients were dying in the hospitals around London – patients dying in lifts trapped between floors, heart-lung machines switching off, ventilators shutting down, even reports of an emergency surgery collapsing into chaos as the lights went out, plunging the participants in darkness. There was a very real sensation that anything could happen that night.

The absence of the Leader only heightened the tension. Gordon had come to learn that without the Party head in attendance, nothing ever got done. The blame lay with the atrophy that had set into the Party mechanisms – as the Leader had drawn power to the centre, some directorships became mere appendages. It was also fear – fear of speaking up, fear of being singled out. Gordon had watched all this over the last decade, learning, biding his time. If the people of London tonight were wondering what would come next, in the Cabinet room in Downing Street, Gordon wondered the same.

Are you ready? he asked himself.

'What do you think, Paula?' Gordon heard Frogmorton say, airily.

'What do I think about what?' Hipwood said, breaking her icy silence.

Frogmorton waved his hand about. 'Place has gone to hell in a handbasket. Can't be much longer before the plebs start rolling out the tumbrels.' He smiled into the shocked silence. 'Unless, of course, you unleash your dogs. What are the Auxpol doing tonight?'

So that's its game, Gordon thought. Undermine, divide, conquer.

Hipwood's lips peeled back in contempt. 'The Auxpol are the spine of the Republic. Without them, the Party would be nothing.'

'This bickering has got to stop,' the Director of Defence said. His face was white, and he nervously tugged at his collar. The lights flickered, and he jumped.

'Oh, do settle down, Phillip,' Gordon said. 'Remember where you are. And who you are.'

'I know where I am, Director,' Phillip shot back.

'More importantly,' Frogmorton said, slyly. 'Where's the Leader?'

The question opened up a silence pregnant as it was pointed.

Gordon cleared his throat and shuffled his papers in front of him. Now was the time to seize the–

'Oh, do settle down, Phillip.' The querulous voice

wandered into the room like an idle thought, just as the Leader appeared.

The directors rose as one, then froze. The Leader entered the room in a heavy iron wheelchair, pushed along by one of his bodyguards. The squeak of the wheels was loud in the silence. Despite himself, Gordon glanced across at Hopwood. The look of naked disdain in her eyes was bloodcurdling.

'Leader? What's happened?' Gordon said, evincing solicitude.

The Leader waved Gordon's words away with a shaking hand. Gordon noticed immediately two things – the Leader's other hand sat in his lap like a dead thing. And that he had slurred his words.

'Just a minor stroke,' the Leader said, with all the care of a child blowing bubbles. 'Hearts not what they once were.' The old man chuckled. Gordon thought it sounded like a death rattle; evidently he was losing control of his faculties, including his speech if that strange slip was any indication. With the Leader's remaining hair forming a cloudy wisp, his head resembled a skull. The grin he gave to Gordon only reinforced the impression.

'Only a stroke?' Hipwood's question cut across the silence like a knife.

The atmosphere, already tense, worsened. The Leader's bodyguards straightened.

'Yes, Paula,' the Leader slurred, quietly. Drool hung from the corner of his mouth. 'It is only a very minor stroke. My doctor has every confidence I should make a full recovery. I have his word. After all, I hold his family in my hand.' That ghastly chuckle issued again.

Gordon narrowed his eyes. He'd heard rumours, tall tales, about the Leader's life span. Some said he would live forever, but those were just the zealots. Believing him to be some kind of saviour. One even claimed that there was a time when the Leader could extend his life through some kind of miraculous procedure, but that option was no longer available to him. Taken away, or something.

Looking at the Leader now, though, it was clear he was just an old man who had lived beyond his years. And was now paying for it.

'Here, here,' Frogmorton cheered, rapping the table with his knuckles. 'Let's have no defeatist talk.'

'Why thank you, Freddie,' the Leader said. His eyes were like dead marbles, boring into Freddie's skull. Freddie's smile only grew broader.

'Speaking of time,' Gordon said, his words as well timed as a stiletto slipped between the ribs. 'We have something of an issue at Battersea, don't we, Paula?'

'The situation is contained,' Hipwood said. 'No doubt your son has already informed you.'

'Was Alastair part of the assault team?' Gordon contrived to appear nonplussed. 'He does know how to keep his cards close to the vest.'

'Oh, please, Gordon, drop the act. You deliberately withheld information from me about the security of a vital piece of infrastructure. You can be thankful the situation isn't worse than it is, after your idiot son blundered about the place.' She took a deep breath. 'Leader, the situation is contained. Elements of Auxpol have secured Battersea Power station, which is fully in our hands.'

The lights flickered again. Gordon almost felt sorry for the woman.

'First the bombings, now Battersea,' Freddie said. His jollity had vanished. In its place, he frowned at Hipwood. He looked like a toad, Gordon thought, with his round body, rugose skin, and thick lips.

Gordon had a flash of inspiration.

'It seems to me that we currently face two problems.' He looked around the table. 'In this very room, indeed.'

'Two, Gordon?' the Leader asked.

'Two,' echoed Gordon, nodding. 'I think we, Paula aside, can all agree that the director's stewardship over her department is wanting. Multiple brazen attacks in less than a week. Despite what she says, it was my son, under my direction, who ensured Battersea was protected. I think we all know what the answer to the problem is.' He finished on a raised voice as Hipwood rose to her feet, face flushed crimson.

'That's going too far.'

A withering glare from the Leader cut Hipwood off. The avuncular personality vanished, replaced by a cold-blooded reptile.

'What's the second issue?' the Leader asked, his grey eyes dead.

Gordon pressed his lips together into a pale line. 'It's one thing to bungle the security of the power supply of the capitol. It is quite another to let into the very heart of power a traitor. Worse than a traitor, in fact.'

There was a murmur of confused concern around the room. The Leader leaned forward, his dead eyes boring into Gordon.

'What do you mean, worse than a traitor?'

Gordon straightened the paperwork in front of him, then looked across the table at the Leader. 'In the last twenty-four hours, based on information given directly to me, I have had my department digging into the archives for evidence of... Well, you can read for yourselves.' The general murmur became more urgent. 'No, hear me out.'

Gordon signalled to an aide standing in the corner, who began to distribute manila folders around the room.

'The evidence I have seen is undeniable, no matter how outlandish it may appear. I apologise for withholding this information for so long, but as you can appreciate, it has taken me some time, and much persuasion, to believe even a tenth of what has been collected.'

'What's this nonsense?' Hipwood said, holding up a blurry photograph.

A large furry creature stood on a snowy plateau, a Buddhist temple in the background.

'That's in the Himalayas,' Gordon said. 'We had explorers in the '50s up there, keeping an eye on Chinese movements. They took that solitary photo.'

'Bloody Loch Ness,' another director said, looking up from a folder. 'I mean, Gordon, really!'

'Let him finish,' the Leader said.

Gordon glanced at him and felt his blood run cold. The Leader looked ready to have Gordon hauled out of the room. He drew himself up. He would have one shot at this, one attempt to convince the Leader. Do that, and everyone else would follow.

'If you turn to the last section.'

There was a rustle of papers. A groan of disgust issued from one end of the table. The looks on the faces of the other directors were bleak.

'When was this taken?' Hipwood asked.

The image, taken from the autopsy Henderson had conducted, showing a mutilated corpse of the duplicates.

'A few days ago,' Gordon said. 'If you read the report, it indicates the corpse is not of this Earth. Yes, they look human, on the margins at least, but the cellular structure indicates it is grown, not naturally born.'

'Grown?' the Leader said.

Gordon went for broke. 'I am advised that these creatures in the photograph have been laboratory grown. They are, in fact, human duplicates.'

'Dead, thankfully.'

Gordon noted that the Leader hadn't ordered him dragged from the room.

'Yes. In this instance. These... things took the place of two men who were bodyguards. I believe... No, I am certain, that there are more duplicates in existence.'

'You said traitor, before,' said the Leader. 'In the heart of power. What did you mean?'

Gordon saw Freddie's head turn like the turret of a tank, his eyes glowering.

'I did,' Gordon said. 'My son, Alastair, has been tracking Resistance fighters and their supporters in the community for many months. He has come across a transmission indicating the Resistance has been receiving... outside influence and assistance.'

'Why was I not told of this?' Hipwood demanded, smacking her palm on the table.

'Because you're a bungler, Paula,' Gordon said, mildly. 'And the mere fact that this traitor is sitting literally feet away from you only underscores my point.'

Freddie began to chuckle as all eyes turned on him. His face lit with a mad joy, the eyes bugging out from their fleshy sockets.

'Fools,' he said, spraying spittle from his engorged lips. 'You know nothing. All you do is sit here and play your games while your nation is a ripe fruit ready to be plucked. You fight amongst yourselves while my masters prepare for victory. I have been pillaging the secrets of the Directorate and feeding it directly to the Resistance. My masters armed and trained and directed them in the assault on Battersea.' He chuckled throatily. 'Truly, this conquest of your nation will be far too easy. And after we have done that, this world will surely follow.' He dissolved into further gales of laughter.

One of the directors sitting next to Freddie placed a hand on his arm, then snatched it back with a cry of pain, as if scorched by the contact.

'He's burning up,' the director yelled. He scrambled to his feet, overturning his chair in his panic.

It was then that chaos truly descended on the room. Waves developed beneath the skin of Freddie's face, rippling and contorting. His features shifted grotesquely before collapsing. His entire body rose and warped. Bones cracked and fissures stitched their way across his skin. With a terrible ripping sound, his face opened up like the petals of a flower, revealing a crimson soaked sucking hole filled with row upon row of teeth.

Rising like a walrus to its full height, the thing that had once been Freddie Frogmorton's duplicate pounced. Hipwood's head and shoulders vanished into the gaping maw. The sound of her flesh and bone pulping beneath the serrated teeth was truly ghastly. With a convulsive wrench, the monster lifted Hipwood upside down into the air. Her skirt fell down, revealing a pair of silk bloomers, which, had the circumstances been different, would've made Gordon laugh until tears sprang from his eyes.

Instead, only horror was in view.

Blood foamed and jetted from the creature's mouth as Hipwood's body jittered and her legs spasmed in agony.

Chairs and side tables crashed aside as the bizarre monstrosity rampaged around the Cabinet Room. Blood sprayed across the portrait of Walpole, making the grim visage grimmer still. The creature trampled a director beneath its heavy feet, the despairing cry cut short with a crunch as her skull was flattened.

Gordon scrambled clear; watching in shock as Hipwood's mutilated body was at last cast aside, wetly smacking the wall before sliding to the heavily carpeted floor. The body twitched one more time, then laid still.

The creature paused, the bizarre head turning left, then right, as if scenting the air for prey. Then it charged again.

Gunfire erupted, a staggeringly loud fusillade in the confines of the Cabinet room. From the corner of his eye, Gordon saw several of the remaining guards lift the Leader's wheelchair and retreat towards the door. The creature bellowed as bullets stippled its flesh. It shrugged Gordon's aide aside, sending him slamming into a wall with bone-crushing force. For a moment, that terrible maw cantered on Gordon, and with all the skill of a born survivor, he began to beat a hasty retreat.

The screaming in the Cabinet Room followed him as he backed after the bodyguards. He pulled his pistol out and fired several times, the creature jerking back when struck. A black, oily fluid spilled from multiple wounds, but nothing seemed able to slow it. Fighting down the panic rising in his throat, Gordon exited the room.

The short corridor led to the Leader's offices. Ignoring the glares from the bodyguards, Gordon pushed his way inside. Thick carpets and wall hangings muffled the creature's bellowing. From his vantage point, Gordon saw it burst through the door from the Cabinet Room, chunks of wood ripping into its flesh. Together with a pair of the bodyguards, Gordon slammed the door shut and began piling heavy furniture against it.

'What's going on?'

Gordon turned at the slurred words. The Leader sat slumped in the wheelchair, one hand feebly waving in the air. Gordon went over to the Leader.

'There is grave danger here, Leader,' he said, staring into the Leader's face. The earlier strength had evaporated. Eyes that had once pierced you to your soul and unmasked every traitorous thought, were now clouded and confused.

'Danger?' the Leader repeated, vaguely. His head nodded. Sweat sheened his wrinkled face.

'You've lived too long, you old fool,' Gordon said, hissing the words through clenched teeth.

There was a massive crash behind him. He turned, pistol aimed. The bodyguards fell back as the door was pushed half open, scattering the furniture. Gordon stepped behind the wheelchair, his free hand resting on the Leader's shoulder.

'Don't worry,' he said. 'I'll see you right.'

Howling its frustration, the creature smashed into the door again, sending the piled furniture tumbling away. A heavy couch fell onto a bodyguard, pinning him to the floor. The creature stepped over the couch, slashed down with a free arm and swept away the bodyguard's head.

Gunfire ripped out again. The creature swung its head left and right. Its teeth shone bloody in the light. Gordon fired, the heavy slugs ripping into grey flesh. This enraged the creature further. It charged forward, smashing aside one of the two remaining bodyguards. He flew across the room and crashed through a window. His despairing scream vanished into the night.

The last of the bodyguards shared a quick, panicked glance with Gordon. Before he could do anything, the creature moved forward. More gunfire, distant sounding with his numb ears. The creature grunted, but ploughed forward, overwhelming the bodyguard. Its teeth macerated his head and shoulders before he fell dead to the floor.

Gordon held his breath. His heart thudded in his chest. The Leader mumbled something. Panting heavily, the creature hunched forward. A constant rain of oily fluid fell from it. The groan it gave sounded like an expression of pain. Despite this, it rallied, rising to its full, terrible height.

'Here we go,' Gordon said. 'Chew on this.'

With a shove, he pushed the Leader's wheelchair towards the creature. The Leader cast a bewildered glance over his shoulder at Gordon, before turning back, just as the creature leaped at him.

Gordon fired, again and again, until the hammer clicked on empty chambers. It was only then that he realised the creature was down, and the room quiet.

Gordon staggered forward. The creature laid in an expanding puddle of black fluid. Its mouth hung open slack in death. Gordon turned to the Leader, who lay half beneath his crumpled wheelchair. Above him, blood had sprayed in a thick swathe across the wall. Gordon took one look at the shattered skull and the blank, dead eyes, and he slumped to the ground, laughing hysterically.

This was how the Auxpol strike team found him when they charged into the room.

CHAPTER TWENTY

SEATED BEFORE a metal table, and strapped into a chair at wrists and ankles, the Resistance fighter glared pure murder at Alastair as he entered the cell, carrying a folder. At some point, water had been poured over her. She sat drenched, her teeth chattering.

The door closed silently on well-oiled hinges. His ears popped as the pressure changed. The cells beneath Leconfield House had a reputation as dark as those managed by the Directorate of Internal Affairs. This warren of interview rooms, holding cells and torture chambers had been carved out of the limestone. Those surviving labour camp inmates were then shot, ensuring the layout remained a secret. This close to the Thames, the walls sweated water, rendering the atmosphere cold and dank.

An audio and visual feed ran back from each cell to a control room on the floor above. Access was only possible by a single set of stairs. Armed guards maintained a watch on the sole landing. It was one way in, and no way out.

Alastair glanced at the camera positioned above and behind the woman. The other camera sat over the door, looking over his head. The lights on both cameras were on.

Alastair smiled at the woman. Long experience informed him that beneath the façade of defiance bubbled a molten core of fear. He stood in a corner beside the door and folded his arms.

'What's your name?' he asked, watching for her reaction.

'Go to Hell.'

'Unusual, but I think I can work with it.'

Silence.

Alastair sighed.

'I assume you've never been questioned by any of the Security forces? What a charmed existence you've led. Do you know how I can tell you've not been questioned by us before? You wouldn't be this defiant if you had.'

More silence.

'This will go far more quickly if you demonstrate a skerrick of common sense and co-operate, you do realise that?'

'Why should I spend what little time remains to me by accommodating you?'

'She speaks! Excellent.' Alastair looked around. 'I'm sure you've noticed it's quite cold in here.' Indeed, his breath plumed around his face. He waved at her. 'Tipping a bucket of water over a prisoner is an old technique. Lowers morale, makes it easier to break any resistance. If you show some sense, talk a little, I can get you some dry clothes. A blanket even.'

'Go. To. Hell.'

'I did say you've not been questioned by the Security forces,' Alastair said, after a pause. 'But we do know who you are.'

Her eyes narrowed.

'The Party runs a police state, Natalie. It's Natalie, isn't it? Not Alice Thompson, as you've been calling yourself for years. Your real name is Natalie Fairbairn. Oh, please, don't look shocked. You may have changed your identity, but short of plastic surgery, your face and fingerprints remain the same.' A smile crept across Alastair's face. It wasn't kind. 'Perhaps if you escape, you can pass on that tradecraft tip to your comrades.'

He slapped the folder onto the table. He glanced up at the camera staring down at him, and smirked.

'Natalie Fairbairn. Born April 17th, 1947, to Peter and Mary Fairbairn, in Surrey. Not quite a child of the Revolution, but close enough, I suppose. You were a primary school teacher before you faked your death. Drowning, was it? Most faked deaths are. Better than risking a fire burning down your apartment building, I suppose. And then there's the matter of procuring a corpse to pass as you. Believe me, Natalie, I've seen it all before.' Alastair tapped the folder. 'It didn't take us long to track your fake name to a cemetery in Highgate. Stealing the name of a baby who died aged six months. Poor form, my dear, don't you think?'

'What do you want?' Fairbairn grated through clenched teeth.

'What do I want?' Alastair pretended to be unsure. He flicked through the folder and pulled out a sheaf of photographs. 'The truth, of course.'

He slapped down a photograph of a middle-aged man.

'Where is your cell based?'

Silence. Another photo dropped onto the table. A woman, hair plain and face careworn. The resemblance with Fairbairn was unmistakable.

'Who do you report to?'

Fairbairn shook her head, spraying droplets of sweat across the images. Another photograph fell onto the pile. A young girl, with eyes as green as Fairbarn's.

'That's your sister, isn't it? I watched your mother take her to school this morning. Your mother looked upset. I wonder why? Perhaps she's the leader of your cell? It's not unheard of.' Alastair leaned forward. 'Your sister's name is June. Imagine how long she would last down here, sitting where you're sitting right now?'

'You wouldn't dare,' Fairbairn said, fear at last creeping into her eyes.

'Why are you fighting us if you didn't think we would dare take your sister in the dead of night and interrogate her? Have you forgotten the propaganda you and your people spread about like so much manure? The lies you tell, the people you kill?'

Rage filled Fairbairn's face. 'Lies we tell? You brainwashed fool. I'm not a puppet of a regime which operates labour camps that work people to death in the Home Counties. I'm not a fascist who enslaved every person of colour in Britain in 1943 and sent them to work and die in the mines and plantations in the Caribbean. What's the death rate there, Column Leader? Sixty percent? Eighty? I'm not part of an elite that enriches itself while the people of Britain spend hours in line waiting to buy a single loaf of bread. You scoop people off the street and torture them simply because they want to live their lives as they wish, and not as the Party dictates.'

'A very pretty speech,' Alastair said. 'I'm sure I've not heard it a thousand times before.'

'And yet you still think what you do is right? You still think the Party is the sole fountainhead of wisdom in this country? Its power rests on the bones of the dead. On the blood, sweat and tears of innocents who number in the tens of thousands. There's absolutely nothing the Party has done in the last twenty-five years anyone could describe as good and decent. And you, you're no better than the people who order you around like a damned pet.'

Fairbairn stopped, her chest heaving for breath. Alastair sighed again.

'So, you won't co-operate? Have it your own way,' he said, gathering the photographs and closing the folder. 'I'm the reasonable one, believe it or not. Outside that door I have two South African mercenaries itching to ask you a few questions. They're not best pleased. One of your friends killed one of their friends at Battersea. When they finish with you, we'll have to scrape what's left into a bucket.'

Fairbairn's eyes widened in shock. Alastair turned and went to the door. He paused, then looked back.

'And when they finish with you, June will be next.'

A few minutes later, Alastair entered the control room.

'She's ready to talk,' he said, closing the door. 'Didn't even need to send Du Plessis or Klaasen in.' He saw Fairbairn on one of the monitors. Her wracking sobs came through the speakers.

Knight turned the volume down. 'Impressive,' he said, without any real emotion. He looked distracted. Given Lewisham's death, Alastair supposed it was warranted. To a point.

'Maybe,' he said, shrugging. 'As long as she talks, who cares?'

'Lewisham would've had something to say,' Knight said, staring at the monitor.

'That's quite enough of that,' Alastair said. 'She's gone, Benjamin. There's nothing you or I can do to bring her back. If you're angry, focus it on people like her,' he said, stabbing a finger at the screen.

The look on Knight's face was unreadable, but after a few moments, he nodded.

'Turn up the volume,' Alastair said, watching as a black gloved interrogator entered the cell.

'Names,' the interrogator said. 'Give me names.'

'I don't have any names,' Fairbairn said with a catch in her voice. 'We never use our real names.'

'Then what use are you to me?' The interrogator's eyes narrowed. 'If you've been playing for time, you're putting off the inevitable. Or did you want your sister brought in?'

'He... The other man, he said wouldn't touch her if I co-operated.'

'Then co-operate.'

'I want assurances,' Fairbairn said, tilting her head to look at the camera. 'I want assurances. In return, I'll tell you about the Italian Job.'

Alastair's head snapped up.

'You'll tell me now,' the interrogator said.

'No,' Fairbairn said, shaking her head. 'Assurances, or nothing. And I don't care who you threaten.'

'The Italian Job,' Alastair said, turning excitedly to Knight.

'What? What did she say?'

'The Italian Job. It's some sort of code name, I'm sure of it.'

'She's dangled a morsel of information in front of us. Enough to indicate she knows something. We give her an assurance, in return for her giving up everything she knows.'

Alastair opened his mouth to respond, when the telephone on the desk chirped. Knight picked it up.

'Who? What do you mean she wants to see him?' Knight glanced at Alastair and shook his head. 'I can ask, but don't be surprised if he bites your head off.'

'Who is this?' Alastair barked when he took the receiver from Knight. A voice he didn't recognise apologised hastily, then mentioned a name. 'Upstairs? In the entrance. Tell her I'll be there in five minutes.'

Alastair handed the receiver back, and stood pensively watching the monitor.

'You've got a visitor?' Knight asked.

'Of all the bloody times,' Alastair said. He turned for the door. 'I'll be back.'

'Sally? What the blazes are you doing here?'

Alastair faltered at the look on Sally's face. Grief warred with anger. She walked briskly up to him and almost collapsed into his arms. Caught in her fierce embrace, Alastair could only awkwardly pat her back while a pair of section leaders looked on, vaguely amused.

'March on, lads,' Alastair ordered.

The section leaders were smart enough to know where they should be, which wasn't there.

'Come on, Sally, what happened?'

Tears brimmed in Sally's upturned eyes. 'One of my friends, she's gone missing.'

'I'm not sure what I can do. Have you spoken with the local police?'

'Oh, they're absolutely useless,' she said, her grief turning to anger. 'They've spent the better part of the day fobbing me off. Surely you can help?'

Aware of the time ticking away, Alastair nodded. Equally aware how public they were, he ushered her up to the reception area, had her signed in and through the gates within a few minutes. Inside, he led her down a short corridor.

'Who is this woman?' he said.

Sally reached into her handbag. She pulled out a photograph and handed it to Alastair.

'Her name is Alice Thompson,' Sally said. 'We've worked together for five years. We were meant to catch up last night and… Alastair?'

He stared at the face of the woman in the photo. There was a roaring in his ears, like the ocean at night, which silenced all other sounds.

'Alastair, let go. Please. You're hurting my arm.'

Alastair pushed Sally through the door, into the control room. A bank of screens confronted them, as did Knight, who looked on incredulously.

'What the hell is going on?' Knight said, rising from his

chair. The presence of a civilian was almost unthinkable.

'You tell him,' Alastair said, roughly. He shook his head in disbelief.

'Hang on,' Knight said. 'Who is she?'

'Sally Wright,' Sally said, mustering as much dignity as she could. She glanced angrily between Alastair and Knight. 'I'm Alastair's... friend.'

'Friend, is it?' Knight said. There was no schoolboy humour to his response, only a vague sense of annoyance.

'She says that Fairbairn is a work colleague.'

'A work colleague? You work with this traitor?' Knight asked, stabbing a finger at the screen.

'Traitor?' Sally lifted a hand to her mouth. She looked shocked. She walked up to the monitor and recoiled at what she saw. 'This is... This is unbelievable. What have you arrested Alice for?'

'Arrested?' Alastair laughed. 'We've taken her prisoner. She's a member of the Resistance. And her name isn't Alice. That's a lie, like everything else about her.'

'I have to see her,' Sally said. 'I have to understand what's going on.'

'Out of the question. The mere fact you know her puts you under suspicion as well, Sally.'

'We could use her,' Knight said, a calculating look on his face. 'She's got security clearance, yes?'

'Out of the question.'

'I do,' Sally said. 'Level four. Surely that allows me to speak with her? Convince her it's in her best interest to talk to you.'

'You've threatened to have this woman's family tortured,' Knight pointed out. 'Even with an assurance from you, she may not give up everything. Maybe your friend can convince her.'

Alastair ground his teeth. Sally's presence upset him in a fundamental way he couldn't quite explain. It was one thing to be with his team, fighting the good fight, it was another thing for someone to whom he had grown attached to find out how he fought that good fight. Of the blood he spilled. Of the secrets ripped from people.

'We don't have time for scruples,' Knight said. 'If she's got information, we need it. Now.'

Unwillingly, Alastair nodded. 'You can visit her, Sally. But you have to convince her to turn. Otherwise I'll personally bring in her family, starting with her sister.'

Pale, Sally nodded.

Alastair signalled to Knight. 'You take her down.'

Knight nodded, and rose from his chair. 'Come with me.'

Alastair had his back to the door when it closed. His gaze was fixed on the screen. After a few minutes, he saw the cell door open. He watched Sally enter, her head turning to take in the grim surroundings. The door closed with a clang, and she flinched. The woman looked at her, mouth agape.

Knight bustled back into the control room, panting for breath.

'Anything?' he asked, standing beside Alastair.

'Not yet.'

Alastair turned up the volume.

'Alice? Is what they're saying true?'

Fairbairn just stared at Sally. Her mouth had settled into a grim line.

'This is a waste of time,' Alastair said.

'Give it time,' Knight said.

'If you don't answer them, they'll bring June in,' said Sally on the screen. 'Is that what you want?'

'They'll bring her in anyway,' Fairbairn said. 'These people… They're monsters.'

'Whatever they are, Alice, is your silence worth June being punished as well?'

'I've done nothing wrong,' Fairbairn protested. 'You want me to give up my friends, is that it?'

'We all have to make sacrifices,' Sally said, drawing herself up.

Fairbairn's head flinched. A tear tracked down her cheek. Slowly, she nodded her head.

'I'm sorry,' Sally said. She reached out and briefly held Fairbairn's hand.

Fairbairn looked at it, then slowly nodded. Sally walked to the door and knocked on it. It opened, and she vanished from the screen.

Du Plessis returned Sally to the control room. She looked calm, but Alastair could see the tension behind her eyes.

'She'll talk.'

'She'd better,' Alastair said. 'We're losing time here.'

The telephone chirped again. Knight picked up the receiver.

'Hello?'

Alastair watched Knight's face go pale. When he did put the receiver down, he looked lost for words.

'What in God's name? What is it, Knight?'

Knight tried to speak, swallowed, then managed to strangle out several words.

'The Leader… The Leader is dead!'

It took Alastair threatening to arrest and intern the men guarding the entrance to Downing Street before he, Knight and Sally were allowed inside the perimeter. Sally had refused to leave Alastair's side and, in his haste, Alastair didn't think it worth arguing about. Amid a gaggle of hysterical staff, dour faced Auxpol officers, Alastair found his father, surrounded by an armed group of bodyguards, fielding questions from the surviving directors.

'Friends, friends, please, calm yourselves.' Gordon raised his hands for quiet, but his words only served to increase the jagged emotions in the room.

A woman collapsed, hysterical, clawing at her face. Alastair exchanged a glance with Knight, who looked at the screaming woman in contempt.

'Not a good start to his leadership, eh?' Alastair said.

Knight looked sharply at him. 'You don't think he would…?'

'Not only do I think it, but he's already in charge. The rest of these idiots don't realise it, yet.' Alastair frowned. Swiftly, he pulled his pistol from his holster, pointed the weapon at the ceiling, and fired.

The explosion in the room silenced everyone. Immediately, Alastair became acutely aware that more than a dozen weapons were pointed at his head.

'That get your attention, did it?' he shouted as he holstered his pistol. 'Any more of this nonsense and I'll have you all hauled off to the nearest labour camp.' Satisfied that the shocked silence signalled understanding, Alastair nodded to his father, who nodded back.

'Friends, this is a terrible moment, for the Party and for the Republic,' Gordon said. 'But rest assured, the reins of power have not slipped from our grasp. As the senior director, I have taken control of the investigation into the Leader's death. No stone will be left unturned in our efforts to expose the perpetrators of this foul deed.'

'He's just announced a purge,' Alastair said quietly.

Sally nodded. 'The king is dead, long live the king.'

Alastair started at the allusion, then nodded, smiling. His father beckoned him forward.

'Come on, let's see what our newly crowned monarch wants.'

The crowd surrounding Gordon cleared a path for his son. Gordon clapped Alastair on the shoulder, something Alastair hadn't experienced before in his life. It felt... good.

'Well done, boy,' Gordon said into Alastair's ear, as the conversation in the room grew loud once more. He glanced at Sally. 'And who is this lovely filly?' He winked at Sally. She winked right back at him, and Gordon laughed.

'This is my... friend, Sally Wright. She works up at the Vault.'

'Oh, keeper of the secrets are we, my dear?'

'There are no secrets in the Republic, Director.'

Gordon laughed. 'See if you can keep this one, boy.' He slapped Alastair on the back. He proffered his hand, and after a moment, Sally took it. 'Pleased to meet you, dear. An auspicious time.'

'Good things come to those who wait, Director,' Sally said.

Alastair's eye widened in surprise, but Gordon laughed.

'Indeed, my dear, indeed. The longer the wait, the greater the reward. Come, let's move to somewhere more quiet. I need an update on your investigation into the Battersea incident.'

'Benjamin,' Alastair said, signalling Knight closer. 'Get back to Leconfield House and find out if that woman has spoken. Radio me if there's any updates.'

Knight nodded, and pushed his way through the crowd to the exit.

Bodyguards formed a wedge and shoved their way clear of the crowd, into a much quieter side room. Several remained on guard outside the door, while two more remained stationed inside. Gordon sank gratefully into a seat.

'What happened here?' Alastair said. 'It looks like a war zone.'

'It is a war zone, boy,' Gordon said. 'Frogmorton…' He hesitated a moment, looking at Sally.

'Don't worry about her.'

'I worry about everything,' Gordon said. Suddenly, he looked very old and very tired. Pinching the bridge of his nose, Gordon closed his eyes for a moment. When he reopened them, he stared straight at Alastair. 'Do you trust her?'

Alastair nodded.

'All right. The thing that was Frogmorton went mad. Attacked everyone in the Cabinet Room, killed Hipwood, killed the Leader. Damn well near killed me.'

'So, it worked?'

'It did,' Gordon said. 'It damn well worked. Why plant something like that in the Cabinet if it didn't take advantage of its position and try to kill the Leader?' He slapped his leg, then leaped from the chair and began to pace around the room. Sally looked at Alastair, an eyebrow raised. He shrugged his shoulders. 'I can do great things now,' Gordon said, talking more to himself than the others in the room. 'With the Old Man dead, we can renew the Party, bring new blood in.' He stopped and looked at Alastair. 'With you by my side, we can do this together. What do you say?'

Alastair didn't hesitate. 'Yes,' he said.

'Good, good.' Gordon rubbed his chin, deep in thought. 'We have to sort out the inauguration. Politics abhors a vacuum. Tomorrow, we'll do it tomorrow.'

'Will you have the support to claim it? The leadership, I mean.' Sally's words dropped like stones into a pond. The ripples rebounded around the room.

'Oh, I'll have the support,' Gordon said. 'They'll embrace me, willingly or not.'

'Power comes from the barrel of a gun, then?'

'Hasn't it always?'

Outside, Downing Street swarmed with people. An alphabet's soup of security services swarmed about, taking names, often from each other. Behind the gates barring direct entry, a small knot of civilians with carefully blank faces watched the tumult.

'Are you excited?' Sally asked, looking around at the commotion.

'I think so,' Alastair said, hesitating. 'Yes. The Party needs renewal. My father will certainly shake things up.'

Sally said something which Alastair missed. He recognised a few members from the Directorate, who were arguing with a pair from Internal Affairs. He felt a tug on his elbow.

'I said, I have to go, Alastair.'

'Oh,' he said. 'All right.' He had hoped they might steal away, spend an hour together. 'When will I see you next?'

'Soon,' Sally said. She smiled, but its warmth didn't match her eyes.

Nodding to her, Alastair watched her push her way through the crowd. For a few minutes, he stood amid the chaos, taking in the energy pulsing around him.

Someone called his name. He turned, recognising a section leader. The fellow came up to him and saluted. He held a squawking walkie-talkie.

'It's Platoon Leader Knight, sir,' he said. Alastair frowned, and beckoned for the device.

'Benjamin,' he said, raising his voice to be heard. 'What is it?'

'It's that damned woman, Fairbairn,' Knight said. Even through the whistle and static, Alastair heard the disbelief in his voice.

'What about her?'

'She's damned well dead. Bloody poisoned!'

Alastair went numb. He turned, shuffling like an old man, looking at the direction in which Sally had departed.

CHAPTER TWENTY-ONE

SHE WAS dead within the hour,' Knight said. 'Du Plessis was with her when she died.'

They were back at Alastair's flat. It was in the early hours of the morning. Alastair and his team had spent fruitless hours searching the area around Downing Street, hoping to find any sign of Sally. Eventually, Alastair had sent everybody home. With Knight not having anywhere else to stay, Alastair had offered him his couch. Despite the hour, the two men were still up.

'Did Fairbairn say anything?' Alastair asked. 'Before she died.'

'Du Plessis said she kept muttering "the Italian, the Italian".'

'How was she poisoned?'

'You can't continue to deny it. We know,' Knight said quietly. He had a sense of the relationship between Alastair and Sally, but also recognised the current moving around them, a dark, dangerous current.

'We don't,' Alastair said, without any conviction.

'I searched her myself, Alastair. No tablets, no bottles. It had to have been...'

Lifting his hand, Alastair cut Knight off. He sighed, then shook his head.

'I've been such a fool,' he whispered. That old, familiar, despairing panic scrabbled in his chest again. He felt the walls loom close. His ruined eye ached, and he longed to pull off the eyepatch and scratch at the scarred tissue beneath.

'Was Sally just an operative? Or...'

'She might've been the leader of the London cell,' Alastair

said. He couldn't believe the depth of the betrayal she had handed him. His hands clenched and unclenched, and he found himself panting. Ignoring Knight's alarmed look, he managed to control himself.

'Sally poisoned Fairbairn because she knew she would talk,' Knight said.

Alastair's shook his head and his irritation drained away. Exhaustion swept over him.

'We'll think more clearly in the morning.'

'We'll be busy,' Knight said. 'The inauguration.'

'Yes,' Alastair said. Word had come through earlier in the evening that his father had cemented his place at the head of the Party. There were rumours that a few executions had taken place to ensure his rise.

'He'll want to take the oath of office as soon as possible. And I daresay even James will be there.'

'Do you think so?'

'Oh yes. Our new Leader will insist, and even James won't be able to ignore such an order.' Alastair raised an eyebrow, imagining that reunion. 'It's ten in the morning, isn't it?'

'Yes. I'm leading a security detail. What are you doing?'

'What does the son of the new Leader do when his father is sworn in?'

Knight shrugged. 'No idea.'

'Neither do I,' Alastair said.

He turned and walked to his bedroom, shutting the door behind him. When he laid on the bed, sleep refused to come for a couple of hours, leaving him to contemplate the shadowy ceiling, and the betrayal that lay across him like a shadow.

Up before dawn, Alastair bathed first and ate a cold breakfast while Knight readied himself. At the kitchen table, Knight ate several slices of toast, while Alastair moodily contemplated his cup of coffee.

'Did you hear the gunfire last night?' Knight asked, pushing his empty plate aside.

Alastair nodded. There were dark patches under his eyes. 'I called into Leconfield House when I woke up. There was more rioting last night. Some of it appeared spontaneous, but some of it was directed. The Resistance won't let the

Inauguration go ahead unmarked.'

'The fools are always looking to blow something up,' Knight said, drumming the table with his fingers.

Raising the cup to his lips, Alastair froze. A thought clicked, then another, and suddenly they were tumbling through his mind in an avalanche.

'Say that again,' he said, lowering the cup to the table.

'The Resistance. Bomb happy. Never saw a landmark they didn't want to strap an explosive to. What they did to Nelson's Column back in '62…'

'Blew it to flinders, didn't they?'

'You've seen the stump. The perpetrators were executed in its shadow.'

'Blew it up,' Alastair said. He rubbed his jaw. 'Let's look over the evidence we have in front of us.' He felt a surge of excitement and began to walk around the kitchen.

Knight frowned at him.

'One,' Alastair began, 'we know for a fact the Resistance is working with a third party from outside Britain, supplying them with bomb making material we've not seen used before.'

'Right,' Knight said. 'The bombings earlier in the week were designed to lower morale and demonstrate the Resistance's fighting ability.'

'Yes. But what if it was really meant to distract us? What if the security forces were looking over "there" while they should've been looking over here?'

'Do you mean they're planning something bigger?'

'Yes,' Alastair said with a sharp nod. 'We have recordings of their meetings, where that code name, Italian Job, is mentioned. There's the chemicals used in the bombs. The attacks were as much a dry run as they were a way to draw our attention elsewhere.'

'It makes sense. I mean, I'd do it that way if I was working against the Party.'

'It's a good thing you're not,' Alastair said. But his gaze was distant, as he thought through the ramifications. 'Second. There's Frogmorton's assassination of the Leader. Causes more chaos, but what else?'

'He has to be replaced,' Knight said. His eyes narrowed. 'Won't the ceremony be held away from the public, for security reasons?'

'You don't know my father,' Alastair said. 'He will want to seal his ascent with the full ritual, seen by as many people as he can summon and to the population at large.'

'At the New People's Parliament.'

'The Chief Justice swears the new Leader in, in a room within the building.'

'Which room?' Knight asked.

'The old House of Lords... Oh God.' Alastair stopped in his tracks, his remaining eye wide. 'I know what they're going to do.' He turned and stared at Knight. 'The Italian Job. Their absolute brazen cheek...'

'Explain it to me again,' Du Plessis said, shouting from the back seat of the Jeep as Alastair raced through London.

Alastair and Knight had arrived at Leconfield House in record time. He had ordered Knight to go ahead with Klaasen and some other men, while Alastair pulled together the main force in short order. Kitted out, Alastair led the small convoy towards the parliamentary precinct.

'The fools are going to blow up the New People's Parliament,' Alastair shouted above the roar of the engine. He saw in the rear vision mirror the look of confusion on Du Plessis' face. 'Don't they teach you lot history down in that God forsaken backwater?' He ignored Du Plessis' angry glare. Alastair was trying to hold together the remnants of his fraying sense of control. Rage filled him, an acid bubbling made him want to lash out. He gritted his teeth and felt them shift in his mouth.

Glancing at Du Plessis' reflection in the rear vision mirror, Alastair continued. 'In 1605, authorities captured a Catholic terrorist named Guido Fawkes just as he was about to ignite barrels of gunpowder hidden beneath the House of Lords in the Palace of Westminster and murder King James and every leading name of the day. "Guido Fawkes" was a pseudonym he took while fighting for the Spanish on the Continent. With a name like that, some of his contemporaries thought he was an Italian.' He shook his head again.

He couldn't get a grip of the extent of Sally's duplicity. She had made a fool of him. *A damned fool*, he thought.

'So, they want to blow up the building?' Du Plessis asked.

'Of course they want to blow up the damned place. Taking in one fell swoop my father and the upper echelons of the Party and Cabinet at his inauguration. With the head cut off, the Party's control of the nation will wither away overnight. The Resistance would step in and install their people to run the show.'

Alastair pulled the steering wheel to the right, sending the Jeep in a long careening turn into a new street. Alastair heard Du Plessis swear.

'Get out of the way, damn it,' Alastair yelled as pedestrians scattered for the footpaths.

He roared through a red traffic light, almost running over a woman. Cars and lorries screeched to a halt and, in one case, ran straight into a shop front window in an explosion of glass.

'Get on the radio and see if you can raise anyone on my father's security detail. The entire building needs to be locked down and searched from top to bottom. We're going to need bodies in the cellars beneath the Parliament if we're going to find them all and stop this madness.'

While Du Plessis spoke urgently into his walkie-talkie, Alastair saw a rapidly approaching checkpoint. He briefly considered planting his foot and ramming through the guard station, but he unwillingly relented.

Coming to a halt with a screech, he wound down his window and watched an Auxpol officer saunter up to the vehicle.

'Identity card,' the officer said.

'I don't have time for this,' Alastair blustered. The scars above and below his eyepatch went white in his anger at being delayed.

'Identity card,' the officer said again, deliberately drawing out the words.

Alastair felt the presence of his holstered pistol at his hip and resisted the urge to drop his free hand on it. He saw another guard approaching the far side of the car. In his rear vision mirror, he saw Klaasen at the wheel of the other Jeep.

Relenting, Alastair pulled his card from his breast pocket and handed it over. The Auxpol officer made a show of looking at the card, then Alastair's face, then the card again, before he handed it over.

'What's your business here?'

'Saving the Republic from damned fools like you,' Alastair snarled. He revved the engine, the sound drowning out the officer's reply.

The other Auxpol guard whistled to his partner.

'Let these ExSec pansies in,' he said, smiling broadly. 'We've got better things to do than nursemaid them during the inauguration.'

Barely keeping his fury in check, Alastair tightened his grip on the steering wheel and watched as the guards moved to the barrier. They lifted it up, and in a scream of burning tyres, the Jeeps raced through.

'Damn fools,' Alastair said as they sped away.

Inside, the streets were empty of vehicles and people. Pigeons roosted on statues and rooftops. The stunted and burned out column of Clock Tower emerged into view at the end of the street. Scorch marks on the stonework testified to the severity of the blaze that had overcome the bell tower in the aftermath of the explosion earlier in the week.

'Has it been only a week?' Alastair muttered, fighting a wave of exhaustion.

At the sight of a uniformed figure emerging from a gate at a run, he slewed the Jeep to a stop in a long skid. Acrid smoke filled the cabin as he and Du Plessis exited, their weapons in hand. Knight went straight to Alastair.

'What's happening?' Alastair barked.

'My team are already beneath street level. They've commenced a search of the cellars. It's a bloody warren down there, Alastair.'

'Can they be reached by radio?' Alastair asked, as Klaasen and a team of four gathered.

'It's spotty, but we've maintained comms since they descended.'

'Good. Radio in and tell them to concentrate on the area beneath the People's Assembly.'

There was chatter among the other men at that point. Alastair turned to look at them.

'We face the gravest threat the Republic has experienced since 1943. Enemies within and without conspire against everything we have built. It has fallen to us, the steel in the spine of the nation, to face them and des—'

Volley fire ripped around them. Men went flying in every direction. Alastair stood his ground, as Knight tried to drag him away. Bullets pinged off the flagstones and masonry, sending stone chips spinning through the air. One cut Alastair on the cheek, which only served to enrage him even more.

Shouting orders while ignoring the gunfire, Alastair ordered Du Plessis and Klaasen to higher ground. The two burly South Africans dodged and wove across the open ground before entering the relative safety of a nearby door. Only then did Alastair allow Knight to lead him to safety.

'Damn them,' Alastair said, panting. He scanned the nearby rooftop. 'There,' he shouted, aiming at a shadowy figure standing in the lee of a leering gargoyle. He fired twice, blowing off a gargoyle's ear with the first, and sending the Resistance fighter toppling forward into a fatal fall with the second.

The firing lessened for a moment, before Du Plessis and Klaasen appeared at both ends of the roofline and began firing indiscriminately at the huddled figures.

In short order, the snipers were cleared from their nests. Several fell to the flagstones, while one hung upside down, its leg trapped by a gargoyle's extended claw. Blood poured from the dangling body. Du Plessis and Klaasen disappeared to return downstairs, while Alastair strutted about, muttering angrily to himself.

'Take it easy, Alastair,' Knight said, coming up to him and taking his elbow.

Alastair pulled his arm away, and rounded on Knight.

'Take it easy?' he shouted. He stepped closer, so that their faces were only inches away. 'There are Resistance fighters inside the Auxpol ring. Sally's here, ready to blow the place sky hi—' Alastair stopped.

The men had emerged from cover, and were warily watching him. His jaw clenched, and he slowly exhaled.

'Come on,' he said, slapping Knight on the shoulder in a show of fake bonhomie. He raised his voice, so the others heard. 'We're going in. Complete sweep of the cellars and vaults beneath the building. We all converge on the grid references on the maps you've been given.'

He glanced at the men surrounding him.

'The ringleader is mine,' he warned. 'As for the rest. Take no prisoners.'

CHAPTER TWENTY-TWO

IN THE old House of Lords, light streamed through Pugin's magnificent stained glass windows, the images rippling like water along the carpeted floor and up the walls. A crowd of people stood where the old seating had once been, now ripped out and carted away after the Revolution. On the dais, where the Throne had once stood, the Chief Justice waited. All along the walls, and especially around the entrance, armed members of Auxpol and the Directorate stood guard, warily watching each other as much as the Party members below.

A team from the Republican Broadcasting Corporation were in place. Television cameras stood ready in a variety of vantage points, while a suited figure, the producer, nervously tugged at his collar. This was to be a live broadcast, and the producer had been informed that if it didn't go off as planned, his next career move would be to the gallows.

The heavy bronze doors opposite the dais slowly creaked open. Armed guards entered the chamber, flowing left and right as Gordon Lethbridge-Stewart, clad in his old RSF uniform, strode in. Beside him, his once-dark hair now a shade of grey, marched Brigade-Leader James Lethbridge-Stewart. Stern face; the epitome of loyalty. The members from the Party parted before Gordon. He nodded to several of them, who hastily nodded back. His head was high, his shoulders straight, his eyes clear. This was the day he had worked towards for decades. Destiny had rewarded him at last, he reflected, as he stepped up to the dais.

The distant chatter of gunfire and a deep rumbling throb through the basalt flooring caused a sudden silence to descend. The guards along the walls stiffened, and the quiet chatter of the assembled watchers stilled. The producer swallowed, his eyes darting left and right. Gordon ignored it all.

He stopped in front of the Chief Justice, who tried to hide his unease.

'Don't have kittens up here, Geoffrey,' Gordon said as a sound man came up, bearing a microphone on an extended boom. 'My son has everything in hand.'

The Chief Justice glanced at James.

'The other one,' Gordon said.

The Chief Justice's smile was tight and strained, but he nodded nonetheless. Who wanted to be executed after presiding over an Inauguration, after all?

Gordon turned. He saw the expectant sea of faces. He heard, they all heard, the sound of more gunfire. The bronze gates closed.

He saw James stiffen, but Gordon ignored him. His eldest son had orders to not react. Alastair would take care of it.

Don't muck this up, boy, he thought, and then began his address to the Party.

The vaults, cellars and corridors beneath the New People's Parliament were a nightmarish warren. Carved from the living rock, their proximity to the Thames meant the atmosphere was warm and damp and often foetid.

Armed with weapons and heavy torches, fighting in those conditions was doubly nightmarish, a kaleidoscope of confused images, glaring lights, flashes of gunfire, the screams of the injured and dying and always, always, the iron tang of spilled blood. Alastair, with Knight watching his back, urged his men over forward, overcoming the Resistance fighters' every effort to stymie their progress.

'Why are they sacrificing themselves?' Knight shouted above the echoes of a recently concluded exchange.

Several Resistance fighters laid every which way, their hastily arranged barricade proving of little use.

'Time,' Alastair said, wiping blood from his cheek. Chips of stone from the wall had lashed his face, testimony to how close a bullet had come to striking him. 'They must need time to complete assembling the bomb materials.'

He was about to say more when a creature, all shoulders

and long, reaching arms burst out of the darkness and charged straight at him. It moved like a tide of flesh, a grey, hulking beast with a shapeless head and a maw that split open to reveal a horrifying assemblage of serrated teeth. Its bellow deafened everyone nearby, even as they began firing at it. A fusillade of lead struck, and it staggered back, as if a wave had caught it across the chest. But it kept on, flinging aside Directorate men as it surged forward.

Fearless, Alastair turned side on, his feet braced. He raised his pistol and emptied the clip into the creature. He felt the pistol's butt recoil into the meat of his hand, felt the jolt run up his arm and into his shoulder. The creature staggered, fell to its knees, and with its arms, tipped wickedly with claws, reaching for him, collapsed dead at his feet.

'Five rounds rapid,' Alastair said calmly to Knight, as he stepped over the corpse. 'That does the trick.'

There was a sudden explosion, and Alastair braced, fearing the worst. A rolling cloud of dust and shards of rock enveloped his position, and when it faded away, he emerged, ghostlike, powdered in white.

'What the hell was that?' Knight asked. He bled freely from a gash in his temple, and looked groggy.

'A trap,' Alastair said. 'Likely a pipe bomb.'

Moving forward, the two men, with several other Directorate troops in tow, came on the ragged, bloody corpses of several of their fellows.

'See,' Alastair said, almost clinical. He pointed to a broken trip wire, lying across a four way intersection. One side of the tunnel had shattered, leaving a pile of rocks covering a broken body.

Knight swore, and spit to clear his mouth. Then they heard the rushing of approaching feet and the Resistance fighters were on them.

The next few minutes was bedlam, a crazed spectacle of men fighting in the near dark, wrestling with each other as beams of light illuminated scenes of bloodshed and death. Alastair dodged a knife thrust out of the dark, felt the blade crease his ribs, before he clubbed his attacker down with the butt of his pistol and shot him in the head as he lay dazed on the ground.

As soon as the attack came, it melted away, leaving Alastair and his remaining men standing alone in the dark.

Alastair heard Klaasen swearing extravagantly in a mixture of Afrikaans and English. Alastair went to him, and saw Knight pulling Klaasen out beneath a pile of bodies. Blood welled from a bullet wound high in his chest.

'Get him out of here,' Alastair ordered.

Knight protested. 'I'm not leaving you down here,' he said, helping Klaasen to stand.

'I trust you to get him to safety.'

Already, Alastair's attention had drifted ahead of their position. He could smell the chemical stink of the bomb materials, and sensed that Sally was close.

Knight opened his mouth to protest, but Alastair cut him off with a slash of his hand.

'Just do it, Ben.'

Without waiting for an answer, Alastair strode away, just as a Platoon Under-Leader Benton hurried up.

'Column Leader!' the young man said. He hastily saluted. 'They're forming up in the entrance to a chamber. We're taking casualties.'

Gunfire drifted up a long corridor.

'Well, why aren't you there helping?' Alastair barked. 'If you can handle a bomb, Benton, I expect you to handle this!' He snapped his fingers. Benton snapped a salute, turned, and trotted back towards the fray.

Alastair pulled out a map and trained his torch on it.

'That's the chamber,' he said to himself. 'That harpy is down in there, waiting for me.'

Pausing frequently, ducking into side corridors, Alastair made his way forward. The remaining Directorate men kept up with him until they reached the outer perimeter of the Resistance defence.

There were only a few left, mostly men, with a couple of women. They were armed with old hunting rifles, and possessed only one torch. They were uncertain, hesitant. One looked behind her, into a darkened entrance. There was a hint of movement, and Alastair's rage bubbled up.

'Kill them all,' he roared, stepping into view and firing.

Gunshots filled the chamber, the concussive blasts echoing and re-echoing until only sound filled the world. When it ended, when the last of the echoes had fled, only Alastair stood, ramrod straight.

He stepped forward, drawn towards the darkness, and felt something hot and wet run down his shirt sleeve. He looked down, and saw blood blooming just beneath his left collar bone.

'Doesn't matter,' he muttered. 'Doesn't matter.'

He kept on, through the arched entrance, and into the chamber beyond.

Deep under the New People's Parliament, in the vaults where Guido Fawkes once came so close to changing history, and while the inauguration of the Leader took place, Alastair finally caught up with Sally.

Alastair staggered along the corridor, splashing through pools of water. His left arm felt numb. With each step, the smell of chemicals grew stronger.

Close, his whirling mind thought. *Close.*

He passed beneath an arch and saw movement. He felt something sweep across his face, felt a burning as nails scratched him. Those fingers caught, and his eyepatch was gone. He felt a piercing pain in his ruined socket, like it had been jabbed by a piece of ice. Then he saw Sally standing not ten feet from him, with a weapon aimed at him. Gas lanterns hissed gently, illuminating the space. On instinct, Alastair raised his pistol.

'I could've killed you,' Sally said, looking him square in the face.

Water dripped down the crumbling walls, and the smell of the Thames lurked in the air. Thick clumps of nitre clung to the upper walls, like knots of pallid rot. Her pistol never wavered. In her other hand, she held a small black box with a switch. With his pistol aimed steadily at her head, and his one good eye focussed on her face, Alastair watched Sally with a welling of emotion that recently had been wholly absent from his life.

Her look of contempt was like acid dripping onto his soul.

'When?' he asked.

The scar on his face throbbed. An old schoolboy shame came over him and he desperately wanted to cover the damaged orbit. But his left arm was numb, and the hand holding the pistol refused to move.

'At *The Revolutionary Arms*,' Sally said, smiling slightly at the memory. 'The son of the Director of ExSec. What a coup that would've been. I had the bomb in the booth and was about to leave, but then I saw you, up close. I recognised you. Only a boy, really. How lonely you looked. How pathetically lost.'

'Please, Sally,' Alastair said, almost begging her. His earlier rage fell away, leaving only this naked need.

'"Please, Sally", what?' Scorn transformed her face. In that moment, Sally revealed herself fully to Alastair.

He almost wept.

'There has to be another way,' he said. 'I can fix this, make it so you aren't investigated. I can—'

'I don't want you to,' Sally said, cutting him off. 'Don't you see? I want to do this. The Republic is a cancer. An abomination. It must die. It will die.'

'Free?' Alastair said. 'We can never be free. The Party is too strong, the people it rules too weak. Cattle like that aren't worth your life. Please, Sally. You don't need to do this. Put down the switch, and we can be together. We can rule this country as we see fit. You and I can kill my father.'

Alastair stopped, shocked by what he had just said.

Sally cocked her head, as if looking at him anew. Then she laughed. The sound was distorted by the low ceiling and the thick walls, becoming a booming cackle tinged with desperate need.

'Kill your father? You could never lay a hand on him. We've people in the Directorate, Alastair. We've people everywhere. I've seen your files, did you know? The one's your father kept about you, from you, all those years ago when he experimented on you. A superman, that's what he wanted to create. With drugs and indoctrination. A republican hero, virtuous and loyal and an inspiration to the people. You've disappointed him so very badly.' She stopped, almost panting. 'I felt sorry for you, did you know? Your father is a bastard, a monstrous, cruel bastard. But you can't kill him. He made sure of that.'

'No,' Alastair said. The hand holding the pistol wavered, only slightly, but both of them saw it.

Sally's smile turned cruel. Her lips parted slightly, and her tongue wetted them with a swift, snakelike motion.

'I saw you that night,' she said, returning to *The Revolutionary Arms*. 'I thought to myself, "what an opportunity". To win my way into your affections. So I adjusted the timer, shoved the bomb further under the table, and waited. And it was so easy. A boy looking for affection, for love.' She held the remote device a little higher, her face transforming into an ecstatic smile of release. 'My little wind-up soldier. I used you, Alastair. I used you and now—'

A shot rang out. The sound filled Alastair's head, spilled out into the world and consumed all other sounds. Its piercing shriek pummelled him, but his hand, after the recoil, was rock steady. Sally, with blood blossoming from her breast, took one step back, then another, wavering, then, in an instant, she collapsed in a tangle of arms and legs. The remote switch flew through the air, rebounded off a wall, and skittered across the flagstones before coming to rest.

A wisp of smoke curled from the barrel of Alastair's pistol. Automatically, he holstered it, tucking the flap into place. Absently, he checked his pulse. It was firm, steady. He took a deep breath, looked down at Sally, and then the world crashed back into place.

His hand went to his mouth, grabbing the flesh, near enough to tearing his lips away. He stood like that, for a few minutes, before he heard movement behind him. He turned and saw his father appear out of the gloom. The ground seemed to shift beneath his feet, and if not for his father's steadying grip on his elbow, Alastair may've joined Sally on the ground.

'Good,' Gordon said, his voice a crooning whisper. 'Well done, boy.'

Alastair had to crane his head around – his father stood on his blind side. With a crash of insight that only shock could unveil, he realised that his father, at every opportunity, always stood on his blind side.

'I… had… no choice,' Alastair said, almost gasping.

'Of course you did,' Gordon said, coolly. He released

Alastair's elbow and stepped forward, looking down at Sally's body. He glanced back at Alastair, a smile on his face. 'Everyone has a choice. This is yours.'

Gordon turned away. Alastair felt the blood drain from his face. His hand dropped to his holstered pistol. For a moment, his fingers scrabbled with the leather flap, gaining purchase only as a phalanx of Auxpol and Directorate men entered the room and formed up around Gordon. One of them was James.

For a moment his eyes locked with Alastair. And all Alastair saw was contempt. Contempt and little bit of shame.

'Leader,' one of the men said, saluting. The others followed suit, their hands flashing up and down, their booted feet crashing on the flagstones. Including James.

'Report,' Gordon snapped.

'Resistance elements have been thwarted in their efforts,' the officer reported. He was heavy set, with an aquiline nose and a high forehead. He glanced at Alastair disdainfully, either not knowing who he was or, if he did, not caring.

'So, my reign begins with success,' Gordon purred.

He spared Sally one last glance, then turned his back on her corpse.

'I want an RBC unit down here to film this,' he said, waving his hand in Sally's direction. He pointed at Alastair. 'You will make yourself available for an interview – I trust you can be reliable enough to put the right gloss on it?'

Alastair nodded, his eye fixed on Sally. Gordon clapped his hands together.

'Excellent. Well then. I have an address to make to the nation. After these tumultuous few days, and with the tragedy of the Leader's death fresh in the minds of the people, now is the time to remind them that while one Leader may be dead, another has risen in his place.' With that, Gordon marched from the room. His bodyguard formed up and followed him out with a clatter of boots and weaponry.

But James lingered.

'I tried to warn you, Alastair,' he said. He shook his head. Pity. And left the room.

The echoes of his departure lingered but a little time, leaving Alastair alone with the silence and his thoughts. He couldn't take his eye off Sally, couldn't allow himself to let go. He remembered their first night together, the feel of her skin and the scent of her hair. His thoughts grew faster in speed and intensity, until he felt his head might burn up like a roman candle.

Anger kindled in his chest and he dropped to his knees beside her corpse. He grabbed both sides of her head and lifted it so it was only inches from his own. His one, good eye stared into her open, empty eyes.

'Damn you. I loved you and you made me kill you.'

He let her head drop and saw blood smeared on his hands. Slowly, moving like he was crippled with arthritis, Alastair groped his way to his feet. He swayed, like a tree in a storm, then, with a sob, he turned and plunged into the darkness.

EPILOGUE

WHEN WILL all this end? How long can the Party maintain its grip on power? What event, or series of events, will precipitate its downfall? When Julius Caesar set out for the Forum on that fatal March day, with the nascent Roman Empire in his grasp, did he know that within the hour he would slump to the ground, fatally wounded at the hands of friends and foe alike? With Europe supine beneath Napoleon's booted foot, who knew that he would be consigned to exile on a remote rock in the Atlantic within a decade? Did the assassination of Adolf Hitler by elements in the German army in 1938 prevent a general European war, or simply delay its possibility?

All that is to say, in the here and now, we can never know what comes next. We can plan, we can anticipate, but in the end, we are groping in the dark as we venture into the future. Healthy one day, dead the next. Facing the executioner's axe on a winter's morning, then pardoned at the last moment. Get off at the next train station, or stay in the carriage and die in a collision a mile down the line. Free will may not be an illusion, but within the roaring chaos of life itself, we are but leaves in a hurricane.

From 'An Unpublishable Memoir' by [redacted]. Retained in the Security Directorate Archives.

Alastair sat in a chair outside the Leader's office. The heavy furniture the previous Leader had favoured had vanished, replaced with a more modern design that emphasised sleekness and lighter colours. No doubt a Scandinavian importer was fattening their invoice to present to the Directorate of Finance,

Alastair thought sourly.

Around him, like shoals of fish swimming with the current, a fleet of civil servants moved about. The leadership had changed, but the machinery of government continued its remorseless march. If he wasn't so exhausted, so mentally and physically drained from the last week, the whole assemblage would've sickened him.

A non-entity in a drab suit approached him, shoes whispered quietly on the polished marble. The look on his face was one of someone performing a task they thought beneath them.

'The Leader will see you now.'

Alastair grunted and clambered to his feet. Straightening his jacket, he glared at the civil servant with his one good eye. The man coloured, turned on his heel, and led Alastair through the outer door.

A fleet of secretaries sat at individual desks, answering phones or clacking away at typewriters. Irene Carson, Gordon Lethbridge-Stewart's principal secretary, watched over her flock of staff like a hawk. She saw Alastair being led in, and raised a hand. The civil servant with Alastair directed him towards her, before turning and leaving the room, his task done.

'Column Leader Lethbridge-Stewart?' she said, her voice carrying across the sounds of the office.

There was a brief silence, and Alastair became aware of at least a dozen heads turning in his direction.

'Yes,' he answered. The buzz began to rise around him.

'Follow me.' She opened a door and led him inside.

A short corridor, guarded at start and finish by Auxpol regulars in their familiar black leather, presented itself. The Auxpol officer at the far end confirmed their identity papers, then allowed Carson to open the inner door.

Where Director Lethbridge-Stewart's old offices were crammed with shelves, themselves crammed with books, the office of the new Leader emulated the new furniture outside. A simple black desk, with chrome trim, sat at one end of a marble clad floor. The bullet holes in the walls had been roughly patched. A lighter rectangular shape on the wall matched the absent portrait of the previous Leader, denoting the swift changing of the guard. To one side, a bank of telexes chattered to themselves, feeding information from around the country into the heart of government. Gordon stood beside one, reading from a strip of paper. On Alastair's entry, he dropped it and turned towards his son.

'Thank you, Irene. Make sure my next appointment is ready. I shan't be long.'

The door closed with a quiet click. Alastair noted a buff envelope sitting on the otherwise empty desk. There was only one chair in the room. Gordon settled himself into it.

'It suits you,' Alastair said, glancing around.

'It does,' Gordon agreed. He pushed the envelope towards Alastair's side of the desk.

'What's that?' Alastair asked, though more for form's sake than anything else. He knew orders when he saw them.

'You've proven yourself... useful, during these last tumultuous days,' Gordon said.

Alastair noticed the cadence of his father's words matched those of his inauguration speech. In the moments after the events beneath New People's Parliament, his father had taken on the manner of someone more Olympian. Distant and august.

'I'm glad I could've been of some small use,' Alastair said, not bothering to mask his sarcasm.

'Watch yourself, boy,' Gordon said. His eyes were hooded as he surveyed his son. 'What is given can just as easily be taken away.'

'What could you possibly give me?' Alastair said, the bitterness of his words a lash. 'I've sacrificed everything to you and your damned cause.'

'What, that girl?' Gordon said. He flicked away a piece of lint on his jacket sleeve. 'Dirty traitor. You can't be pining for her, surely?' When Alastair remained silent, his father shook his head and sighed. 'After too many years of drift, the Party is in strong, capable hands at last. My predecessor had become lax and allowed too many people too much latitude. That has stopped.'

'Yes.' Alastair was growing tired of the conversation. 'I've seen the lists in *The Times*. You'll have the devil's own the time replacing all those people you've ordered executed.'

'The herd must be thinned for the new blood to rise,' Gordon intoned. 'It will serve as a salutary lesson to their replacements. Succeed, and they live. Fail… Well, you did say you read the paper.'

'And what of my position?' Alastair said. 'The Resistance may be on the run, but they are still out there. We broke up one cell, but that isn't the only one left. And the aliens. Are we going to let them off the hook just like that?'

'You expect too much, my boy, if you think everything can be tied off in a neat bow. The most important thing to understand is that the position of the Party is as it ever was – firmly in control. Auxpol and the other security services can spend their days and nights combatting the Resistance and keeping an ear to the ground for any outside interference. My main concern is ensuring the supply of energy around the Republic. If we succeed in that, we renew our faith with the people and maintain our control over them, and the nation.'

Reluctantly, Alastair picked up the envelope and opened it. There were two pages inside. He began reading the top page, and despite his exhaustion, his heart leapt at the information contained in it. He glanced at his father, who nodded, once. Placing the top letter on the desk, Alastair began reading the second.

He recognised the form, the stamp, and the signature. He read the instructions, all the way to the bottom. The earlier joy drained from him. He made a cursory effort to keep the dismay from his face. When he finished, he dropped the page onto the desk.

'I'm a soldier, damn it,' he said, leaning forward with his knuckles on the desk. 'You're asking me to be a damned desk jockey.'

'Not any desk jockey, boy,' Gordon said, his nostrils flaring. 'My desk jockey. The Director of Defence has agreed to your promotion. Take it and be glad. I know what you want, Alastair. You want to take over at Eastchester. But for now, James is well-suited to that role. You will run a different labour camp. In the meantime, you will prepare. Be patient, and you will end up in Eastchester. That project is the key to keeping the lights on in the Republic. But Stahlmann only causes division. I don't trust him to get the job done, but until he is fully set up your brother will serve as a nursemaid. And then, I will need someone I can trust.'

'Trust? Me? You've never trusted me, Father. You've only sought to control me, use me to further your own ends.'

'And hasn't it worked beautifully,' Gordon said, leaning forward and picking up the stamped orders. He glanced at them. 'Project Inferno we're going to call it,' he said, dropping the letter on the desk. 'It's critically important his drilling effort isn't derailed by Stahlmann's own personal weaknesses. Indeed, *when* you take over as camp commandant, you'll be responsible not only for keeping Stahlmann on a short leash, but ensuring no subversive elements infiltrate the facility to undermine his work. Nothing can be allowed to interfere with our efforts at energy independence. Understood? Good. Dismissed.'

Seething, Alastair barely restrained himself from leaping across the desk. The raw hatred in his expression was matched by his father's smile of contempt. Restraining himself with a visible effort, Alastair turned and marched to the inner door.

He wasn't quite there yet, but at least Eastchester and Project Inferno were now within his reach. It would do. For now.

'Alastair,' his father called.

Alastair froze.

'Don't fail me,' the Leader said softly. 'Don't you dare, Brigade-Leader Alastair Gordon Lethbridge-Stewart.'

Concluded in *Ghost of the Schizoid Earth*
Coming 2021.

FROM THE HAVOC FILES

LETHBRIDGE—STEWART

ASHES OF THE INFERNO

Andy Frankham-Allen

This story is set after the television story
Doctor Who: Inferno

FIVE DAYS now, but tonight was the worst. He lay there, awake, long into the night. All around him he could hear the screaming. No, not around him. It was coming from inside him. Every day since Tuesday, the same screaming seemed to follow him, a background sound, but always there. But he couldn't place it. No single voice. Something much worse. As if the world itself was screaming. And only he could hear it.

He sat up and pulled the bedcover off him. No, he couldn't do this for another night. He lifted his legs over the edge of the bed, his arthritic feet looking for his slippers, when something caught his eye. Something in the corner of his bedroom.

He peered closely, not quite sure what he was seeing. A form of some kind, like a shadow of a person; ill-formed, not exactly there, but also not exactly *not* there either. Ghosts and spectres; hardly news to him, and most definitely not something to be bothered by. He'd seen more than his share of the unexplainable in the last quarter of a century.

He listened carefully. A sound came from the shadow. No, not a sound, a voice. The words were hard to make out.

Not.

Leave.

He closed his eyes, attempted to block out the ambient sounds around him.

You're not going to leave us here!

He staggered back, his ears ringing.

He knew that voice. Knew the anger in it. But he hadn't heard it in years, not since…

He approached the shadow, sure of who it was now. And the closer he got, the more distinct the form became. The green and khaki uniform, the gun belt strapped over the shoulder and down the chest, the black hat with the familiar blocky emblem. But still the face was indistinct. On the left arm though, something was very clear; a black oval badge, with the letters R.S.F. in white. The Republican Security Forces.

A phrase jumped to the front of his mind; Unity is strength!

He swallowed. This wasn't right. He hadn't heard a peep from that world in fifteen years. Perhaps he was getting too old, seeing things…

But no, something was pulling at him. He looked at his arm in surprise; it was lifting of its own accord. The feel of the uniform under his palm. It was more than a ghost; the man was really there in his bedroom with him.

As if just touching the form made it real, the face of the man became clear. Just for a moment, and then it was gone, and he was in his bedroom on his own again. But it was long enough for the panic and fear on the man's face to linger in James' mind.

The face was well-known to him; he had seen much of it in the last five years, but not like that. The eyepatch, the scar peering from behind.

And the words, still they echoed around him. His past was calling out to him.

James Gore turned away. He knew what he had to do.

James waited in the common room, not at all patiently. He still liked to think he was in control, but he knew he wasn't. Not anymore.

If he'd been in control then he wouldn't be where he was, safe in a retirement home for ex-government officials. Well, he supposed, he should call them *un*officials, after all every one of them had worked for the shadier arms of the British Government, the areas almost nobody knew existed. All of them had secrets, and all of them were being watched. Closely.

James looked down at the papers on the small table before him. Years of research and experiments, and about the only thing he'd kept on him over the years. The answer was there, he was sure, but he needed more information. And somehow he knew his expected visitor had access to it.

There was a knock on the door and he looked up. 'Yes?'

The door opened and a young man entered. As ever, young Rhys Rubery was dressed smartly, and offered a friendly smile as soon as he saw James. As a rule, James didn't much care for young people; even growing up he preferred the company of older people, but young Mr Rubery was different from most. He had about him a certain deference that James found appealing. Mr Rubery called the people in the retirement home 'important people', which was certainly better than 'old codgers', a term James had heard thrown in his direction on more than one occasion since he'd taken residence in the home. Of course, Mr Rubery, like all the others who came to help out, knew nothing of the men who lived there. Important people indeed – *once*!

'How are you today, Mr Rubery?'

The young man shook his head, but his smile didn't waver. 'Call me Rhys,' he said, not for the first time. He laughed. 'Mr Rubery is my dad, and I don't think I want to become a teacher.'

James knew this. Over the last few months, since Rhys had started helping out, they had spoken a lot. 'How did the flying lesson go?' James asked, thinking of Rhys' intention to become a pilot.

'Yeah, it was good, thanks. Thank you for arranging it.'

James waved the thanks away. 'Anything I can do to help. Not often you come across someone of your age who has such definite plans for their future.'

'No point wasting time,' Rhys said with a shrug. 'Have to make the most of the time we have, right?'

'Quite right too. Achieve your goals, Rhys. Never let anybody stop you.'

'I won't.' Rhys looked back at the open door behind him. 'Someone is here to see you, by the way. Looks a bit like you, actually.'

'Excellent.' James got up out of his chair, and crossed the room to the mantle and carefully placed a small photograph there. 'Bring him in, please, Rhys.'

'No problem. See you later.' Rhys left the room.

James remained facing the mantle, deliberately keeping his back to the door. He had to maintain some semblance of power. It was a foolish game, he knew that, but it was one he had perfected so much in the fifteen years he'd been on this world and he didn't intend to let go of it now. Especially not with his visitor.

He heard the footfalls on the floor, soft and precise. He smiled, careful to keep his back straight. He waited, knowing how much it would annoy the man who had just entered the room. Eventually, after some moments, the visitor cleared his throat.

'Well, you summoned me?'

'Quite so,' James said, and turned slowly. 'How are you,

Old Man?'

It was an old joke, one established a world away, and one the man before him didn't care for. James was the elder brother, however in his world Alistair had died when they were kids. And then, twenty-five years ago, Alistair had returned, only now he was older – older, in fact, than James himself. Things had changed since then. Ten years after Alistair returned home, James had followed him, but the temporal shift had seen him enter Alistair's world ten years too early. By the time they had met again, James was the elder, but still he continued the term of endearment, in the hope that he'd persuade Alistair that they were still allies. The results had been... *interesting.*

Brigadier Alistair Lethbridge-Stewart regarded James coolly. 'Too busy for small talk,' he said.

'You surprise me,' James said sarcastically. Alistair was dressed in the beige uniform of UNIT; a secret organisation barely two years old. The public secret behind which the Fifth Operational Corps hid, James knew, although he'd never let on to Alistair that he knew. Secrets had been his stock-in-trade for many years now, and he wasn't about to give them up now that his brother was working for the United Nations.

'I assumed your days of summoning people were over,' Alistair returned, with equal sarcasm.

'As a rule, yes, but these are exceptional times.'

Alistair raised an eyebrow in an all too familiar way. 'You have no idea. What do you want?'

James nodded. He indicated the two chairs in the room. 'Please.'

For a moment it looked as if Alistair was about to walk out of the room, but after a brief shake of the head, he deigned to sit. Once both were comfortable, James asked him, 'How well do you remember Deepdene?'

'Not well, as you should know. Barely flashes most of the time.' Alistair frowned. A thought had crossed his mind, and it wasn't a pleasant one. 'Why ask this now? We haven't talked about this in over four years.'

James knew to what Alistair was referring, their first meeting in this world, James' attempt at a distraction while Owain Vine and Edward Travers were wired to the Gateway.

James didn't regret what he had done; he had made a choice and, right or wrong, he stood by it. He leaned forward and opened the small box on the table before them. 'Cigar?' he offered.

'Not while I'm on—'

James waved the excuse away. 'Oh come on, Alistair, it's just you and me here. No cameras. Who's going to report you?'

'Very well.'

They lit their cigars and sat back, for a moment seemingly almost content in each other's company. James knew it wouldn't last, but he felt inclined to try and continue to build the bridge between them. In truth he knew that Alistair was not his brother; his brother had died in '38, over twenty years before he first met the man before him. But the Brigadier, as he was known by almost everybody these days, was the closest thing he had to young Ali-stare. Certainly more so than the fifteen-year-old boy they had found within the mirror…

'How is the wife and little Kate?'

Alistair took a deep drag of the cigar and puffed out the smoke. 'Fiona is fine. Both are keeping well.'

'Good. Perhaps one day you could bring them to…?'

'No,' Alistair said sharply. 'Despite what you may think, you are *not* related to them. You're barely related to me.'

'And yet you took my son as your nephew.' James waved it away. 'Old arguments. The point is, you still came when I asked you to.' He let that point sit between them for a moment. 'Alistair, I'm getting too old for this. Can't we put the last five years behind us?'

Alistair nodded slowly, and sat forward. 'It has nothing to do with old age. This has everything to do with your power… Or rather, your lack of it. We took everything away from you. The Vault, the Red Fort…'

'Yes, and look at me now!' James snapped. He held a hand up. 'Do you remember Alastair? That is, the younger version of you from the world between this one and the next?' It was clear from Alistair's expression he did not. 'Surely I told you about him?'

'You mentioned him once, I believe. But that was over four years ago. I can't be expected to remember every detail of our first proper conversation on this world.'

'Be that as it may, you might recall I mentioned he was taken in by the Director, my world's version of our father. He was twisted, indoctrinated, subjected to all kinds of mental manipulation. The drugs we put in you were nothing to what the Director used on him.' James closed his eyes, thinking of the last time he'd seen Alastair, happily playing the role of commandant of a labour camp. 'He knew nothing of where he came from,' James continued, opening his eyes slowly. 'He was our father's pet project. The perfect fascist soldier; the man I would never be. He never questioned anything, didn't even wonder why he aged faster than everybody else around him.'

James waited for Alistair to speak, but he said nothing, just continued to puff on his cigar.

'I saw him again. Last night. Same twisted face, same old scar.'

Now Alistair did speak. 'Last night? He's here?' The idea clearly disturbed him. As it should. James had recognised the rank on Alastair's epaulettes. He'd reached the rank of brigade leader, and only the most sadistic, zealous soldiers reached that rank. The Glorious Leader's work on creating the perfect son was completed, clearly.

'At first I thought it was simply the after image of a bad dream,' James explained. 'But the more I thought about it, the more I considered that sound I've been hearing the past week... It was no dream, Alistair.' He looked his brother in the eyes, and his haunted face was reflected back at him. 'That other Earth, the one I came from, is in trouble. Something catastrophic has happened. I can feel it. And... That other version of you, he spoke to me. Accused me of leaving him there.'

A look came over Alistair, one James wasn't able to read at first. It was, James realised after a few moments, dread. Alistair knew something.

'Have you seen him too?' he asked.

'No,' Alistair said shaking his head. 'Not me. But...' He looked around the room and lowered his voice. 'What I am telling you is top-secret, and must not be repeated to anybody, not under any circumstances.' He waited until James agreed. 'For the last few months my people have been running security on a top secret drilling project, one that, if successful, could have meant a great deal of good for the world at large. But, of course, something went very wrong. The details are a bit beyond me, but from what I can gather, during the course of the last week my scientific advisor went missing. He returned yesterday, quite out of his head. At least so I thought at first.'

James was vaguely aware of this advisor. The Doctor. He had heard murmurs of the man these last few months, murmurs which suggested he was the same chap who had helped Alistair defeat the first attempted incursion by the Great Intelligence. Only, it wasn't the same man. Nonetheless the Fifth had standing orders to secure the man's help, should he return. And, as best as James could work out, that's exactly what Alistair had done.

'Hang on. This advisor of yours, he has a time machine, correct?' James smiled at the look Alistair gave him. 'Come now, you think I am completely without contacts? Obviously they're not as good as they used to be, but if what I hear is correct…'

'Yes, it *is* the same man.'

'This mysterious Doctor who helped you in the Underground?'

'Yes, him. Anyway, in this instance, so he claimed, he not only travelled in time, but he travelled to a version of Earth that ran parallel to this one. A world in which he met a version of me, a version who wore an eyepatch and was…' Alistair stopped and frowned. 'It was your world, wasn't it? That man, this other version of me, was the boy we apparently rescued from within the mirror?'

'Yes. What else did the Doctor tell you?'

'Well, you have to understand, James, I'm still not sure I believe it. Of course I trust him, to a certain extent at least. But he is an alien, and we only have him working with us because… Well, better with us than them.' Alistair stood up. 'Do you know, I think I had almost forgotten about all the madness with Deepdene? I never really quite accepted it, even back then. The drugs Kyle had me pumped with. But…' He shook his head and began to pace the room. 'It was all true. And now your world is dead.'

'My… Wait.' James wanted to believe he'd misheard, but he wasn't that old. 'Alistair, please, tell me exactly what you've been told.'

Still pacing, Alistair explained everything he understood about the Inferno drilling project; the primordial gasses released and the effect they had on people, and worse… On his world, the world of Brigade Leader Lethbridge-Stewart and James' father, the great leader of the Republic, James himself had overseen the early stages of what was then called Operation: Mole-Bore. It never occurred to him that it would happen on this world too. Alistair explained that in James' world, the drilling was well in advance, and it had cracked the crust of the planet. The last thing the Doctor had seen was the world engulfed in lava and flame.

James sat forward and placed his head in his hands. The sound he had been hearing… He was right. It was the sound of the world screaming. But not this one, no, it was his world. Screaming as it died.

'So, I am all that exists of that world.' The finality of it was too much to put into his head. James had lost people before, of course, loved ones, friends, and every one of them had been hard to process on some level, but this… This was too much.

Of course his son was out there, but his quantum signature now matched Alistair's world – no doubt a result of arriving on this world pre-puberty – whereas James was still a product of his own world.

He stood up. 'Where was this Inferno project? I'm assuming Eastchester, like in my world? Can you take me there?'

Alistair blinked in surprise. 'Don't be absurd,' he said. 'It's top secret. I can't just turn up there with you, even if you do already know where it is.'

James walked over to the mantle. 'Do you remember this?' he asked, removing the framed photograph and showing it to Alistair. It depicted three boys, two of a similar age and one younger, standing outside a small village cottage.

'Well, of course, I gave it to you.'

Alistair had kept the original, but in a rare moment of familial solidarity he had produced a copy of the photo as a gift for James shortly after he had fallen from grace. 'You told me it was so I never forgot the boy I was.' James forced a smile.

'Of course, I was never really this boy. The world I grew up in, although similar, was not this world. But I remember this picture being taken, too, not long before you died.'

'Yes, you have told me this before, but I don't see what relevance it has on—'

'I *am* your brother, Alistair. On some level you know this. We've been… well, not quite enemies, but we have been in opposition for almost five years now.' James shook his head. He handed the photograph to Alistair. 'At that point we were the same person, your James and me. We lived the same life.'

'Then you remember more than me,' Alistair pointed out. 'I don't even remember this.' He shook his head at the picture. 'I know it happened, the evidence is here. I have heard many stories from Ray, but I still remember none of it.' He sighed and shrugged. 'Maybe you are my brother, or at least the closest I have to him. But that doesn't mean I can simply stroll in to the factory grounds with you. There is a lot of mopping up going on there, which I should be supervising, and would be if not for your summons. There are many eyes on that place still, not least Sir Keith's lot at the Ministry of Science; many questions are being asked after what happened yesterday.'

James knew he wasn't explaining things well. He *had* to go there. He hadn't known that when Alistair arrived, but now he knew his world was dying… James couldn't explain it, all he knew was something was pulling him there.

He walked over to the table and picked up the folder of papers. 'Look at these,' he said, and handed the folder to Alistair.

His brother replaced the photograph and accepted the folders. After a few quiet minutes of looking through the papers, he eyed James. 'What am I reading?'

'Research,' James explained, taking his seat once again. 'Ever since I arrived here I've spoken to some of the finest minds in the world, trying to understand how the Axonite brought me here. Ironically the biggest breakthrough came five years ago, after you visited my world. I spoke to a Russian scientist who helped to bring you back, and he explained—'

'Very well,' Alistair said, cutting him off. He too sat back down. 'What has this to do with Inferno?'

'Well, according to what I've discovered, there are certain points where my world and this intersect. It's all to do with

200

the position of the Earth's orbit of the sun, rotation of the Earth and...' James waved it all away. 'Scientific gobbledygook that I'm sure will be of no interest to you.'

'Quite.'

James smiled at Alistair's expression. 'According to my research, there are two further intersections, one of which must have been this past week. And the Doctor's machine somehow moved through that intersection.'

'Okay, say I accept that, and to be honest I see no reason why I shouldn't. I still don't see why any of this means I need to take you to this intersection point.'

'I am quantum locked to my world.' James leaned forward urgently. 'I have heard it screaming all week, and last night I saw your Republic counterpart. This Inferno project may be over, but the intersection is still open.' He raised his hands to stop Alistair from interrupting. 'I can't really explain why, but I need to see my world. If it really is over, I need to see it.'

'And if you could, what would this achieve?'

'I believe the Americans have a word for it; closure.'

Alistair sat back and steepled his fingers. For a moment he considered, his eyes moving from James to the papers and back again. 'Like burying a relative,' he said softly.

'Yes, exactly that. If my whole world is gone, everybody I ever knew dead, then... I have to say goodbye.' James paused. 'Um, what I really need to do is speak to your scientific advisor. He could fill in the blanks, tell me what I need to know.'

'Absolutely out of the question,' Alistair said with a snap. 'He knows nothing about you. He thinks he's in the loop, but really he's kept in the dark about a lot of things, and I have orders to maintain that illusion.'

'Thought you trusted him?'

'To a point.'

James smiled grimly. It was as he thought. 'Then, failing that, I need to go there myself. Surely you can see why?'

'And this is your last chance?'

'Well, there should be another intersection in a couple of years, but what will be left of my world by then? Alistair, as your brother, or least what remains of him, I implore you, please let me do this.'

James immediately recognised the driver of Alistair's staff car. His former adjutant back in the days when he commanded the Fifth, William Bishop. Aka, Mr Anne Travers. James nodded at him.

'Isn't this a bit beneath you, Major?'

Bishop looked back at James as the older man climbed into the back seat. 'The Brigadier called in a favour,' he explained. 'If anybody asks, you're an advisor from the Fifth. My presence should help convince them of that.'

'Ah. Thought he'd call on that... Oh, what's that chap's name? Benetton or something.'

'I believe Sergeant Benton is already occupied,' Bishop said, and looked to Alistair for confirmation.

'All my men are,' Alistair said, and got himself comfortable in the passenger seat. 'Right then, shall we?'

The drive to Eastchester was relatively quiet, with only the occasional bit of small talk passing between them all. Clearly Bishop still held James responsible for what happened to his wife's father, which was fair. But James had to wonder; what good did it do to hold a grudge for so long? He thought to ask, but opted not to, after all he had held on to his own anger for a long time. James wouldn't have minded so much, after all it wasn't as if Edward Travers was actually dead.

His ruminations were interrupted by Alistair's announcement that they had arrived.

They passed through the gate with little resistance. Alistair was still in command of security at the plant after all, and the corporal at the gate wouldn't dare question him.

The car drove through the plant, which was just like any other mostly-run down oil refinery. Full of tall chambers, with gantries and walkways joining them. Pretty much the way James remembered it from his own Earth. They stopped outside the main building, and James got out. Alistair poked his head through the open window and provided Bishop with instructions before the car pulled away again.

'Now then,' Alistair said, standing straight, swagger stick held in his hands behind his back. 'You are not at liberty to explore. You will remain with me at all times, do I make myself clear?'

'Yes, sir.' James threw him a salute, which elicited a raised eyebrow in response. 'Now, where's this hut?'

With a hearty throat clearing, Alistair set off. James followed. His instinct was to be chatty, to brazen it out, but there was a strange air around the processing plant. If James had to name it, he'd call it 'funerary'. A gloom, pressing down on everything. The feeling only increased as they neared the hut. From the outside it was no different than the other huts scattered around the plant. Usually used for storage purposes. Often forgotten about until needed. But this one had seen a lot of use in the last few weeks. Alistair lifted a small device and pressed a button. With a whine the doors parted. He looked back at James.

'This is where it all happened, apparently.'

Still slightly sceptical. James couldn't really blame him. Dealing with aliens was one thing, dealing with the possibility that there were copies of you out there, living a version of your life... It played on the biggest frailty of humanity. Ego. The sense of uniqueness at the heart of every man, woman and child. The belief, often unspoken and unrealised, that there will only ever be one person exactly like you in all of creation. It was a feeling James had been confronted with twenty-five years ago when he'd questioned the drug-addled Alistair. When he'd learned of Alistair's past; where James had died in 1938. For a brief moment James felt a little jealous of Alistair. Because of the drugs they had given him, Alistair's memory of those events were blurred, often unreal and mostly unremembered, which meant that, despite what he had been told, he never really believed the idea that there was more than one of him out there. Even now James could tell that his brother didn't really accept it, not deep down where it mattered. On the surface he did certainly, as he accepted most things, but deep down he didn't believe it to be true.

James had no such recourse. He had accepted it, and for some time the realisation had messed him up. Of course, that was a long time ago now. These days the notion that another version of him had lived and died on this Earth was as normal to him as having to eat.

With a deep breath he stepped into the hut and looked around. He wasn't sure what he had expected, but it was just a normal hut. Shelves and walls were bare, although the dust patches did rather suggest that stuff had recently been moved. He closed his eyes and attempted to block out the sound of Alistair standing behind him.

There. It was slight, but he could hear the scream. Even as muted as it was it pierced his soul. He tried to ignore the feeling he experienced in the pit of his stomach, ignore the nausea rising in him.

'You're not going to leave us here!'

James' eyes snapped open and he spun around. For a moment the other version of Alistair stood there. Ranting, his face covered in sweat, his one eye wild. He had his gun out, pointed at someone standing behind James. Now other voices joined him. James struggled to make them out, but he could only hear Alastair's.

'We helped him. We've every right to go. I'll give you until three.'

James stepped towards the brigade leader. 'Alastair, can you hear me? You have to stop this, whatever's going on, you need to calm down.'

But Brigade Leader Lethbridge-Stewart didn't respond. He simply counted down, his voice tipping over to hysterical.

'What's going on?' asked the Brigadier, stepping through the shadowy form of his other self. 'James, snap out of it, man! There's nobody else here.'

'He's there,' James said, his voice barely a whisper. 'Out of the way, Alistair!' He roughly pushed Alistair aside and reached out for the brigade leader. A gunshot rang out and a look of shock spread across Alastair's sweaty face. 'No!' James tried to grab hold of him, but the spectral form vanished with a strange green mist.

The world seemed to tilt around him. James staggered, saw the floor come crashing towards him.

The next moment he was facing the ceiling, Alistair looking down at him, surprise written all over his face. So much like that other face; no eyepatch of course, and a neatly clipped moustache. But in all other ways the face was identical.

'I failed you,' James said, now seeing the fifteen-year-old boy in front of him. 'I should have tried harder, got you away from the Director.'

'James, snap out of it. Where did that wound come from? James!'

For a moment everything was black, but then Alistair was looking down at him. There was a pain in his stomach. James lifted his head. Alistair's hands were covered in blood, pressing down on James' stomach in an attempt to staunch the wound.

'It went right through him,' James said. Alistair clearly didn't understand. But James did. For the first time in fifteen years he understood perfectly. He may have left his world, but he was still connected to it. For fifteen years it had held onto him, and when his world died, it pulled him back. Like some primal force it refused to die alone. If the other Earth had to die, then so did he.

'I should never have come here,' James said. Breathing was difficult. He reached out for Alistair's hand. 'I'm sorry. I should never have come here. Forgive me.'

Whether Alistair forgave him or not, James never knew. He didn't know anything ever again.

Lethbridge-Stewart returned home late that night. The shutting down of the Inferno project had a long way to go, but only a skeleton security crew was needed for the rest of it. He'd left a small unit there, with Captain Miles overseeing them. He thought about returning to HQ to discuss James, but on the way realised he couldn't tell anybody at HQ about him. Certainly not Miss Shaw, and most definitely not the Doctor.

He shook his head and walked into his house.

No, he was proving to be an expert at compartmentalising his life. His current command, and all that entailed, was separate from his former command. The link between the two was known only to a select few at HQ, and even less at High Command. His work life and home life never met. Once he had made the mistake of trying to combine them, but he'd learned the cost of such integration, and it was a price he considered far too high to repeat the mistake. His wife knew nothing of what he really did, which did put something of a strain on his marriage, but it was a strain he was managing.

He walked through the house, said hello to Fiona and walked up the stairs to his daughter's bedroom. He poked his head in, but she was fast sleep, her blonde hair dark with sweat. He crept into the room and opened the window slightly. With a sad smile, his kissed her gently on the forehead and left her room as quietly as he had entered.

He came to his own bedroom and sat on the bed. Before he knew he was going to, Lethbridge-Stewart reached for the phone on the bedside cabinet and dialled a number he knew he didn't ring enough.

'Hi, Dylan,' he said as soon as the other end of the line was picked up.

'Oh, hi, Uncle Alistair. Been a while. What's up?'

Brigadier Alistair Lethbridge-Stewart smiled at the sound of his nephew's voice. There was nobody else in his family he could talk to. Nobody else who knew about James. Everybody else was gone; his father, his mother, Owain, and now his… brother. Yes, Lethbridge-Stewart realised, his brother was dead. Died right in front of him. Again.

He thought back five years to when he had first learned of the existence of James. So much had happened since then, more than he could ever really talk about. And in that time he had lost a lot of people, but never like this.

He supposed, he thought with an odd abstract detachment, this was how it must have felt in 1938 when James had first died. He thought of his mother, and wondered if he had been any kind of support to her when she had lost her son. He couldn't remember, of course. It must have been awful for her, for them all.

He told Dylan what had happened, and together they remained silent, mourning a man who had been many things to them. To Dylan, a father… once. And to Lethbridge-Stewart, a brother… of sorts.

And, Lethbridge-Stewart finally admitted to himself, everybody needed support when losing a loved one.